TESTED

Tested

The Soulmates Series
Book Two

Liv Rancourt

Cover Art: Amy Caldwell
Editor: Meg DesCamp

ISBN-13: 978-1-7368520-3-3

This book is for everyone who's glad they're not
the same person they were in high school

TABLE OF CONTENTS

GLOSSARY

Ádh mór balbh – good luck, dumbass
Affaire du cœur — love affair
Amore mio — my love
An marbhdhraoi — a necromancer
Beurteilung — *assessment* – werewolf term for resolving conflict with a fight to death
Dia á sábháil — Oh my God
Meascach — halfbreed
Mo bhanríon — my queen
Mo chath — my battle
Mo chontúirt — my perils
Mo leannáin — my lovers
Mo mhuirnin — my dear, my darling
Mo rúndiamhra — my mysteries
Mo rúin — my secrets
Mo shíorghrá — my soulmate
Tá mé ag siúl fear marbh.- Dead man walking

.

PART ONE: MO LEANNÁIN

CHAPTER ONE

CONNOR

An marbhdhraoi. A necromancer. That's what the guy needs, and I'm not one. I say it with conviction, under my breath, staring at the pile of rags wrapped around a clay pot. The pot holds an oversized rosemary shrub, the plant's scent dominating but not entirely concealing the smell of death.

"Sorry, Mr. Goldsmith, I've never tried to get rid of a revenant before." A couple of poltergeists, sure, and one case of demon possession that almost started a gang war, but never a simple revenant.

Mr. Goldsmith, a lanky seventy if he's a day, frowns at the pile.

I nudge the wrinkled fabric with my toe. "Your best bet is to burn this stuff."

"But don't you want to take fingerprints or something? How else are you going to figure out who did this?"

This is a skeletal revenant who's made a habit of appearing shortly after sunset and upsetting Tippy and Top, Mr. Goldsmith's matching pair of apricot Pekinese. His house, deep in the Laurel Canyon, is surrounded by sage scrub and eucalyptus that do little to protect against supernatural practical jokes.

Assuming this is a joke.

I'm formulating a response when the ground lights surrounding the patio buzz on. The sun's kissing the western horizon, which means Trajan is about to rise, if he hasn't already. "I'm a private investigator, not a cop, and not a warlock. The best I can do is make some phone calls and make sure this is some kind of a prank and not something more serious."

Revenants are more annoying than anything else. Frightening, given to popping up when you don't expect them, and apparently distressing to pampered canines. If someone wanted to cause real trouble for Mr. Goldsmith and his pups, they'd have sprung for a full-price, brain-eating zombie. Between his description and the lack of the residual aura a zombie would leave, I'm confident it'll be an easy fix.

Borrowing a pair of extra-long barbecue tongs, I pick up each piece of fabric and carry them to the patio's central fire pit. Mr. Goldsmith grumbles more than he helps, but it's a small job and easily accomplished. One quick squirt of lighter fluid and the flick of a match and the bespelled clothing goes up with a bright, clean flame.

Another success for Connor MacPherson, Private Eye.

I promise I'll follow up and Mr. Goldsmith hands me a check, his lips pinched. "If that thing comes back, I want a refund."

"Mr. Goldsmith, if that thing comes back, I'll hire a necromancer to remove it for good." A city as big as LA has to have more than one necromancer. Tray'll know one, or his friend Stone. I pocket the check and head for the Prius, my mind shifting from work to anticipation.

I'll be home with my men as soon as LA traffic allows.

My men. Mo shíorghrá and mo mhuirnin.

The idea still makes my mind spin. I'd returned to LA absolutely certain I'd never again be with Trajan Gall, but in less than six months,

I'd been proven wrong. Not only do I have Trajan in my arms and my bed and my heart, but I share those spaces with David Collins, too. The werewolf brings a lightness to our relationship. Trajan and I had been strong on our own – until I'd gone and fucked things up – but David makes us laugh as well as love.

Trajan is back to calling me *amore mio*. David just calls me pookie, despite my protests.

I'm not a phouka, not that there's anything wrong with them. Anyone who lives with a werewolf is careful about putting down four-legged shifters of all types.

The traffic on Laurel Canyon Boulevard is surprisingly light. The unincorporated areas of LA don't have streetlights, and the heavy blanket of darkness weighs on me. "It's only eight o'clock, guys," I murmur, both hands on the steering wheel. "Where is everybody?"

A car cruises up behind me going much faster than the thirty mile an hour speed limit. The driver pulls into the lane next to me but drops back before I can get a good look. The driver is male and the vehicle is a luxury SUV.

And there's something about the driver's aura that feels familiar, although he's gone so quickly I can't say why. Maybe I'm just making stuff up; leaving the protection of the Elites has me feeling twitchy. I can't call up Dante and ask for whatever toys I need. The wizard's a grumpy fuck but he was the closest thing I had to a partner and sometimes I miss that.

Then David says something outrageous and Trajan smiles and it's worth it.

I'm still musing about my lovers when the SUV's headlights crawl right up my tailpipe. He's so close I can't see the lights anymore, just the vehicle's broad black hood filling my rear view mirror.

A phalanx of cars come at us from the opposite direction and I use the glow of their headlights to get a better look at the vehicle behind me. There's another flicker of familiarity, but it's not enough for me to connect it to anything.

The SUV drifts back, then floods my mirror with his high beams. I duck, squinting against the glare. My grip on the steering wheel tightens. Most roads in the Laurel Canyon are steep and winding, and whoever is behind me is making it impossible to see.

He cuts the lights, or rather, he scoots up close to me again, close enough I can no longer see his headlights.

And then he taps my rear bumper, hard enough to make me jump. The hell with the speed limit. I give the Prius some more gas and switch lanes to get away from him.

He follows. *What the hell?*

This has all taken a minute, maybe less. I navigate a downhill curve, willing my heart rate to slow. I'm in the right lane, doing about fifty. The SUV's on my tail but he hasn't tried to hit me again, and I'm pretty sure we're going to get stopped by a red light in a quarter of a mile or so.

Damn.

The road takes a bend to the right and I keep close to the shoulder. He's close, too close. I speed up, but there's only so much a Prius can do. I hear an echo of David's laughter. He's been after me to get a car *with more balls*, as he says. Right now, I see his point.

We're approaching the intersection, the lights glowing a couple hundred yards ahead of us. Red from the stop light. Red from a car's brake lights. Red from my anger at whoever's tailing me.

The Prius might not be the fastest car on the road, but I'd bet money it'll corner better than my shadow's tank. I slow down to about forty. With luck, I'll be able to lose myself in the canyon before the SUV can make the turn.

I tense. The car is still stopped at the light ahead of me. The shoulder is narrow, maybe too narrow for an SUV. I'm going to pull around the stopped car, scoot along the shoulder, and make a tight turn. I draw a long breath in through my nose. I don't know who's after me, but I can lose him.

I slow another ten miles an hour, pulling closer to the shoulder. As I'm making my move, the damned SUV comes for me, giving my bumper a solid tap. Instead of making a tight turn, I lose traction in the gravel shoulder and spin out. Relaxing into the Prius' motion, I manage to avoid the other car but broadside an electrical pole hard enough to trigger my airbags.

My brain whites out for a beat or two and when I blink, I've stopped moving and the car is filled with white powder. I can't breathe. My seatbelt has caught me in a vice grip and there's a gently deflating bag of nothing in my lap. I manage a sip of powdery air.

My lungs rebel.

I'd cough except I don't have any air to expel. My ribs are burning and, lightheaded, I try to open the door. *Fresh air.* If I can't see the air, I'll have a better chance of breathing it.

The door opens some six inches and stops. I manage a gasp. Someone is standing there. Someone…their aura glowing green with streaks of silver.

Brodie.

"Jesus, man. Are you okay?" Brodie takes a step away from the car and helps me pry the door open.

I manage to draw in enough air to cough. That's the best response I can come up with right now.

"I mean, I was just playing."

Brodie is taller than me by an inch. Tipping my head to meet his gaze makes my neck hurt, so I don't even try. I shake my head. That hurts too. "Text." The word comes out mangled.

"What?" Brodie Kerr, Captain of the Elites, has the balls to look sincerely confused.

If I could find my gun through all the white powder, I'd shoot the fucker. Instead, I coax some more air into my lungs. "Next time, send me a text."

He just grins at me.

Where's my gun?

Traffic is crawling past me, although I'm not taking up much of the lane. He takes hold of the driver's side door and starts to shove. "Put it in neutral," he says, and I manage that simple task.

When the Prius is fully on the shoulder he steps aside and, after a struggle with the seat belt, I manage to crawl out. Brodie makes like he's going to put an arm around me and I flinch. "What was that all about?" I ask, holding an arm tight across my ribs.

"We need to talk."

I pull myself up as close to straight as possible. "I'm unclear why driving me off the road was necessary to bring about a conversation."

Brodie's grin broadens. His father is a djinn and his mother smoked a whole lot of grass. The combination gave him a decidedly unique worldview, a headful of blond dreadlocks, and cast-iron nerves. Now that my mind is a little more focused, I understand why playing chicken down Laurel Canyon Boulevard at night would appeal to him.

I sag against the car. "All right. You've got my attention. Talk."

"It's Poole, my dude." He cuffs my shoulder. "He's got a job for you."

Poole, the head of the Elites. The closest thing I have to a father figure. The one person who could destroy the little island of peace I'm sharing with Trajan and David. "I can't." Because I'd blown it once and wouldn't take that chance again. "He knows my answer, so I don't see why he's still asking."

He tosses a few skinny dreads that have broken free of the bundle at the back of his head. "What'd you do tonight, MacPherson?"

I shrug and then wince because it hurts. "Went to see a man about a dog."

He laughs at that, arms crossed to show off his biceps. "Shit. A guy like you is too good for whatever that bullshit is. You've got skills, man, and it's killing all of us that you're not using them."

I rub my eyes to get rid of the powder. I don't answer, because there is no good answer. He's not wrong. I do miss being part of the Elites. I miss the challenge, the camaraderie. Poole was the first one who ever said my gifts were worth something, and that validation changed my whole life.

But it was the Elites, and specifically Poole, who ordered me to fool Trajan into thinking I was dead, and I can't chance doing that to him again. That's too high a price.

"I'm doing fine, and my answer's not going to change." A cop car pulls up, light flashing but no siren. "Now get out of here before I tell them how you drove me off the road."

Brodie's smile has dimmed. "Don't be like that."

"Don't *you* be like that." I shrug, palms up. "I gave the Elites eight years. Time for me to do something else."

"You're making a bad decision." He sobers completely. "You can't just walk away."

The cop is headed our way. "I suggest you do walk away before your name ends up in a police report."

With a look of disgust, he takes off. It's hard to maintain your image as a member of a supersecret supernatural SWAT team if you end up in some yokel's accident report. He swaggers when he walks, possessing a confidence I recognize.

I used to walk like that, before I saw up-close how badly I'd hurt Trajan. Apricot Pekinese might not present the same level of challenge, but with time, I'll get hired for more complicated cases. I fish my phone out and send David a text.

Remember how you said I needed a new car?

CHAPTER TWO

TRAJAN

I'm one hundred and seventy-five years old, and some days I feel every minute of it. Other days – like today, for instance, with David parading around in a pair of shorts so tight they're giving me an anatomy lesson – I don't feel much older than the twenty-five years I'd spent on earth before I ran across a vampire.

That vampire is Jacques Betancourt, my maker and the owner of this palatial mid-century modern house in the Hollywood Hills where David, Connor, and I have been staying. Jacques felt guilty after our little dust-up with David's uncle and invited us to stay in one of his safe houses, so I picked the best of the lot. While I've known Jacques long enough to know he's liable to change his mind on a dime, it's working for us. For now.

The main entrance is on the middle floor, with the bedrooms upstairs – one bedroom windowless for vampires. Downstairs there's a media room, a weight room, and a large patio with an infinity pool. The coordinating elements are space and light, wood and stone, and the distant Pacific Ocean.

The sun set an hour ago, the last whisps of amber fading from the horizon. David spent time at the pool before I rose this afternoon and his warm golden skin smells like cocoa butter. He's fluttering around the kitchen, and all of a sudden I'm very hungry.

I lean in the doorway, taking in his smooth thighs and the multicolored hair he's got tied in a knot at the nape of his neck. I've never fed from David without Connor present, and yeah, Connor's supposed to be home any time, but I'm hungry *now*.

"You're lurking." David points a knife at me. He's chopping tomatoes, cubes of red surrounded by a spreading puddle of juice at one end of the cutting board.

"You're right."

He glances up at me and I shift my gaze to his throat. Setting the knife down, he wipes his hands on a towel. "Is there something I can do for you?"

His smirk says he's got at least some idea of what I want. I brush a hank of hair out of my face, the same hair that's been falling in my face for a hundred and fifty years. "I figure since you're making Connor dinner, you might be willing to feed me, too."

I'm not usually so bold, but damn. He looks edible.

He shakes a finger at me. "When Connor gets home you can both eat."

"Sure. We'll stretch you across the table and he can feed you strands of spaghetti while I take blood from your groin."

David covers his mouth, but not before he whimpers. "Oh," he gulps, "my."

I stalk toward him. "Or I could take a taste right now."

His phone buzzes, making him jump. "It's Connor," he says. "He's going to be later than he thought, which is good because then the sauce will have more time to cook down. I can make the pasta once he texts me to say he's heading home because he said he'd text and I don't know why I'm babbling except with you looking at me like that I don't know what else to do."

"He's going to be late? That's too bad."

"Are you really that hungry?" He's got his arms crossed like he can't decide whether to be pleased or irritated. "I mean, I guess you can feed." He tips his head to one side. "But no sex. No peen until Connor gets here."

I shrug, coming close enough to touch him. "Pretty sure he won't mind."

"I am too, but until I hear him say it for himself, I don't want to assume."

Tugging the hem of his shirt, I pull him closer. Connor's been threatening us with a sit-down where we discuss our rules and whatnot, but I'd been trying to side-step the issue. I have no words for what we're doing and I'm a little afraid I'll say something wrong by mistake.

I reel David in, his back to my front. He's shorter than me, and a whole lot warmer. Werewolves tended to run hot, and he was no exception. He rocks his hips against my cock, at least until I hold him still. "No sex, you said."

"Yeah, but the two are inextricably linked."

I chuckle. "They're what?"

"Inextricably linked. In my mind, vampire bite equals orgasm. I'm not sure I can do it any other way."

I keep my hands on his hips, holding him still, and trace circles on his neck with my tongue. I won't feed a lot. Just enough to take the edge off. An appetizer to the main course I'll have when Connor gets home.

I settle on a spot right above his carotid artery. He holds his breath and I pierce his skin.

David shudders in my grasp. The werewolf's blood is sweet, and spicy, distinct from other tastes. A lot like him. He's trying to hump the air, but I hold his hips still. I swallow once, twice, then lick the wound to close it, turning my bite into a kiss.

I hold onto him until the strength returns to his legs. When I'm sure he can stand on his own, I step back. He shakes his head like he's trying to clear the fog of sex.

"And now you're going to tell me to keep cooking." He shakes his head again, but this time he's laughing.

I try and parse what he needs, a little surprised at myself for being so forthright. I don't usually give in to impulses like that, especially since we started playing house with Connor. "I won't lie. I liked having you all to myself."

With a slow pirouette, he turns to face me and puts both hands on my chest. "I liked it, too, but…"

"But?"

"Next time Connor says, 'We should talk,' we really should."

He's grinning as he says it. I laugh, because every time Connor raises the subject of ground rules, one of us finds something else to be busy with. "Okay."

"Now get away from me so I can calm down." David adjusts his shorts around the bulge in his crotch. "Don't you have end of month reports to run or something?"

Laughing, I brush a strand of hair away from his saucy grin. The blue of his eyes makes me think of the daylight sky, a sight I've been denied for one hundred and fifty years. That thought sobers me, because there are two ways I can think about it. I can dwell on the sadness of what I've lost.

Or I can be grateful to have the gift of this young were who stepped in and gave me a reason to see what the one hundred and fifty-first year will bring.

"Go cook." I give him a gentle shove. "I'll see about the September reports."

I'd set up an office in a room on the main floor, one of the only places in the house without a view of the Pacific. David had been majoring in finance before the abrupt end of his college career, and I'm hoping he'll express an interest in helping manage my business empire.

I settle myself at my desk and laugh. "Empire" implies something much bigger than my assortment of apartment complexes, shopping centers, and the Santa Monica condo I'm currently renting to one of Jacques' minions.

I also own The Club, a vanity purchase I made so my friend Sheena had a safe place to practice her passion. She's a Dominatrix, one of the best, and along with the club manager and the head bartender, she takes care of The Club's day-to-day operations. My role is pretty much limited to opening my checkbook and the occasional scene when Sheena determines a client could benefit from fucking a vampire.

Might not be an empire, but it's not bad for a man who got his start card sharking on a Mississippi paddle-wheeler.

I'm negotiating a truce between a lawyer with a lawsuit on his mind and the manager of one of my shopping centers who swears the floors were dry that day when I hear Connor come in. After sending a DM to the manager, basically saying *Fix this*, I leave the office to greet the other reason I'm still alive.

Connor MacPherson, the man who loved me and left me and returned from the dead.

Connor, whose suit coat is smudged with white powder and who's got an arm around David as if he needs the support.

"What the hell happened? You look like you've been rode hard and left out in the desert."

Connor's smile has a false note. He doesn't smile all that often, and the one unfortunate byproduct of our history is that I don't always trust him as I should.

Especially when he smiles.

"Wrecked the Prius." He says it apologetically. "My client was in the Laurel Canyon, and the roads up there are so dark, I almost missed a turn and spun out on some gravel."

"Aw, dude." David hugs him tighter. "You need a shower and a shot of scotch, and not necessarily in that order."

Connor tips his head to brush a kiss on David's hair. "Thanks, *mo mhuirnin*. I'll take the scotch neat if you're pouring."

David gives him a squeeze and slips out from under his arm, leaving me staring at a weary Connor. "You sure you're okay?" I manage words, the fear of losing him relaxing its grip enough for me to force them out.

"I'm sorry, *mo shíorghrá*. I didn't mean to upset you."

"Upset me?" I huff a bitter laugh. "I'm not sure I should be your primary concern here. Do you need to get checked out? X-rays or something?"

"Nah." His smile is back and it's no less false. "Like David said, a shower and some scotch will fix what ails me."

He heads for the stairs, moving as if his joints ache and he's afraid of jarring something loose.

"I'm glad…"

He pauses on the bottom step, giving me a look that's hard to interpret.

"I'm glad you weren't badly hurt, *amore mio*," I say. It's not all I want to say, but it's all I can manage.

I'm still standing in the foyer when David scoots past with a tumbler of clear bronze liquid. I want to ask him if he thinks we heard the whole story but fear still has its grip on my vocal cords.

Because I either trust Connor, or I don't. When I made the choice to let him back in, I did so knowing I took a risk.

Maybe the three of us do need to have a conversation.

We put it off for two nights, maybe three, giving Connor time to recover from the injuries he denies having. He doesn't have obvious damage, but he still moves like everything hurt.

I occupied myself with convincing Lawsuit Lawyer that he'd be better off spending his time harassing other small business owners. His blood tasted the way cell phones smell – and they don't – so he tasted like nothing. I also planted a thought that I hoped would lead him toward more socially conscious choices, and I took his card so I'd remember his name if he turned up in the news for helping an old lady save her home from Big Business.

David uses the time to shop for Connor's next car.

"Hey, Connor. This place is open till ten." David points at the laptop screen from his perch on the end of the big sofa. Beyond him the window shows the last fading dregs of sunset smeared across the horizon. Connor sits on the couch's opposite end, while I have a chair furthest back from the window.

Connor leans over to take a look at David's laptop. "Really not sure how practical a Porsche would be." He settles back into the sofa cushion. "I'm looking for something electric."

"Tesla, here we come!" David laughs at his own joke and starts tapping the keyboard.

Connor catches my eye and groans, and I chuckle, too. The energy between us is calm, comfortable.

So, I toss a grenade into the room. "If we're close enough to choose each other's cars, maybe we should figure out what we're not comfortable with."

Straightening slowly, Connor gives me an appraising look. David's eyes are wide and his hands freeze on the keyboard.

"I mean"—if vampires could blush, I'd be doing it now—"the other night I needed blood, and since you weren't home, David and I..."

David is blushing hard enough for both of us. "I was going to tell you, but you'd wrecked your car and I figured that was enough drama for one night."

Connor shifts his gaze from me to David. "It doesn't upset me if Trajan feeds from you without my supervision."

Damn. I cross my arms, ready for battle. "Sarcasm makes it sound like you do mind."

"Okay, it does bother me that you waited three days to say something."

David rounds on him. "Did you hear what I just said? You'd totaled your car, and since then you've been walking around here like a strong breeze would knock you down. Forgive me for not adding to the burden you're obviously carrying."

That's my saucy wolf. "And we're telling you now."

Connor closes his eyes, hands fisted in his lap. "Okay." He shakes himself, as if letting go of whatever bad humor has had hold of him. "You're right. I appreciate that you gave me time to get my head out of my ass. I do mean it, though." He gives me a meaningful glance. "If you're hungry and I'm not around, it won't bother me if you feed from David."

"Would it bother you if I had sex with David?"

The wolf in question gives a little squeak.

Connor's expression relaxes. "Would it bother you?"

Suddenly on the spot, I drop my gaze and do my best to consider the question honestly. "I don't think so. You're both important to me and I want you to be happy."

David clears his throat. "I don't think it would bother me, either. You both have done so much for me – are *doing* so much for me – that I don't have room to complain."

Connor and I both protest that. "You absolutely have a right to how you feel about this," Connor says.

"Besides, a youngster like you shouldn't be trapped by two old geezers like us." Somehow putting those words together makes me more nervous than talking about who sleeps with who.

"Aw, Tray, come on. You're not a geezer, and neither is Connor." David's smile is tinged with sadness. "Without you two, I'd be dead."

Again we pelt him with a chorus of protests.

"I'm serious, though." He shouts us down. "And even if you hadn't stepped up to be my de facto pack, I'm old enough to know what I want." He clears his throat as if he's nervous. "And what I want is you, both of you, for as long as you'll have me."

We're all silent, David's words wrapping around us, filling me with warmth. It's Connor who breaks the spell.

"It's going to take work, this relationship," he says. "Circumstances are going to change, and feelings are going to change. We'll have to be honest with each other, maybe more honest than we've ever been."

It crosses my mind that I could challenge his honesty by asking what had really happened the night he wrecked his Prius. Instead, I take a different route. "So here's something I've been wondering about for a while."

"Oh yeah?" His smile shades to something with more tension.

I take a second to decide how to frame what I want to say. When we first met, Connor gave me a Reader's Digest version of his history: an upbringing in the country, an estranged mother, a young boy who found himself in the big, wicked city. But when the three of us moved in here, he'd shut down David's teasing by confessing to an unexpected supernatural background. "I've never met anyone else who claimed to be Tuatha Dé Danann. What did you mean when you told us that?"

"I'm not surprised you haven't met any others. There aren't many of us, and we tend to live in less populated places."

David leans forward, so eager I can tell he's been curious about this too. "Is that why you're from Montana?"

"Yeah. We lived up in the hills on like ten acres, with a couple other Tuatha families."

"LA must have freaked you out." I can see the gears turning in David's head, so I poke at the most obvious inconsistency. "I mean, it's not a rural, isolated place."

Connor laughs, but it's as if a wall has gone up. His eyes are guarded and his smile is gone. "I'm only half Tuatha."

"And what's the other half?" David asks.

After a long pause, Connor answers. "Don't know," he says. "I could be the product of a virgin birth, for all the info Mom gave me about my father."

He says it lightly, like he's trying for a joke, but something – *shame?* – undercuts the humor. Puts a stop to my questions, too. David doesn't say anything. He just gets up and goes to Connor, pulling him out of his seat and into a hug.

There's nothing wrong with never knowing your father, but Connor's said so little about his background that this revelation feels bigger than it might otherwise. I take a step toward them, my arms open. The sun has set completely, and the big windows are filled with city lights and the glossy darkness of the Pacific Ocean.

"Group hug." David whispers the words. The two of them come close and I wrap my arms around them. Connor's smokey scent brings me comfort, while David's tight little body gives me heat. I close my eyes and bask in my senses.

Yeah, getting Connor to trust us with his story is going to take as much work as getting me to trust Connor. Hell, this whole relationship is going to take work, but I do believe it's worth it.

CHAPTER THREE

C onnor gone again?" I swear I don't know why, but that's the first question I ask every day when I rise.

David just laughs at me. It's been a week since we had our little heart-to-heart chat, and while no one has tested our new ground rules, Connor's been gone so much I'm getting close. Chalk it up to life experience, but I have the feeling that if any of us pair up for feeding or for sex or for just running to the grocery store, the one left out might be surprised by his own response.

"Left about an hour ago," David says, "something about a revenant who's angry his clothes got burnt."

"Sure." My phone chimes with a reminder. "Oh, I'm supposed to meet my real estate agent to check out a property I might want to rent. Do you want to come with me?"

David looks down at himself. He's wearing a long cotton skirt – or maybe trousers with incredibly wide legs – and a chartreuse crop top that'd be open in the front except for a single button at the center of his chest, right between his nipples. The button is painted with a smiley face. "Do I have to change?"

I can't help but laugh. When we first met, David used fashion as a weapon. Now it's just…who he is. "Nope. The agent I'm meeting is human, but she prides herself on dealing with the supernatural. You'll add to my vampire cred."

David's natural glow is squelched for a heartbeat. "Sure. If nothing else, I'm good as a vampire decoration."

I start to protest, but he waves me off. "Give me a couple minutes and I'll come with you."

He skips off – literally – before I can come up with a proper response. Of course he's more than a decoration. Whenever I'm not worrying he's too young for a committed relationship – and a menage, at that – I fret about how to keep both him and Connor safe. If I dig deeper, I might see how those two impulses are related.

After we look at the property, David and I could go test drive a couple SUVs. The car might belong to Connor, but David's opinion – or rather, his ability to express that opinion – matters more than anything else.

I retreat to my room and pull out a pair of black jeans and a silk jersey tee the color of café au lait. I slick my hair back – not quite hitman mode, but close – and wait for David in the kitchen.

He reappears wearing a more subdued version of his earlier outfit. The cotton skirt has been replaced by artfully torn jeans, and he's got a white muscle tee under the smiley button top.

"Very nice." I give him an approving once-over. His hair falls in long layers around his face, the colors made brighter by the inch or so of dark roots. We pile into the Range Rover I bought to replace the Escalade some asshole blew to bits. The new ride isn't as big as the Escalade, but it's just as imposing, so I like it.

We work our way to Santa Monica Boulevard, David listing every restaurant he'd like to try, which could be perceived as rude – vampires don't eat – if he weren't so damned enthusiastic. As it is, I just imagine how he'll taste after he has some of that blah blah blah at Chez Wherever.

Our destination is in West Hollywood, a storefront right off the Sunset Strip. The space has a professional kitchen, and while it's been vacant a while, I want to see if the real thing equals my imagined potential.

Parking proves to be a challenge, so we're some five minutes late to meet the real estate agent. Fortunately, she waited, and is tapping furiously on her cell phone when we walk up.

"You're Glory?" My question's rhetorical. I'd researched her on-line and seen pictures as well as testimonials from other supes she's worked with.

"I am, and you must be Trajan Gall." She extends her hand, her dark skin making the lime green nail polish glow. Her hair is a bundle of tiny braids pulled back from her face, and her white suit has been tailored by an expert.

We shake hands and I pull David forward. "This is David Collins. He'll be working with me on this project, so if you need anything during daylight hours, he'll be your contact."

They shake hands and she smiles with delight. "You're so warm. Were? Shifter?"

David snorts a laugh. "Wolf."

He manages to layer a lot into that one word, and Glory's eyes widen. "Collins…wolf…Oh."

I tighten my grip on his elbow to keep him from running. "Let's take a look at the space, okay?"

Glory unlocks the front door and holds it open for us. The air smells like stale grease and old meat – or something funkier than old meat. Dead meat? It's not a great first impression. She follows us in and turns on the overhead lights, two banks of fluorescent bulbs that cast a harsh glare.

The room is a generous rectangle with two doors divided by a shadowy hallway at the rear. There's a window with a wide shelf at its base next to the right door, a pass-through from the kitchen. Glory heads for the kitchen door, heels clacking on the linoleum floor, and I follow.

David stays by the entrance.

Glory waves me into the kitchen, and the further I go, the stronger the smell becomes, strong enough to make me blink. I gesture at David, who hasn't moved. I don't know why he's chosen this moment to pout, but it's annoying.

There's a row of appliances along one wall, their stainless-steel surfaces worn but relatively clean. Whoever takes over this space won't be able to run a high-volume establishment. There's not room for more than three people in the kitchen. Glory starts to list the features, highlighting what the advertising copy emphasized. No new information, given the research I'd already done, so I turn my attention to her.

For a human, she sure doesn't give off much energy. I debate whether I should try to mess with her mind, just to see if I can, but decide against it. She carries on, leading me out of the kitchen and down the hall.

"The restrooms are the last two doors down there but check out this storage. It's really —"

"Don't." One word. Not loud, but David freezes both of us in place, Glory with her hand on a doorknob and me with my chin hanging open.

"Pardon me?" Glory's tone shifts from warm to frosty.

David closes his eyes and inhales. Exhales. "There's something in there."

"What? Dust bunnies?" Glory swings the door open.

"Nope," I say, gagging as the smell hits me. "More like a dead body."

David comes up behind us. "I tried to warn you. I could smell it as soon as we came through the door."

The body in the closet is a woman, or mostly a woman. She'd been petite, and she lay naked – either her attacker had stripped her or the magic had done it – with long black hair covering her face. My mind skates over her wounds, grabbing hold of the fact that she'd partially shifted. Her lower limbs and long, plumed tail are those of a fox. "Kitsune, I think."

"Oh no." Glory starts sputtering. "You all knew we were going to find this here. I should have known better than to mess with —"

"Quiet." I don't speak any louder than David had but I add a little vampire mojo to shut her off. "We didn't know there'd be a dead body in the closet, but I do know what we're going to do about it."

"What?" David asks.

"Call Connor, unless one of you wants to explain a half-shifted kitsune to the cops."

Glory already has her phone out. "I don't know who Connor is, but Adam Smith is the supernatural liaison for the LAPD. I'm calling him first."

She spins on her heel, phone to her ear. I've heard of Smith. He's a new addition to the local police force and no one I know can decide if that's a good thing or not.

David's got his phone out, too, and he's texting someone, most likely Connor. We'll just have to see who gets here first.

The cops win, but not by much. Two uniformed patrolmen take one look in the closet and back away, pretty much the response I expected. They decide to wait in their car, leaving us to make polite conversation while we wait for the higher-ups to show.

"So I'm guessing you won't be interested in renting this place?" Glory's gotten over her irritation, and she's scanning her phone's screen. "Because there's a similar listing in Culver City that you might want to see."

I'm not sure whether to laugh or to applaud her for her persistence. "As long as it's not the scene of a recent homicide, I'm up for a look."

She laughs and tucks her phone away. "I'll do what I can."

"I do think it would be nice to have a coffee shop or something, or a pub with appetizers and beer, someplace where supes would feel comfortable."

David's been standing with his hands on his hips, looking out the window. "Really?" He turns to face me.

"Yeah, and I thought maybe you could run the place."

He grimaces, but before he can otherwise respond, an older guy with the shaggy hair and orange-peel skin of a surfer strides through the door. His suit coat fits like he borrowed it from someone bigger, his jeans hang low on his hips, and he's wearing flipflops instead of shoes. He heads for Glory first, hand extended. White tape wraps around his palm up to the base of his thumb.

"You're the one who called me, right? I'm Adam Smith."

They shake hands, Glory conjuring up her practiced smile. "Yes, Detective. We met at the fundraiser for street kids' services last month."

"That's right." He whips out a small spiral notebook and a pencil and starts making notes.

"And who are you two?" He glances from me to David.

We introduce ourselves and he scribbles some more. He doesn't react to David's name, but I get a side-eye.

"You run that kink club down on San Pedro Street." It's not a question, so I let a shrug be my answer.

"Are you thinking of expanding operations up here?" His suspicion is palpable, his gaze direct. For all of his middle-aged surfer vibe, I can see why the LAPD hired him.

"Nah, we'll keep the whips and chains where they are. I'm more in the market for a place that's open to all types." *Except maybe elves. Elves are assholes.*

"Huh." More scribbling. "So you all just happened to check this place out and accidentally found a body?"

"More or less." The interview is interrupted when Connor blows through the door.

"Smith." Connor reaches out to shake hands with the detective.

"What are you doing here, Mack? Awfully quick to have the Securitas involved."

They shake, and Connor shrugs. "David texted me. These two are my" — he pauses for a heartbeat — "boyfriends." Connor's got his chin raised like he's daring Smith to say something.

For his part, Smith scribbles another note and flips the page of his notebook.

"Besides, I'm not with the Elites anymore. I've got my private investigator's license."

Smith looks up from his notebook with a smile. "Fuckin' a, man. That's the best news I've heard in a long time. I've been saying for years that we need somebody at the street level."

Connor's grin is a little more tentative. "Have you seen the body?"

"Not yet." Smith stuffs his notebook into his jacket's inner pocket. "Let's go."

With that, we all head for the storage closet. The body hasn't moved, which shouldn't surprise me, but it does. Smith squats down, still making notes, and Connor leans over his shoulder.

"Is that a knife?" Connor points into the closet. "Maybe the murder weapon."

"Hmmph." Smith's response doesn't confirm or deny. "I'll get the homicide team in here and send you copies of the evidence reports."

Connor nods. "Thanks." He glances at me. "Do you recognize her?"

It's a fair question. Of all of us, I've spent the most time in Los Angeles, and have the most contacts in the supernatural community. "I can't tell with her hair in her face like that."

He hums. "Yeah, but we can't touch her till the evidence team gets here." He takes out his phone and snaps a couple pictures. "Why don't you two head out and I'll bring you photos later. Is that okay, Smith?"

"They'll need to give statements. Glory too."

Connor gives us an apologetic shrug.

"We'll wait outside. Get some fresh air." I nudge David and head for the door. Glory follows.

The Santa Ana winds have kicked up, swirling the dry air and exhaust together, but it's better than the smell in the restaurant. Glory busies herself with an iPad that she's pulled out of her purse, so we leave her to her work. David's got his arms crossed and his chin tilted, very much the angry young wolf I first met.

"It's not like I set out to ruin your night." I try for humor but it falls flat. David flips the hair out of his face but otherwise doesn't respond. "We should be done in time to go to a club later, if you want."

He gives an exasperated snort. "Did it ever occur to you to ask me if I wanted to run a restaurant of some kind before dragging me out on this escapade?"

I blink, unsure of how to respond.

"I mean, I get that I should be doing more to try to find a job, but don't feel like you've got to create a pet project to keep me occupied. I'm your boyfriend, not a child."

"Sure, I get that." I feel like I should apologize, though I'm not sure what for. We stand there until an SUV with LAPD on the side and an incident van pull up. Smith is the guy in charge, but Connor's got enough pull to make our statements a priority, so after another hour or so we're ready to go. Glory's already gone – so much for being agent to the supes – and by the time we get to the Land Rover, David's mood has improved.

"Wanna watch some *Dancing with the Stars* when we get home?" His grin suggests he's got more than dancing on his mind.

I meet his grin with one of my own. "Sure, puppy. Whatever you say."

We can sort out his feelings later.

Part Two: Mo Rúndiamhra

CHAPTER FOUR

Connor

Once the homicide team takes over, I step back. I manage to get a photo of the victim's face, and I send it along with a description of the crime scene to a contact in LA's office of the Securitas. A murdered kitsune isn't a big enough event to bring on the full force of their authority, but giving them a warning seems prudent.

On my way out, Smith reiterates his promise to keep me in the loop.

"Thanks, man. I'll message you if I get an ID on the vic." I give him a quick salute and head for my rental car. It's a Ford Taurus and I've managed to keep it hidden from David because I'm afraid he'll die laughing. Literally. I hit the rental's keyfob and it chirps at me. David's got his heart set on a Tesla. For me.

Not in my lifetime.

Parking the Taurus a block away from the house and fibbing when David asks what I rented is getting tiresome, though. I'll have to come clean at some point.

Before I put the car in drive, I shoot a text to Sheena. She's been around this town as long as Trajan has, and since I'm out, I may as well run the photo past her to see if she recognizes the murdered woman.

Because that was the other detail I gleaned from the crime scene. As if finding a half-shifted kitsune in the closet of a vacant storefront wasn't suspicious enough, the victim had ligature marks around her neck and a vicious stab wound in the center of her chest. Definitely not self-inflicted, even with a knife half-covered by her body.

Sheena responds from The Club, on a break between clients, and she can talk if I can get there in the next thirty minutes.

Is it possible to get anywhere in LA in less than thirty minutes?

I'm not sure but I give it a try.

The Club is in the Fashion District, exactly thirty-five minutes from the WeHo storefront. I manage to talk my way through the front door without flashing my badge – which is now a paper PI license – and find Sheena seated at the bar. The room's black and red color scheme is a little obvious for my taste, but Sheena in Domme attire fits right in.

Despite a black leather dress that's more skin than fabric, she's the one spot of true beauty in the scene, but Sheena's an Amazon, which means she's lethal. She's about three inches taller than I am, which puts her at 6′ 5″ and when our gazes connect, her expression shifts from *hostess with the mostest* to *I might have to kill this man someday*. Trajan may have forgiven me for faking my own death, but Sheena has not.

For that matter, I haven't forgiven myself, and I'm not likely to any time soon.

And the more time we spend together, the more likely I am to give her a reason to kill me, so I've got my phone out before I hit the bar. The bartender's busy with a trio of waitresses at the other end, and the seat next to Sheena is empty. I stay standing, although she's unlikely to be intimidated by such a lame attempt at control. "How's business?"

She gazes at me through eyelids heavy with kohl. "Busy night." She gives me a quick once-over. "You looking for a spanking?"

"Nah," I chuckle. "I just came from a crime scene."

"Look at you." She applauds, but it's mocking. "The cops already calling on our junior private eye."

I take a practiced inhale. She's trying to get under my skin, and I don't blame her. Still, I'm not going to react. "Actually, Trajan went to check out a restaurant space he's interested in leasing, and he and the agent found a body in a storage closet."

Sheena's aura shifts from glossy green to red with concern, her loyalty to Trajan undeniable. "Damn it. I hope the cops aren't blaming him for it." She nudges the barstool next to her in my direction, as close as she'll come to an invitation to sit.

I stand. "Not at all. The victim was a kitsune, we think. She half-shifted when she died, and none of her injuries are consistent with a vampire attack."

"That's good. Shit. Hang on." She taps the bartop with a long fingernail. "That came out wrong. I'm glad he's okay, but I'm sorry for the woman who was killed. Do the cops know who she was?"

Now I do climb onto the bar stool. "That's actually why I'm here. I don't want to upset you, but I took a photo of the victim and I'm wondering if you would take a look, see if you can ID her."

"What time is it?" she asks the bartender. He's hovering as if he wants to talk to Sheena but is afraid of interrupting.

He looks out over the room. "Your next client is in the lobby."

"Shit." She turns to me. "Can you text it to me?"

I could, but if the picture starts making the rounds before the family is notified, that would be bad. "Can I meet you later?"

"I'll come by the house after I get off." She shoos the bartender with a flap of her hand.

She stands, and so do I.

"So make sure you and Trajan aren't too busy with your hot little wolf to entertain a friend."

"Text one of us when you're on your way so we don't embarrass you."

Because I may struggle with the finer points of this private eye gig, but I'm one hundred percent behind entertaining David and Trajan.

The scene at my Taurus rental flattens the happy little seed Sheena had planted. Brodie Kerr is leaning against the passenger door, arms crossed, eyes downcast. He glances up as I approach.

"What's up?"

Brodie's grin has a manic edge. "Waiting on you to finish getting reamed."

I keep my mouth closed and let my body language say *Fuck you*.

"Nah, I can tell you weren't having fun in there. You're too uptight."

Brodie might have been the closest thing I had to a friend in the Elites, but he could still be an irritating motherfucker. I let a couple heartbeats pass before I speak. "Was there something you wanted?"

"Same ol', same ol'. Da boss wants you back."

Da boss. Poole. I inhale slowly. "And what do you suppose has changed since the last time we had this conversation?"

"Everything, man. Everything."

"What?"

"Let me ask you something. When you saw that dead girl tonight, who's the first person you called?"

I don't answer. He already knows too much.

"I'll tell you who. You called the downtown office and filed a just-in-case report." He rocks his shoulders like he's going to start rapping at me. "Now, why would you do that if you don't want to come home, baby?"

I fight the urge to put my fist through his face. "We're done here."

"Are you sure? Are you sure you're sure?"

Ignoring him, I circle the vehicle to the driver's side door. "You might want to stand clear," I say, opening the door. "Got things to do."

He flutters his lashes. "Gonna go see your vampire sweetie? The one who's up to his ass in the missing elven princess case?"

I freeze, halfway into the car. Gripping the top of the door, I glare at him over top of the car. "What?"

"Now I gotcha, but you know what? I'm not going to say anything more until you talk to Poole."

His tone might be light, but his eyes are dead serious. He's got me, all right, and he knows it. The missing elven princess had been my case and leaving it unsolved bothers me more than I'm willing to admit. Still, I play for time. "Stand back. Don't want to run you over."

I climb into the car and slam the door. A man with more common sense than me would watch him to see where he goes next.

A man with more common sense and a better hold on his temper.

I come home to a quiet house. I pause in the foyer, scanning for any trace of my lovers. Flickers of David's golden aura grace the stairs to the lower level and if I close my eyes, I can hear the faintest sound of manufactured applause.

Trajan and David are on the big black leather couch in the media room. David's curled up on his side, his head in Trajan's lap, and he's snoring softly. Whatever's on the big screen involves bright colors and people dancing and Trajan's running his fingers through David's hair like there's nothing else he'd rather do.

I pause in the doorway and Trajan turns to me and smiles. "We made it through three episodes before he crashed."

"I didn't crash." David pops up, his hair flattened on one side and his eyes sleepy. "Trajan said he'd poke me if Gianni got cut."

"That was a while ago." The affection in Trajan's eyes warms me even though it's hard to see. I can't remember if he ever looked at me that way.

"I'm sorry to disturb you." My voice is gruff, humbled.

David scoots his butt to the top of the couch. He swings his legs over, landing lightly on his feet. "You didn't disturb us," he says, his grin going feral. "We were waiting for you to get home so we can take your mind off work."

He stalks towards me. Trajan also stands, arms crossed over his fists to make his biceps bulge. "Puppy here wanted to play but we decided to wait until you could join us."

My breath is coming faster. "I still need to" —

David drops to his knees in front of me. "Need to shut your mouth is what you need to do."

He goes to work on my belt while Trajan fucks me with his eyes. The power Trajan exudes when he goes vampire has always been an aphrodisiac. There's part of me, buried and deep and rarely acknowledged, that understands death. That controls it, even. Trajan's presence has always resonated on that level, and desire scrambles whatever rational thoughts I'd intended to share.

My cock swells when David yanks down my zipper and pulls it out. He swallows me whole, and I get hard so fast my vision blurs.

There's something I do need to tell them, but I'll be damned if I can remember what it is. My senses are overwhelmed with the wolf's hot mouth and the vampire's cold strength. I want Trajan. I want David. I want them both.

"David promised me he'd get you ready so I can fuck your ass," Trajan says and at the same time, David tugs on my balls. He's got the other hand wrapped around the base of my cock and he's bobbing and sucking with such intensity I'm not going to last.

David releases my balls and works his way to my hole, his tongue laving the head of my cock. Pleasure shimmers over my skin, raising goosebumps. I start to thrust – can't help it, really – and my trousers slip down to the floor. David's got a finger inside me, flexing and bending, loosening me up. Trajan grins, and his fangs show.

"*Dia á sábháil*," I gasp. *Oh my God*. My eyes flutter closed, and when I open them again, Trajan's standing at my side. He licks a stripe on my bared throat and David growls.

"Bend over the back of the couch, puppy." Trajan nips my throat and murmurs, "We got him ready for you earlier."

David's out of his jeans and bent over, ass in the air before I can process the reason the air is cold on my dick. He reaches back with one hand and spreads his cheeks, showing me the plug. "Who's gonna take this out of me?"

Trajan's busy pulling off my hoodie and I toe off my shoes. "I will," I whisper. Stepping out of my jeans, I drag the vampire toward David.

Removing the plug makes David growl again. His ass is so beautiful, round and golden, after hours spent down by the pool. I want to bury myself in him, but I move slowly, because after the way he sucked me, I'm ready to explode.

Trajan's pulled lube out of somewhere and I gasp at the cold intrusion of his fingers. He knows my body well and knows he doesn't need to waste time. In moments, his fingers are replaced by the blunt head of his cock ramming into me.

I groan, long and low. Pleasure and pain mingle, impossible to differentiate. David's impatient whine cues my next move. I thrust into him slowly, every move threatening to send me over the edge. When I'm in as far as I can go, Trajan hauls me upright against his body.

"Now make him come," he hisses, and, holding tight to David's hips, I start to thrust.

Trajan's cock is a lead pipe in my ass and he's wrapped his arms around me like a vise. The only part of me that can move is my hips, and I give David all that I have. He's working his own cock, hand moving with blinding speed, and soon he starts to buck and groan.

I'm barely hanging on when David stiffens and yells, ropes of come splatting on black leather. Then Trajan starts to move, and as the vortex begins to suck me down, he bites.

I'm gone.

My heart stops beating and the world goes white. All I know are the surges of pleasure burning a bright path from deep in David's body to the vampire's teeth in my throat. I pour out everything I've got until my knees get weak. Trajan kisses closed the wound in my throat and bends me over so I'm cradling David in my arms. The vampire grasps my hips, thrusting at an easy pace while I return to my body.

He speeds up and so does my heart. I nuzzle David's neck, losing myself in the scent of his body wash and the product in his hair. Trajan thrusts harder and I arch my back, giving him all I can. His fingers dig into me and he moves with a speed no ordinary human could survive.

Faster than he's ever fucked me before.

But I stay in position, holding David close and letting the vampire use my ass. He needs it, and so do I. When he reaches his peak, it's cataclysmic, waves of pleasure that resonate through all of us. His legs give way and we slide to the floor in a heap, spent and sweaty.

"First one who can stand has to go get us a wet towel," David murmurs, burrowing in closer to me. Trajan's spooning both of us, our legs tangled together.

"That was some welcome home," I manage, and we all laugh. Then I remember what I'd meant to say up front. "Uh, Sheena's coming over after her last client."

Trajan snorts a laugh, and David mutters "Buzz Killington" under his breath.

"Yeah, uh, I have a picture of the victim to show both of you."

David throws a wild punch that lands somewhere between my ribs and my kidney, and Trajan starts laughing for real.

"All right. Playtime is over," Trajan says. "Detective MacPherson's back on the job."

"Wouldn't you rather have time for a shower before she gets here?"

They both groan. The biggest shower is on the upper floor. It's going to be a while before my legs will be strong enough to manage two flights.

CHAPTER FIVE

DAVID

The last – and I mean *the last* – thing I want to do after getting so very well fucked is to make polite conversation with Trajan's bestie and look at photos of a dead woman. That's what's on the agenda, though, and I suppose I should be thankful Connor remembered she's coming before Sheena actually knocks on our door.

I will say, though, that pretending to be too weak to walk and having a vampire carry me up two flights of stairs makes up for some of my aggravation. I dress in a Hang Ten hoodie and a sarong instead of jeans, because while Connor's pretty cool, his dick is big enough to leave a mark. My bits appreciate the flow of air as I jog downstairs, just in time to get the door for Sheena.

She stalks in, wearing a black leather Domme dress and smelling like cigarettes, which makes me bite my lip. *No smoking or the vampire complains.* Hell, he does more than complain, enough that I've pretty much quit smoking.

"There's already chatter," she says with no other preamble.

Connor's facing the big windows, his copper curls still damp from the shower. "Chatter about the murder?"

"Sort of." She drops onto the couch next to Trajan and gives him a kiss. "Guy came in right before closing and said there are all kinds of rumors."

"Like what?" Connor's bleak expression matches Sheena's somber tone.

"The usual. Drug deal gone bad. Revenge. He was pretty convinced this was only the first, though."

"The first of how many?" I ask, settling on the chair closest to Connor and adjusting the sarong to keep from flashing Sheena. She wouldn't appreciate my boy parts except from a professional standpoint, but still.

Connor comes over and leans against the arm of my chair, fingers teasing the back of my neck.

"He didn't say, and he wouldn't tell me why he thought so," Sheena says.

Connor's hand stills, as if he's making a conscious decision not to punch the nearest available object. "One is already too many," he says, his voice firm, determined. He holds his cell phone toward Sheena and Trajan. "Recognize her?"

I crane my neck so I can see too and immediately regret my choice. The face in the picture is grey verging on purple and spattered with blood. Retreating to my chair, I leave the rest of them to it.

Trajan and Sheena give the photograph a long look, then glance at each other. "Maybe one of the Nosakas?" Trajan murmurs, and Sheena nods.

"Could be Adeline, although I can't imagine why anyone would do that to a middle-aged kitsune whose gravest sin is probably parking on the wrong side when the street sweepers come."

"That's your best guess?" Connor's all business, which is impressive given it wasn't so long ago that he pounded my ass. He swipes his phone and glances up at Trajan, as if he's giving him one last chance to change his mind.

Trajan shrugs in response. "There aren't that many kitsune families in the area."

"Not much to go on, except for those earrings," Sheena observes. "Pretty sure Adeline

Nosaka likes her diamonds, so that could be her."

I hadn't noticed her earrings, but then I didn't take more than a glance. Connor murmurs something about texting Smith the name, and I ponder identifying marks. My bum is tender, but that's not the kind of thing a guy shows the public. When I was part of my family's pack, I didn't need marks. Any wolf who met me would sense my affiliation at a glance.

But now I'm a lone wolf with a self-made pack. I shift and the sarong spreads open, showing off one of my thighs. I could put a tattoo there, something with symbols for each of us. Connor could be the sun and Trajan the moon, but then what am I?

That *is* the question of the hour.

Connor announces that he's going to accompany Smith to talk to someone from the Nosaka family and Sheena says it's time for her beauty sleep. I respond with something suitably snarky and then I'm left with Trajan and we're staring at each other across our beautiful living room. It's too early for bed and even with my wolf's ability to heal I'm not ready for another round of bumpin' uglies.

"Wanna watch more—"

"I didn't mean to make you angry." Trajan interrupts me. Shuts me right up, in fact.

He shifts in his seat as if he can't decide whether he's uncomfortable or not. "I'm ready to diversify and while restaurants are relatively high-risk, running a place aimed at the supernatural crowd appeals to me."

This is Trajan the cold and collected business-vampire talking, not the lover or the hitman/bodyguard. I miss the hitman, tbh, but I square my shoulders and try to respond as David-the-alpha-were-and-finance-major. "I'm not saying you shouldn't do exactly that. I just"—I shrug—"don't want to be handed something I didn't earn."

His expression is still forbidding, but something in his gaze softens. "Oh, you'll earn it, puppy, but take some time and think things through. There's no rush."

"All right, well…" *I guess it's not the time to suggest more Dancing with the Stars.* "Let me do some reading and I'll let you know."

Trajan heads for his office and off to the laptop I go. To do some reading. And not to play Half-Life 2.

Absolutely not.

I wake up an hour or so before sunset. Trajan's still asleep but Connor's already gone. He's left me a note, though.

Going to meet with Smith. Text me if you're willing to play junior investigator.

Text Connor? *What would I say?* My hand reaches for my phone on autopilot, but rather than text him I stand there staring at nothing. Trajan wants me to run a restaurant and Connor apparently meant it when he offered me a chance to be his partner. I'm torn between saying yes to both because Connor and Trajan have done so fucking much for me and refusing them both because I don't want another hand-out.

What do you want to do, David? My mind poses the question like I'm my own internal therapist. What do I want to do?

My phone chirps, startling me so badly I almost drop the damned thing. It's Sheena.

Get dressed. I'll be there in twenty. Try to look like you're related to the American Alpha.

I stare at my phone, unable to decide whether to text her back with a request for more information or to do what she says because otherwise she'll kick my ass. Deciding to treat this as a handy reason to avoid making a real decision, I jog up the stairs to my room.

My closet, however, doesn't want to play ball. From her snarky comment about how I should dress, she probably wants some kind of business suit. With my wardrobe spread between Seattle and LA – and a goodly chunk having gone up in smoke – the pickings are slim. I really miss my Fleuvog boots, because the stacked heel made me taller than pint-sized.

Sadly, they're just a memory. Besides, I *am* the son of the American Alpha, no matter what I choose to wear.

I settle on a pair of jeans so tight I need the slits in the knees to bend my legs, and a vintage polo in watermelon pink. I pull my too-long hair into a knot at the nape of my neck and put on a pair of tortoiseshell Ray-Bans and a pukka shell necklace. *Voila! Make it '80s, but NOW!*

Sheena texts me to say she's in the driveway and I stalk outside, because stalking is all I can do in these jeans. She drives a late-model CRV with a black box of I-probably-don't-want-to-know-what in the back seat. I climb in, ignoring her obligatory eye-roll.

"Your Mama taught you to dress like that?"

I give her all-black ensemble a snide once-over. "Yup."

My Mama taught me all kinds of things. She'd also reconnected me to my bank accounts and credit cards. Getting cut out of the pack had done a number on my finances, but she'd fixed it, saying I might not be pack, but I'm still family. I have a little savings and some room on my Visa. Getting a job is important, but I have time for Sheena's adventure.

She doesn't say much as we wind down out of the hills and onto Wilshire Boulevard. I can't help but fidget, and after one irritable huff too many, I snap. "Where the hell are we going?"

"Downtown."

"Well thank you very much. I feel so enlightened now."

"I have half a mind to take you to a Men's Wearhouse and make you buy a decent suit."

"Hey, my bits are covered. That'll have to do."

She huffs again and I count to ten. I mean, there's cryptic and then there's rude. "Is there a reason you're not telling me where we're going?"

"Because, sunshine, I'm a little nervous about our reception."

"That's...on point." I shoot her a sidelong glance. "Would you care to elaborate?"

"I'm not completely sure I can. I got a text from Lydia saying she's been called out by the leader of another pack and asking for back-up."

Okay, now I'm confused. "Lydia the lesbian biker chick?"

"Biker chick," she snorts. "I wouldn't say that to her face."

We roll on down Wilshire into Koreatown. "When you say someone called her out, what does that mean, exactly?"

"You're the werewolf. You tell me."

"I think it means someone wants to take over her pack."

"Maybe. I'm not sure." She negotiates our way around a driver who's a good fifteen years too old to be on the road. "Her pack is small, and she controls an area from Santa Monica Boulevard to the north and the Ten to the south, then Western Avenue to La Cienega. Apparently the Los Feliz pack wants a chunk of her territory."

I shrug, because yeah, werewolves gonna werewolf. "They offer her anything in return, or just threaten to kill her?"

"That's what we're going to find out." She pulls onto a side street and parks the car.

We're surrounded by three and four-story buildings housing every kind of business imaginable. On our immediate block, there's a mission, a sketchy looking hotel, a "wild foods" juice bar – whatever that means – and something called the Feather Palace. I elbow Sheena and point to it. "Might have to check that one out when we're done here."

"Whatever." Her frown is more serious than her eye roll. "I just want you present. Keep your mouth shut and when it's time, do your alpha mojo thing."

Alpha mojo thing? I'm not entirely sure what she means. If I'm called on to shift, more than likely my wolf will cooperate – *maybe* – but if all she needs is attitude, I can do that no problem. She heads for a warehouse with a faded sign saying *Nix Toyz* over the door. I follow her, throwing an extra swing in my stalk.

The place is big and fairly empty of anything that it would take to run a business. Instead, there are two clusters of people, each having staked out a section of the dusty floor. Lydia and three of her wolves are in the corner closest to the door, near a window where the late day sun glints off their black leather and chains.

Lydia's dark hair is streaked with grey and the skin around her eyes is creased, as if she's spent a lot of years staring at the sun. Her posture mixes cautious and bored, grounded in an inarguable pride. Her wolves share that pride, and together they're an imposing group.

The other group is busier, less organized. There's at least eight of them, none of them older than thirty, and at a glance, it's hard to tell which one is the alpha. I stare at them until they're all staring back, and that's how I figure it out. Seven of them look annoyed. The alpha looks amused.

He's not much older than me, but taller and rangy. He must be good in a fight or he wouldn't have four guys hanging around like some kind of Greek Row chorus.

And he must be good in bed or he wouldn't have a trio of women cat-clawing each other to be close to him.

Lydia'll take him without breaking a sweat.

Still not sure what I'm doing there, I trail behind Sheena. When Lydia catches sight of me, her lips twist in annoyance. "Jesus, Sheen. What'd you drag him in here for?"

"Back-up," Sheena says tersely, and we slide into position behind Lydia's weres.

"Hey, I called for a sitzung," the Los Feliz alpha says. "That's for wolves only. Tell your loser friends to wait outside."

Oh, my wolf does not like his tone of voice. Not at all. I don't say anything – Sheena told me to keep my mouth shut, so I do – but I let my gaze tell him he's a suckafish punk and his wolf would piss himself if he ever came across mine.

"Ground rules say I can have guests of my choosing, and while I don't remember choosing that one" – Lydia glares at me – "they can stay."

I meet her heat with a cocky grin. It's clear she doesn't want my help and I know darned well she doesn't need it. Maybe I'm only making Sheena happy, but whatever, I'll stay.

"All right, Lydia Sanchez, let's get this over with." The Los Feliz alpha speaks to Lydia but he's side-eyeing me. "I formally notified you of my intent to take control of the area around the Hollywood Forever cemetery, as far as North Highland Avenue and Wilshire Boulevard."

"And I told you to go fuck yourself."

Her stone cold tone makes me smile for real.

"Is that right? I should go fuck myself?" He steps into the neutral zone, one of his girlfriends hanging on his arm. "I think you could come over here and tell me how you really feel."

He's smirking like he has this in the bag. There's as many kinds of alphas as there are wolf packs, and I'm going to enjoy seeing Lydia turn this one into puppy chow.

Lydia strides forward, her three wolves maintaining their position. I like their discipline, especially compared with the lax and jeering frat boys from Los Feliz. Their alpha takes a moment to suck face with the girl on his arm, then sends her back to the others.

"We gonna do this?" he asks Lydia, hands clenched like he can't wait to throw the first punch.

She laughs. "No."

"Now see, you guys. The cemetery is ours."

Lydia reaches over and grabs a fistful of his shirt, dragging him forward till they're face to face. "The cemetery is mine, you little fuckwit. Do some goddamn homework before you challenge someone who might fight first and answer your questions after you're dead."

He shoves away from her. "What the fuck? I gave you notice the way I'm supposed to."

"Land's assigned by the Were Council, dumbass. There's one for the city and another for the state, all the way up to the American Alpha."

"American Alpha." His snort grates on my nerves. "You think the American fucking Alpha cares about your little piece of LA?"

With a not-very-apologetic grin at Sheena, I pull out my cell phone. "Want me to call him and ask?"

"Oh sure. Call the guy in charge."

I aim my comment at Lydia. "I could, but you don't need the help. Besides, watching you teach Spunky over there a lesson will be fun."

The Los Feliz alpha roars at my insult, but Lydia laughs. "You're trouble, Collins."

"Yes, ma'am." I bow in her direction. Sheena pokes me, hard enough to let me know she's exasperated but not hard enough to leave a bruise.

"Okay," Lydia says. "Here's what I'm going to do for you, son."

The Los Feliz alpha starts yelling at her, but she raises her hand and shuts him up. *See, that's how a real alpha operates.*

"You and your friends go back to your overpriced condos and get on the internet and look up the rules around claiming another pack's territory. You'll find you need to petition the City of Los Angeles Were Council, and if they approve it, you'll take it to the LA County Council. If they approve it, and that's a big ol' *if*, then you and me can negotiate a fair price."

He draws himself up like he hasn't just had his ass handed to him. "Or how about we just settle it in the ring."

The up and down look Lydia gives him should have flayed the meat right off his bones. "I don't think you want that, boy. I'd hate to mess up that pretty face."

"You're joking. I'll take you down, old woman, without even breaking a sweat."

Lydia and I share a glance, and I springboard off that little nudge of energy. My wolf and I might still be discovering what we can do without the Collins Family Pack around us, but it's harder to argue with genetics.

And I come from generations of alphas.

I stalk to the center of the floor, and without raising my voice, I tell the Los Feliz pack to kneel.

Three of the guys drop immediately, averting their eyes as if they can hide from their other pack members. I don't repeat myself, at least verbally. Instead I catch the eye of one of the girls and nod. She bends one knee and then the other. One of her friends tries to pull her back to standing, but I nod at her and she kneels, too.

That leaves one of the frat boys and the third girl. Without the strength of the Collins Pack around us, my wolf's retreating. I fight him, holding on and bringing them down with a raised eyebrow.

Then I turn to the pack's alpha. He's way more resistant than the others, and though I'm not as strong as I was when I so rudely bopped into Lydia's lesbian bar and made her kneel, I'm still a Collins. He and I get locked in a stare-down. I'm mostly faking it at this point, but damn. He breaks away from my gaze, and I've got him.

Slowly, moving like somebody's grandfather, the Los Feliz pack alpha kneels to me.

"Now apologize to Lydia, or you can meet me in the ring."

He doesn't look up, but he responds, "I'm sorry, ma'am," with enough sincerity that I let it go.

Lydia looks at me and grins, tipping her head toward the door.

"Now get the hell out of here, all of you," I say, and the Los Feliz pack scrambles to their feet.

They take off, all except the alpha. He stops in the door and glares at me. "We're not done," he says in a tone that's probably meant to be threatening.

I don't even respond.

I can't. I'm ready to keel over I'm so tired, which makes it hard not to be bitter about what I've lost. The previous version of David Collins had more power than he knew what to do with. Now I'm just a lone wolf with alpha tendencies.

"Let me know if he gives you any trouble," I say to Lydia. "He'll be fun to fuck with."

"Punks. Both of you. I don't need some pretty boy fighting my battles for me."

"Oh honey, no." I raise my hands in surrender. "You would have hurt that guy without trying. I just got annoyed at his disrespect."

She snorts and turns her glare on Sheena. "I asked for back-up, not this." She waves at me like I'm a cat or something.

"Stick a sock in it, Lyd." Sheena takes my arm and starts for the door. "Every wanna-be in this city thinks you're an easy target, and I figured for once we'd show them the kind of allies you really have."

"Ally, huh?"

"Always," I say. With Lydia and her wolves following us out the door, Sheena hustles me to her car.

CHAPTER SIX

CONNOR

I pull my rental car into the driveway even though I know David'll give me shit for it. The sun is mostly set but none of the lights on the main floor have been turned on. Even if Trajan hadn't risen yet, I can't imagine David sitting around in the dark.

He's not. I find a note on the side table in the foyer, the same place I'd left a note for him.

Kidnapped by Sheena. Be in touch soon.

I scratch my head at that one. *Sheena?* I suppose if I don't hear from him by midnight, I'll know who to call.

I crumple up David's note along with the one I left him and head for the kitchen. Smith and I had spent most of the afternoon interviewing various Nosakas. David's sense of smell might have been useful, but Sheena must have made him a better offer.

Though I can't quite imagine what that could be.

Poking through the cupboards, I find the coffee maker. If I'm going to spend the night retracing Adaline Nosaka's last steps, I need a boost.

The coffee maker burbles along, spreading its heavenly scent, and Trajan's footsteps thump down the stairs. His eyes are heavy with sleep and his hair, which is never completely tame, threatens to revolt.

"What's up?" His voice is raspy, as if he really has just risen.

"Making coffee so I can work all night."

He comes up behind me and wraps an arm around my waist. I lean into him, grateful for his strength. We'd been an odd match from the beginning, both of us secretive and neither one of us particularly demonstrative, but this – his cool presence with its essence of death – had always bolstered me.

"Where's David?" he murmurs, lips against the skin behind my ear.

He flicks me with his tongue and I gasp. "Dunno."

"Hmm." He drifts down, nuzzling along the side of my throat. "Odd of him to take off."

"Yeah." I say the word on a sigh. "Said Sheena kidnapped him."

Trajan stills, then snorts a laugh. "Do I want to know the details?"

He eases away from me, and I worry that I killed the mood. "I don't know any more than that. I left him a note asking if he was willing to help me and Smith, and he said he'd text me later."

"So I guess it's just you and me, then," he purrs in my ear.

The mood is definitely not dead until the coffee maker gives one final, exultant gurgle and goes silent. I pour myself a cup and reluctantly turn so I can lean against the counter. "Part of me feels bad for pushing him into the investigator thing, if that's not something he wants to do, but damn. We could really use his help."

"Cops don't have another wolf on staff?"

"Not one who was present at the crime scene and not one who's as powerful as David." I sigh into my coffee mug and we stand silent for a moment. It's comfortable, being here with Trajan, and not something I want to lose.

"Didn't you say you could take the form of a dog?"

I inhale a tense breath, frustrated that I hadn't told Trajan the truth from the beginning. I'd kept my nature secret out of a lifetime of habit, but now I have to admit that if we're going to make this work, I need to open up, at least a little. "Yeah, but it's not the same thing. David has two natures. It's natural for him to go from one to the other. For me it's more of a process." *Something I'd rather not get into in any detail.*

"He's said he relies on us to hold himself together when he shifts."

I smile to lighten the mood. "Glad to know we're good for something."

"He got pissed at me last night, too." Trajan rakes a hand through his hair as if he's going to be able to calm it down without some water and product. The vampire's aura is hard for me to read, but there are flickers I take to mean frustration. "He took offense at the fact that I'd made arrangements to view a possible restaurant rental without asking him if he'd like to be the manager first."

"But if you wanted to open a restaurant, you wouldn't necessarily need him, would you? I mean, The Club runs without you sleeping with the manager."

"Sure, but I guess I phrased it badly. Anyway…" He gives up on his hair and braces himself against the counter with his hands. His latent power is so apparent, even when he's as relaxed as he is right now, and I'm drawn to it.

Drawn to him. No matter what the cost.

"I guess we'll just have to wait and see when he gets back," I say.

"Yeah. We'll have to wait and see."

It's still too light out for Trajan to go into the living room, so we settle on either side of the kitchen's center island. For a minute I feel bad that I've got coffee and Trajan doesn't have some vampire equivalent, but then I remember how well he fed last night and let it go.

"So, I'm also thinking about buying a house, something big enough for the three of us."

I pause with the mug at my lips. "That's a big step."

He rests his elbows on the stone countertop, hands held palms-together as if he's praying. "The odds that one of us does something to piss Betancourt off are better than even, and I'd prefer we don't find ourselves out on the street."

"Can't argue with that." I weigh my next statement carefully. "I got a stack of cash when I left the Elites, so I could go in on it with you."

He doesn't answer right away and when he does, it's as if he's speaking in the middle of an internal debate.

"But if you contribute, David will want to, and what twenty-three-year-old has..." His words trail off, and I'm left with the feeling that there's more he doesn't want to say.

Which might be okay.

My phone chirps and it's Smith, wondering if I can meet him at some place called the MessHall

Kitchen in Los Feliz. One of Adaline's cousins is the manager and is willing to talk to us. I finish my coffee, pretty sure I need to respond to Trajan's offer in a more constructive way. Living in Betancourt's house gives our whole relationship a temporary feel. Buying something new? That's permanent.

"However we finance it, we should probably talk with David first."

Trajan grins at me from behind his praying hands. "I believe we've both learned that lesson."

"It'd be nice, though, having a stable place to live." I stand, pocketing my cell phone. "Your condo was big enough for both of us, but with three…I think a house would be better."

"Me too."

"I gotta go."

Trajan keeps his seat but reaches out for me. We clasp hands and I lean in for a kiss. Even that light brush of lips lights a spark in my belly. I lean into him, laughing softly. "I am yours, *mo shíorghrá*. Wherever you go, I will follow."

He holds my hand tighter. "What I want is for us to be together."

"Me too."

We're silent for a moment, letting our eyes do the talking, and then I make a break for it before one of us drags the other onto the floor. Climbing into the rental, I feel a twinge of disappointment that David's not around to make fun of my Taurus. "Ah well," I murmur. "He'll make up for it later."

Maps of LA designate our neighborhood as the Bird Streets. Not only are we high up in the Hollywood Hills, but the streets have names like Warbler, Thrush, and Skylark. Our house is on the rather un-birdlike Doheny Drive, and to get down to Sunset Boulevard, I have to navigate a steep, hairpin turn. At the center of the turn, a black SUV with tinted windows is parked across both lanes.

Poole is at the wheel.

Colonel Parker N. Poole, Commander in Chief of the Elites. I stop the rental car because he's not going to get out of my way. Hoping none of the neighbors need to get past our little roadblock, I climb out of the Taurus.

"Poole." I nod a greeting. He's got the classic square jaw and flattened nose of the Marine he used to be. Still has the regulation buzz cut, although the Securitas doesn't require it. Too many of its members can change their appearance at will.

"I'm angry, Mack, and I know you know why." He speaks the way some men shoot bullets, blunt and direct. "Though Brodie's such a flake I should have known I would need to talk to you myself."

"Yes, sir."

"I want you at headquarters in an hour or less. That's assuming the traffic in this hellhole will let us get anywhere."

My heart sinks. Smith needs the help a lot more than the Elites do. "Yes, sir."

Poole throws the big SUV into gear and pulls a U-turn, heading down the hill. Thankful we didn't cause any accidents, I follow. I also text Smith to tell him I'll be late.

Headquarters is on the ninth floor of a shiny silver office building near the Staples Center. I park in the lot underneath the building. There's a security guard in the lobby but Poole must have cleared me with him because the guard just waves me on. The elevator holds the aural shimmer left by all the beings who've used it, and I get off to face a bank of windows, just as the sun drops below the horizon.

Darkness reminds me of Trajan, and I get a bad feeling. A really bad feeling.

The door to headquarters is unlocked, the lobby empty. The lights are dim, although down the hallway to the right, there's an open door with light spilling through. I head in that direction, following the sound of voices.

I find Poole sitting at one end of a long table in a room that could have been the setting for a mid-century war movie. The furnishings are utilitarian at best and the walls covered with maps and black-and-white photographs. Poole's wearing an uncharacteristically formal black suit and tie, and the reason for his formality is seated at his right hand.

Ananda Pendragon, the Morrigan.

Shocked beyond thought, I can only bend a knee, sinking to the floor, my left hand raised to my forehead in respect.

"Get up, *meascach*." Her voice echoes as if three women spoke at once.

Halfbreed. I stand slowly, regretfully, not at all ready to face a living god, even if she is my many-times-great-grandmother. As a direct descendent of the Morrigan, my mother had a rebellious phase and briefly broke free of her family's control.

I'm a souvenir from those days.

"This one is your best?" Ananda Pendragon directs her question at Poole.

"Of course." He looks surprised. "I wouldn't waste your time with less."

"I see." She nods and turns her attention to me. Her eyes are as dark as her midnight hair and her fingernails are scarlet. When I was a child, I'd had little contact with the old ones, the living gods. My mother and her parents had kept me separate, a blemish on the beauty of the Tuatha Dé Danann. My interest in joining the Elites had come as almost a relief, as if my family hoped a glorious death in battle would redeem the half of my soul that didn't belong to them.

Not that I have a clue who the other half belongs to.

Ananda Pendragon's dagger-like finger points at me. "Listen, *meascach*. There isn't much time. There's a clan of vampires in this city who are determined to upset the balance between the races. They have kidnapped an elven princess, and if she is not returned safely, there will be war."

"Yes, *cathaoirleach*. I was assigned the princess's case before—"

Poole interrupts me. "We will make finding the princess our top priority."

"It's not already?"

"Of course, ma'am, but we also have—"

"You have nothing else. *Nothing*. If the elves declare war on the vampires, the whole world will suffer. I'll come myself and destroy every vampire in this city before I let that happen."

Facing down a god is intimidating, but still I have to ask, "How do you know it's the vampires who have the princess?"

She gives me the kind of look someone would give a dog who decided to sit up and speak. "Because it's written in the wind."

The wind? "You're going to destroy all the vampires in LA because you dreamt one of them was involved?"

Poole eases back in his chair. He might be holding his breath, too, because only an idiot questions a god.

Ananda Pendragon straightens. Her hair begins to float, like she's caught in a breeze no one else can feel. "You will die too, *meascach*." Instead of the echoes of three women, this time her voice holds a chorus.

"I *will* die, at some point. We all will, except you, *cathaoirleach*, but threatening to destroy people when we have no actual proof they're involved is a problem."

"Mack." Poole whispers my nickname.

"I'm sorry, Colonel, but if I'm going to be of use to you, we need to be working from the same playbook."

"You will do as you're told." Power fills Ananda Pendragon's voice.

I stand. Maybe growing up hidden away from the family gods had been a good thing after all. While the Morrigan frankly terrifies me, getting pushed around just pisses me off. "And why do you care, Ananda Pendragon, if the elves and the vampires start a fight? There are only a few Tuatha in the city of Los Angeles." Not remote enough. I'd always figured they didn't like the competition from so many other supes. "And as far as I know, you don't like either the elves or the vampires. What's your stake here?"

She stands, too, her hair going wild and her eyes glowing red. "My reason doesn't matter to such as you. Find the princess or I'll start killing vampires, and…" — she draws a sigil in the air — "one called Trajan Gall will be the first to die."

A door appears to her left, glossy black and surrounded by flames. She pushes it open and steps through, leaving us surrounded by sickly-sweet smelling smoke.

"You know," Poole says, drumming his fingers on the table, "if you had just come the first time Brodie asked, we might have avoided some of this."

"If he hadn't wrecked my car, I might have been more agreeable."

"What?"

"Nothing." I sink into a seat, though I'd rather run. "So I'm really looking for the same princess who went missing two years ago?" Because calling us the Elites implies we're good at what we do.

"Yes. Princess Tatiana Ivanova."

"And no one picked up the investigation?"

Poole presses his lips together and stares off into space. I give him a couple beats to answer then move on to my next big point. "Does all this mean I'm back on the team?"

"Well, yes and no." After a heavy exhale, he pulls a pen and a business card out of his pocket and scribbles something. "Here."

I take it from him. The business card is his – Colonel Parker N. Poole etc. etc. – and the phone number on the back has a San Francisco area code.

"You are not back on the team, Mack, but you have all the resources of the Elites at your disposal."

"Do I get to charge you my private eye rates?"

He huffs a laugh and puts the pen back in his pocket. "I want you to work fast, and I want you to keep this investigation a secret, especially from your boyfriend."

"What?"

"Your memory can't be that bad. You're the one who uncovered a possible link between the princess and Jacques Betancourt."

"But Trajan won't tell Betancourt anything."

"Are you sure? One hundred percent?" Poole's aura hardens, turning a grim grey. "If a vampire's maker demands something, the vampire has no choice but to comply. I'm asking you to honor the oath you made to my command."

The oath I'd sworn when I was nineteen and had nowhere else to turn. He looks at me expectantly, but I can't force out a *Yes, sir* to save my life. Instead, I manage a tight, "I don't like this." More accurately, I hate that he's playing the oath card.

The last time Poole thought I'd made Betancourt's radar, I'd had to fake my own death.

Poole blinks, the faintest glimmer of pink threading through the ominous grey of his aura. "I know I'm asking a lot, but you're the closest link to Betancourt that I've got. And I have to say"—he shrugs—"your great-great-whatever grandmother is scary as hell. I don't want my team to have anything to do with her if I can help it."

I clamp my jaw shut to keep from popping off with an inappropriate opinion.

He takes my silence as agreement and tries to smile. "Now get the hell out of here and go find that princess."

Since I still can't trust myself to speak, I head for the door.

"I'll email you a packet with what little information we've gathered since you had the case," he says. "Don't hesitate to call me, but I'm serious when I say you need to keep this a secret."

I leave without giving him the satisfaction of a response. I text Smith on my way to the car. He's on his way to talk to the restaurant manager and we decide I can meet him there. Google says it'll take me twenty minutes to get there on the freeway but like a good Angeleno, I take surface streets.

Rolling along Sunset Boulevard gives me time to think. I need a strategy, one that honors the promise Poole demanded without betraying Trajan's trust. I mean, I'm not happy about any of this, but Poole's not wrong about the influence Betancourt has over Trajan.

Although two years ago I'd believed Poole when he said he had intel that my cover had been blown. To keep me – and indirectly Trajan – safe, I needed to "die." But if Jacques Betancourt really knew I'd been investigating him, he'd have taken me out of the game as soon as I reappeared.

Which means that either Poole's intel was wrong or that Betancourt had nothing to do with the princess's disappearance. Regardless, disappearing two years ago was a waste of time and effort.

Not that I can tell Trajan any of that.

The harsh reality makes me grimace. An hour ago, I wished I'd been honest with Trajan from the start and now I'm back in the business of keeping secrets. *Just like last time.*

Promising myself I'll tell him as soon as it's safe, I start mentally organizing the information I have so far and wondering if the team has learned anything useful over the last two years. More importantly, in a battle between the vampires and the elves, who wins? And why does the Morrigan care anyway? Maybe Smith has heard a rumor that might help. With that in mind, I turn right to head for the MessHall Kitchen.

I need to find the princess before she destroys my life.

An hour or so later, Smith and I leave the artfully deconstructed restaurant after having a non-productive conversation with one of Adaline Nosaka's cousins. He'd been polite and appropriately saddened by his cousin's death, but he had no idea who would have done the deed.

"Do you want to divide and conquer tomorrow?" Smith tugs off his blazer, revealing a white shirt with a Hang Ten logo embroidered on the left breast.

"What do you mean?"

"We start in the morning and one of us goes back through the list of Nosaka's friends and relatives and the other chases down the owner of the strip mall where the body was found."

I press the key fob and the rental car chirps to life. The strip mall's owner had been suspiciously vague about both his whereabouts and his willingness to be interviewed. "Let me try David again. If he'll agree to go with me to interview the owner, he might catch a scent that'll be useful."

"David's your…"

"Boyfriend," I say with confidence. "David Collins. He's a werewolf, and—"

"Oh yeah, the Alpha's son. I heard he had a dust-up with his uncle last spring."

I suppress a sigh. David's reputation precedes him.

"I mean," Smith continues, "you're right about him being a good tracker. If you can bring him on, that'd be awesome."

Something about Smith's enthusiasm makes me think he's been feeling a little lonely as the only supe at the LAPD. Which makes me ask, "What is your gift, if you don't mind my asking?"

Smith's perma-tan skin turns smooth and grey, his head elongates, and a double row of razer sharp teeth turn his grin into the fearsome mouth of a shark.

His mouth opens and I take a reflexive step away. In a flash, Smith is back and grinning at me.

"On land it's mostly a party trick but watch out if you come across me in the water," he says.

"I will."

He laughs louder. "Nah, Mack, you're good. I mean, being a shark shifter got me this liaison gig, so I can't complain."

We say goodnight after promising to connect in the morning.

CHAPTER SEVEN

Trajan

Scrolling through my playlists, I find a Handel opera featuring Orlinksi, a young countertenor who is both too beautiful and too talented to be human. They say he is, though I have to think there's fey blood somewhere in his family tree.

After spending most of the night working with Smith, Connor's out the door as soon as I rise. He said something about talking an adolescent nymph out of her neighbor's pool. David has gone for a run, so I have Jacques' huge house all to myself. There's business I could be attending to, but instead I lounge on the big sofa facing the windows. Looking out over the city to the ocean's swath of velvet black, I use the remote to turn the volume up as high as it will go.

Truth be told, I'm feeling useless. I'm a vampire, damnit, yet I've been following after my two lovers like some kind of undead cheering squad. I'm not hungry. I have all my needs met. So what is it I want?

I want to deserve someone as young and beautiful as David Collins and I want to trust Connor the way I used to.

That's the real rub, right there. The lack of trust.

He says he's going to interview a suspect and I wonder if he'll come back, or if I'll be called to view his falsely lifeless body at the city morgue. Tonight, when he got called out, I came close to inserting myself into a situation where I had no business, simply because I couldn't bear to see him leave.

I tap my thumb against the smooth leather seat. I need to move past this or I'll ruin everything.

"What the hell is this?"

David's voice breaks the spell of my thoughts.

"Can you turn it down just a little? Jesus."

I turn the stereo down and he grins at me. "Sorry."

"I mean, I'm sure it's the good stuff, but maybe we don't need quite so much of it."

Sighing, I pat the seat next to me. "Come watch the ocean and talk to me."

He plops next to me, massaging his neck with one hand. He's warm and slightly damp, and when I scoot him around and take over the massage, his head drops forward as if someone has cut a puppet's string.

"Our next house needs to be on flatter ground."

"Mmhmm."

David exhales. "Although it is nice to be able to go running without a wet suit. At this time of year, it's pouring rain in Seattle."

He's keeping track of the weather back home. "You miss it."

"Some." He stiffens and I dig with my thumbs into the thick bands of muscle running up the back of his neck. His answering groan tells me I hit the spot.

"We could visit."

He's silent for a beat. "At some point I'll need to clean out my apartment and pack up the rest of my clothes."

I spread my hands to focus on his shoulders. "Maybe after Connor's not ass deep in murder."

"Yeah." He stretches under my touch. "I wonder if they're making any progress."

"Me too." I don't share the rest of my uncertainty because it's pointless. Just because I don't trust Connor doesn't mean David shouldn't. "We could run over to the club, if you want. I need to talk with the manager." It's a conversation that could happen by text, but I don't want to deal with hours of unoccupied time. I'll spend too much of it wondering what Connor's really up to.

David catches my hands and pulls me closer. I rest my chin on his shoulder, and we sit quiet. "What?" I ask. His mind has gone somewhere else, and I wish I could follow.

"Nothing." He squeezes my fingers. "Let me grab a shower and we can go."

He hops up from the couch and has hit the stairs before I can respond. I follow him more slowly and while he showers, I do my best to dress like the owner of a fairly successful sex club. I even break out an Armani jacket, which was a good call. David's shiny green trousers, ruffled yellow blouse that started life in a woman's closet, and bright white kicks could have stepped off a high-fashion runway.

"God, you're gorgeous," I murmur, and he flashes me a megawatt smile.

"And you"—he lays his palms against my chest—"are the sexiest hitman I've ever seen."

I rut against him a couple times, playing, although it wouldn't take much to make me want to slide him out of those slick trousers and have my way with him. "We better go."

He rises up on his toes and kisses me. "C'mon, Guido. You've got a club to run."

Arm in arm, we head for the Range Rover. Me, an overpriced assassin, and him, a vision of youth and beauty.

Traffic is typically awful, so we have plenty of time to get lost in our own thoughts. David's put something jittery on the stereo, amplifying my nerves. "Well, we're here." I park next to our bartender's pickup truck and turn the engine off. "Are you ready?"

"Why wouldn't I be?" David's confidence rings false.

"Because this is the first time we've been here together in a long time."

He shoots me a wicked grin. "And the last time we were here together, you damn near jacked me off at the bar."

I laughed, a little embarrassed. "Yeah, but you were so horny."

"True." He shakes his head, flipping a wayward lock of hair out of his face. "Are you going to try the same thing again tonight?"

I let my smile grow more serious. "Not tonight. I do want to show you off a little, though, and maybe see if you're into it."

"Into what?"

I laugh at his wide-eyed surprise. "Follow me and see."

One thing Sheena and I agreed on when we opened The Club is that it should have a little of everything. We allow more sex than some BDSM clubs, and although we stock toys for our guests to use, we allow them to bring their own, too. Supernaturals are welcome, as long as they don't harm the humans, and our bouncers and dungeon monitors are very good at keeping everyone in line.

Tonight's doorman is new, though he recognizes me and waves us in. The familiar stark interior greets us and I scan the crowd, looking for anyone I recognize.

The Club has a good-sized common area. A single bartender presides over the long bar, which is easy to do because all he serves is soda and water. Even though it's Sunday night, customers fill the high-top tables and a few stand against the wall. On our way by, I wave to the bartender and nod at the bouncer lurking in the corner, keeping an unobtrusive eye on things.

The manager's office is upstairs. A U-shaped upper balcony overlooks both the common area and the hallway to the scene rooms. We have the occasional guests who want to get it on in the common area, but most prefer the rooms.

You have to be something of an exhibitionist to play in front of an audience.

We reach the front office, where a bouncer sits in front of a bank of screens, fed by the security cameras in each room. He's supposed to be keeping an eye on the action, though our arrival has him shoving his phone out of sight.

Most of the rooms are empty, but one monitor shows a scene in progress. A man is bent over a horse with his hands in cuffs and a spreader bar between his legs. A statuesque brunette – not Sheena – is wearing a strap-on, high heels, and a thong, and she's giving him her best.

David slows, then stops in front of the active screen. The sound is turned low, but the man's muffled grunts still carry, although the woman's low commands are harder to hear.

"If you ever wanted to try that, you know…" I let my words fade. I can't read his expression, although the tell-tale bulge in his jeans hints that he's not totally opposed to the idea. The woman reaches down and grabs her play partner's balls, hard enough to make him cry out. David twitches as if he's feeling the man's pain.

She thrusts in all the way, then unbuckles the belt and steps away, leaving the dildo in his ass. Coming to the front of the table, she bends over in front of him and spreads her legs. He starts to suck her pussy through the thong and David makes a face.

"I mean, you wouldn't have to play with a woman."

Below, the woman pivots on her heel. She grabs a fistful of the man's hair, jerks his head up, and slaps him, hard. She's shouting something about how worthless he is and he takes it. She hits him again, hard enough to leave a pink splotch on his cheek.

I'm keeping an eye on the scene but I'm also watching David. He frowns, his gaze locked on the screen.

"You choose your partner and the role you play."

He shoots me a puzzled glance. "Why would I do that?"

"Might be fun to explore your kinky side."

That makes him laugh. "I spend most nights as the filling in a Tray and Connor sandwich. That's kinky enough for me."

His dismissal leaves me both frustrated and pleased. I can't deny that having him in bed with me and Connor is one of the great pleasures in all of my long life. Still, I worry that he'll wake up one day and hate us for trapping him when he should be getting his ya-yas out.

Unless I'm one ya and Connor's the other. "Come on," I say, and lead him into the rear office. The manager and I have a brief conversation. He and David haven't met before, but the conversation is about money, so I'm okay with David listening in. I'm still hoping he'll agree to represent me during daylight hours.

The scene has wrapped up by the time we leave the office and we make a silent trip to the car. Only when we're well on our way to the house does David speak.

"Why do you run a club like this?"

"Because I wanted to have a reason to meet people and, you know, stay in touch with what's going on. Customers might not want to visit a fine-dining restaurant run by a vampire, but for a sex club, my nature would be an attraction." My answer surprises me a little, but that doesn't make it any less true.

"Makes sense," he says, "but you must get off on it a little."

Do I? I shrug. "Connor isn't into kink at all, and I was completely happy in a monogamous relationship with him." *Except for the lies.* "If you were to say you wanted to try this or that, I'd help, but if you don't, no problem."

David spends the rest of the drive staring out the window. When we get back to the house, he turns to me, his expression serious.

"Do you like getting tied up and smacked around?"

"Nope."

"That's what I thought." He unbuckles his seatbelt. "I'm pretty sure I'd hate it, and I don't want to do something to someone else if I won't let them do it to me."

"But what if that someone else asked you really, really nicely?"

He gives an exasperated snort. "I'd tell them to talk to Sheena."

"But you're okay with bottoming for me and Connor." Which is a different thing, but not entirely unrelated.

"As long as you don't tie me up first." His grin is the first spark of humor he's shown since we got to the club.

I hold my breath, waiting to see how he'll handle my next question. "But do you ever want to top one of us?"

His eyes turn sly and a little embarrassed. "Maybe."

With that, he jumps out of the Range Rover. I follow, amused by his reaction. I rarely bottom, but if David Collins asked me really nice, I just might.

CHAPTER EIGHT

Next time Trajan casually asks me to run to the club with him, I'm going to be busy getting a manicure or organizing my lipsticks by age and brand or something.

FFS.

It's not like I don't enjoy sex, because *hello*, I totally do. Watching that relatively ordinary-looking guy taking it in the ass from a woman whose big hair had come straight out of 1988, though? Not my thing.

Although Trajan's little unconscious squirm when I said I might want to top him is the high point of my night. Such a funny guy, my vampire. Trying to be all tough and hitman-adjacent, but underneath the brooding stare and the hair product, he's kind of a cinnamon roll.

I'd topped guys before, and I might do Tray under the right circumstances. In the meantime, there's a dead kitsune and who knows what all murder and mayhem to try to solve.

The next day I get up as soon as I hear someone moving around. I'm in my own room, for once, and the sun's still up so those footsteps must belong to Connor. I throw a silk robe over my nonexistent sleepy-time clothes and find him in the kitchen, making one of his gourmet smoothies. I make a face at the color – a vaguely beige shade of grey – but when he offers, I grab a glass.

"Don't tell me what's in this," I say, and take a swig. It's…not bad. I can almost feel the vitamins and minerals racing to buff my muscles. He looks tired, no, more than that. Weary. His hair is damp and combed straight back from his face and his stubble is as long as George Michael's on the cover of Faith.

Because yes, I am familiar with the classics like that.

I let him take a couple swallows before hitting him with my questions. Or at least some of my questions. There are some things that I don't want to ask unless I've had time to soften him up first. But then he beats me to the punch.

"What's on your agenda for today?"

"I was just going to ask you the same thing. If you need a sidekick, I'm happy to play Boy Investigator."

He gives me a sharp nod, as if he's satisfied with my offer. "Always happy to have a partner, but maybe" — he gives me a once-over that's way too hot — "put some clothes on. I have an appointment to meet with Adaline Nosaka's best friend, and I was hoping you could come with me."

While I can't imagine a reality where I'd be helpful in that kind of situation, I down the rest of the mystery smoothie and head for the stairs. Adaline was a respectable woman, so her best friend must be, too. With that in mind, I comb my hair into a neat ponytail at the nape of my neck. I put on jeans that only have one knee ripped out and a vintage motherfucking pinstriped button-down.

A pair of penny loafers complete the look in a way that makes me smile, and I strut downstairs, already grinning because I know Connor will be amused.

Connor's waiting for me in the kitchen. "You ready to" — he pinches his lips together and I know he's trying not to grin — "go?"

"Lead on, Sherlock."

He does, and as I follow I wonder how he managed to find a pair of plain khaki pants that fit his ass so beautifully. His own button-down broadens his shoulders and his brown belt narrows his waist.

"There oughta be a law," I murmur.

He glances at me. "What?"

I just laugh. Then we get to his car and I laugh harder. "You willingly rented a Ford Taurus? I can't even with you, Connor MacPherson. Don't you have any pride?" Connor just smirks at me, the saucy bastard, making me roll my eyes. "Clearly you have none whatsoever. What am I going to do with you?"

It's a rhetorical question and wisely, he doesn't answer. "You cannot expect me to ride in that thing."

He notches his hands on his hips and fakes a scowl. "Okay, I'll make you a deal. When our murderer is safe in jail, you and I can go out and test drive a few new vehicles."

"Oh honey, we most certainly will."

We climb in and I sniff at the stale scent, hoping Connor's sexy whiskey aroma will take over soon. There's a dark spot on the floorboard, a spill left by a previous occupant. Connor's not terribly talkative, other than to tell me that first we're visiting a contact he got from Stone, so I spend the drive imagining what could have left that stain. Blood, most likely. From there, I progress to reasons blood gets spilled, and then I move on to the body we'd discovered.

That leads me to all kinds of unpleasantness, and I'm grateful when Connor pulls into the parking lot of a strip mall on Ventura Boulevard, because *wow* my thoughts got depressing.

"Do we have a strategy? Like, is one of us the good cop and the other the bad cop?"

"Not sure."

"Well look, let's keep things simple. I am definitely the good cop. Remember that." I climb out of that sad Ford Taurus. If Connor responds, I don't hear him.

Of course, once I'm standing in the parking lot, I have to wait for him because I don't know where we're going. He gets out and inclines his head toward a place called Ron's Books and Trinkets.

"Trinkets? I want a trinket," I say, and follow Connor's lead. He opens the door for me and I can't help rubbing up against him on my way by.

"Behave," he says through gritted teeth, but before I can come up with an appropriate response, I'm overcome by the scene in front of me.

There are books. Like, hundreds of books. They fill shelves and they're stacked on the floor, and there are boxes under a window that I know intuitively are filled with more. There's also a rack of vintage postcards and one of old baseball trading cards, and a whole shelf dedicated to comic books.

And that's just what my first glance takes in. "This is crazy," I whisper.

Connor pats my shoulder on his way deeper into the store. There's a counter running down the left wall, and that's where he's headed. I follow, although I really want to poke around more slowly. The dusty smell of old books and the dim lighting have me intoxicated.

A display of vintage jewelry near the cash register catches my attention. There's a Black man behind the register, Connor's apparent destination. As we close in on him, the old book smell gives way to another.

Magic.

I glance at Connor but his expression hasn't changed.

"Excuse me," Connor approaches the counter. "I'm wondering if I could ask you a few questions."

The witch? Warlock? Whatever he is, he waits a couple heart beats, as if he's weighing Connor's request. I mean, we're the only people in the store. It's not like he can't afford to take five minutes away from pricing the pile of junk spread over the counter.

I might even buy some jewelry if he plays his cards right.

"What can I do for you?" he says finally. He's short and stocky, a Dead Kennedys tee stretched tight over his belly.

Connor introduces us and hands him a business card. "I got your name from Stone Parata. He said you hear a lot of things, and you might know something about a murder victim, Adaline Nosaka."

The witch – or whatever – listens to all of that without giving us his name, and when Connor finishes, he doesn't move for a good fifteen seconds.

"You said his name is Collins?" The witch speaks to Connor but points at me.

"Mmhm."

"Weird." His expression takes on the barest glimmer of humor.

"Why?" I ask, more annoyed than anything else.

"Someone told me a wolf from the Collins pack has a target on his back."

"I'm not part of the Collins pack." The words hurt to speak out loud.

The witch's grin turns mocking. "Well then, pretty boy, it can't be you."

I keep my eyes on the pile of old pipes, strings of plastic pearls, and silverware that might be real silver that covers the countertop. Mentally, though, I'm weighing the odds that I am the Collins with the target on his back, and whether one of my uncle's allies is looking for revenge. Dad would have cleaned house after the *beurteilung*. He couldn't afford not to.

Right?

"Who told you this?" Connor asks.

The witch gives him an expectant look but doesn't volunteer any new information. After a minute or so of this stand-off, Connor gives an exasperated snort and pulls out his wallet. He lays a couple of twenties across two old pipes that look like they're made from real corncobs, and asks the question again. "Does that help your memory?"

The witch pockets the money with a smirk. "Whoever he is, he's probably in the wind by now."

"What else have you heard?" Connor asks. "Do you know anything about Adaline Nosaka?"

"Now that's an interesting question." The witch – who still hasn't given us his name – runs his fingers through a box of rhinestones near the cash register. "I don't know who did her, but word is she's only the first."

Connor's intensity would wilt a lesser – or smarter – man. "The first victim?"

"So they say."

"Tell me more."

I lean forward, arms crossed, hoping I can motivate him to answer. Better than standing there like a bump on a log.

The witch blows a kiss at me, which makes me recoil. Connor heaves another sigh and puts two more twenties on the counter.

"I appreciate your generosity"—the witch snatches up the money and stuffs it away—"but that's really all I know. Adaline Nosaka might not have been quite as nice as she seemed, but she didn't deserve what happened to her, either."

I give him my best bitchy look. "You owe us."

"What?" The witch doesn't seem to be impressed by my efforts.

"Connor just gave you forty dollars and you responded by saying you didn't know anything else. That means you owe us information." I raise my chin, daring him to hit me. "That also means we'll be back."

I take that as my cue to leave. Connor doesn't follow right away, but he's out by the car soon enough that I didn't miss anything important. The car chirps and I climb in. Only when we're both buckled into our seats do I turn to him. "So?"

"What happened to you being the good cop?"

"He annoyed me."

Connor occupies himself with checking left and right before backing out of our parking spot, but he's grinning as he does it.

"Wonder what else he was selling in there."

Connor's grin fades. "What do you mean?"

"The whole place stank of magic."

He guns the engine, jerking us out into a break in the flow of traffic. "Didn't notice."

"Really?" His frown wipes the smile off my face.

"Not a whiff." He might be trying for humor, but he misses the mark. "I didn't *smell* anything except mildewed books and maybe some incense."

"That's odd."

"Look, I'm not like you. When I was with the Elites, I carried a fucking sensor so I didn't miss shit like that."

"Good thing I'm around, then." I give him finger guns, but his expression says he's not sold on my admittedly snarky reassurance. "Maybe they'd let you borrow one?"

"Won't need to as long as I've got you around."

He says it lightly, like he wants me to think this is no big deal. We break with our surface-streets-only tradition and get on the freeway.

The silence between us stretches long enough to make me twitchy, and I jump when Connor finally speaks. "I should have seen something in his aura, anyway."

"His what?"

"His aura." Connor's staring hard at the road ahead of us. "The energy surrounding him."

"You can see that? I didn't know that was a real thing." I chew on my lip for a second. "What's mine look like? Is it pretty?"

"Gorgeous," he says, his lips twitching into something like a smile, and I finally feel like I can exhale. I want to ask him how he learned to see auras and what the skill is good for and a couple hundred other things, but he's finally lost the crease between his brows so I save my questions for later.

Connor MacPherson, Private Eye and Super Enigma. I thought the vampire was supposed to be the mysterious one. Compared with Connor, though, Trajan's an open book. We lapse into a more-or-less companionable silence. I spend time wondering which Collins werewolf the witch meant and how much Connor really misses the Elites, and Siri tells us how many miles we have till our exit.

When Siri declares that we have reached our destination, Connor parallel parks us in front of a gracious hacienda style home in Pasadena. He hasn't said anything, but the clipped way he shuts off the engine makes me think he's still frustrated.

"Okay, when we go in there, let me talk, and I want you to memorize everything you see and hear and smell."

"Whatever you say, Sherlock."

I can be a good Watson. Promise.

The front yard is small and well-manicured. Small boxwood shrubs line a slate path leading to the front door, a heavy slab of oak with a circular knocker in the middle. Connor reaches for the knocker and the door swings open.

"Oops." Nothing good ever came from a door that opens by itself. The smell of death rolls across the threshold, so that when Connor takes a step forward, I grab him. "Better call the cops, first."

He gives the door another nudge. "Is it that bad?"

I force myself to take a deep inhale. "Worse."

He mutters, "Calling Smith" and pivots so he's facing the street. I grab my phone and shine the flashlight through the open doorway, without actually going inside. The foyer has a door on each side. Through one there's a couch and a flat-screen TV, and the other door is closed. Directly ahead, there's an arched passageway leading deeper into the house. I can't see anyone, but there's a puddle on the floor that from my angle looks an awful lot like blood.

"Worse than that, even," I whisper.

CHAPTER NINE

Two hours later, I've come to a startling conclusion. Murder is boring. Connor called Smith, who made us promise not to leave the scene. Apparently, Pasadena has its own police force, but not a supernatural liaison, so the three of us – Connor, and Smith, and I – get plenty of side-eye while the incident team rolls into gear.

By some miracle, Smith gets permission for me to view the victim. "You don't have to stay in there long. In fact, it'd be better if you got in and out as quickly as possible. I need you to tell me if you smell anything similar to Adaline Nosaka."

To say I don't want to go into that house is an enormous understatement. More accurately, I'd rather shave my head and buy a Taurus than go into that house.

"Sure. Just give me a minute."

I spend some time communing with the boxwood hedge, then nod at Smith. "Ready."

Only the hedge hears my spoiled little boy rant about having to do things I don't want to, and the hedge isn't talking.

The mood in the house has changed. Instead of emptiness, there's hubbub. Instead of dim spaces, the rooms are lit by harsh halogen spotlights.

Instead of a lively interview with Adaline Nosaka's bestie, there's the body of a selkie in her human form, her face covered by her pelt.

Maybe I should take Trajan up on his offer.

Gathering my 'nads, I stand next to the body. I shut my eyes so nothing distracts my sense of smell. Under the broad swath blood leaves across my senses, there's a salty ocean scent that's likely the selkie herself. Humans, but no more than I'd expect from the incident team. A trace of smoke which might be Smith. I'd smelled something similar near Adaline Nosaka, but then he'd been at that scene, too.

No one scent says *Hi, I'm your killer*, which is frustrating. I try for another couple minutes, then give up in disgust.

I suck at this.

Smith is busy with one of the homicide detectives. I catch his eye and mouth, "Nothing," and at his nod, I beat feet away from the scene.

A small crowd has gathered on the street in front of the house. I find Connor standing in the middle of them, chatting up one of the neighbors.

"First Adaline, and now Monica. This is just so sad."

The woman at Connor's elbow looks to be the same generation as Adaline, although she reads to me as wholly human. Connor's expression reads as sincerely sympathetic. "They've been friends a long time," he prompts.

"Oh my gosh, yes. I think they went back to high school."

"You knew them both?"

"We're in the same wine group. Ada has a knack for choosing great wines, and Monica has a knack for drinking them." She doesn't seem to notice she's referred to the two dead women in the present tense.

Connor asks her whether their husbands get along and gets a dissertation on Monica's dating life and how her first husband and Adaline's only husband are still close. "Monica and her ex had something of a competition to see who could bring the youngest date to wine group."

The crew from the medical examiner rolls a gurney into the house and Connor's informant grows quiet. "I'll miss them," she says, her eyes growing damp. "They were perfectly lovely, and now they're gone."

She breaks off and, giving Connor a watery smile, she leaves the little cluster of neighbors.

"Do you suppose she knew they were supes?" I ask.

He watches her go, his frown thoughtful. "Is she?"

"I didn't pick up anything but human."

"Me neither." He scratches at his George Michael facial hair. "Should have asked her if she knew who might want to hurt them."

Given that my knowledge of detective work is limited to a few episodes of NCIS, I'm hesitant to volunteer anything, except I'm me, so I do. "See what house she goes into and we'll stop by tomorrow and ask a few more questions."

"Good thought." He pulls out a small notebook and pencil and jots down her address. "Smith is going to have a long list of people to talk to, so he'll appreciate the help."

He catches my elbow and leads me gently out of the cluster of people. "Did you get anything in the house?"

Speaking quietly, I share my lack of useful information. We head for Smith, who's following the loaded gurney out of the house.

Blood and ocean. The body snags my attention and I draw in a deep breath, hoping to pick up something new, something valuable. A Tesla Model S pulls up to the curb next to us and a guy climbs out. He's older than me, but not by much. "Monica? What's going on?"

A pair of Pasadena detectives intercept him and Smith waves us toward the street. We walk half a block or so, where we won't be overhead by the neighbors. Though most of them are fixated on the scene with the young man, who's getting increasingly hysterical and blocking the gurney from its destination in the ME's van.

"Divide and conquer?" Connor asks Smith.

He nods, his mustache drooping. "I'll let the locals do their thing. Their lead guy promised to send me copies of all the statements they take, and I figured you and I could make a second pass tomorrow."

"Sounds good."

The sun set an hour or so ago, but as Connor and I amble toward his fancy Ford Taurus, weariness washes over me. I'd been awake till almost dawn with Trajan, then primed myself to leap up as soon as I heard Connor moving around. Kinky sex and murder; it was a lot to take in. Underneath the tired, though, I'm angry. *Who murders a selkie?* That's some serious bullshit. "It feels weird to take the rest of the night off."

"Who said anything about that?" Connor hits the keyfob and the Taurus cheeps back at him. "We might have to wait until the human police work through the interview list, but there's plenty we can be doing."

"Such as?"

"The victims have been friends since high school, and it's unlikely their murders are unrelated."

"Huh. Yeah." I stop to do some mental math. Given the victims' approximate ages, there are forty-some years of friendship to sort through to find a motive for their deaths. Connor puts the car in gear and I start mentally organizing a web search.

We're heading up Doheny Street when he shoots me a glance. "I'm going to drop you off, and then I have something I need to take care of."

"Anything I can help you with?"

"Nah." He sounds casual but there's tension in his jaw and across his shoulders. I try to come up with an argument that'll get him into the house with me, but I can't.

Connor doesn't even get out of the car. He drops me off in front of Jacques' big house and promises he'll return soon. I'd give something expensive to know what his little errand is about.

Don't worry about it, David. I just need to check on one thing.

And I wouldn't worry, dumbass, if you hadn't told me specifically not to. Connor never defends himself against my mental snark, which is probably just as well.

Inside, I find a note from Trajan saying he'd gone to view another possible restaurant space. I'm amused by how consistently we leave notes to each other, like we're an old married couple…or thruple, I guess. At any rate, I'm not accustomed to rattling around this big ol' barn by myself. I grab my laptop, an old UCLA sweatshirt, and a bottle of seltzer and settle in at the wrought iron café table near the pool. The air is cooler than it had been during the day, but for someone who'd grown up in Seattle, the mid-sixties temperature is almost warm.

Jonesing for a cigarette it's not worth the hassle to smoke, I keep my hands busy by starting a spreadsheet. I make a page for Adaline and a page for Monica, and, working down the columns, I start with demographics. Both of them have left breadcrumbs online, and after some initial confusion regarding married and maiden names, I start digging.

I find plenty of information about Monica. She'd been a swimmer as a young girl – hello, selkie, that's cheating – with a high enough profile to have a Wikipedia page. She was born in 1964 and she graduated from the Westridge School, a private girls school in Pasadena, in 1982. She attended USC with a partial scholarship for swimming, and she competed in the Olympic trials in 1984 but did not make the team.

And she ended up a crumpled heap on the tile floor of her lovely Spanish-style home. I shake my head, not at all sure I have the chops to play this game.

Once I've captured as many of Monica's details as I can, I shift my attention to Adaline. She was born the same year – 1964 – but she graduated from Beverly Hills High. She doesn't have a Wikipedia page, but I find her name on an alumnae bulletin from ten years or so ago. The bulletin refers to her as Adaline Ito Nosaska, and lists her husband as Brandon Nosaka.

I drill down and find Brandon Nosaka runs a chain of sushi bars, which might explain why Adaline's body had been found in an empty restaurant. I make a note to ask Connor whether anyone has talked to Brandon. Someone must have, either the police or Smith or Connor himself, and I'm curious about what he'd have to say.

From there I move to social media. Adaline's Facebook profile is set to private, but fortunately Monica had much blurrier boundaries. I find her on Facebook, Instagram, and Twitter, and Adaline figures prominently in her list of friends.

I find pictures of them drinking wine, shopping, working out, and going to the beach. Every shot is well-lit and artfully composed, as if Monica had a stylist for her Instagram feed. There's even one of those Throwback Thursday posts with high school versions of Monica, Adaline, and two other women.

Which is cool, and all, but doesn't do much to help me understand why they'd both been murdered.

I'm still at the table poking round the internet when Trajan sticks his head out the door. "I thought I saw a light down here."

In a white button-down worn open at the neck, he's looking rumpled and sexy, more businessman than hitman. His hair, though. I shake my head. A raggedly-cut hank falls across his brow, the cross he has to bear in return for eternal life.

"Hey, Tray." I set the laptop aside and rise. We come together at poolside like one of us is a magnet and the other is steel, and once he has his arms around me, I allow myself to relax. "We found another dead body," I murmur against his chest.

His arms tighten around me and he brushes his lips against my forehead. "Where?"

"We went to talk to Adaline's best friend, a woman called Monica Johnson. We were supposed to meet her at her home in Pasadena, but she was dead when we got there."

He doesn't move to release me, and I don't let go. "It's driving me crazy. I want to know who and I want to know why."

We hold each other for several long minutes before his voice rumbles against my sternum. "Where's Connor now?"

"I don't know. He said he had to check on something."

Trajan eases back a step so he can look me in the eye. "What something?"

"He didn't say."

His frown makes me uneasy, or else it bumps up against my existing uneasiness. This is crap, so I go for the heart of the thing. "Do you trust Connor?"

"I want to." His murmured answer rings another alarm bell. "Do you?"

I brush the hair out of his face, aware that this is a tricky moment. It'd be real easy to side with Trajan, to make it us vs. him.

Which would eventually tear us apart.

On the other hand, I know exactly where Trajan's coming from. "I think I trust Connor as much as I trust anybody. I'm just not sure he's telling us everything." It's possible for me to hold two parallel truths simultaneously.

I'm good that way.

"You hungry?" I murmur, still teasing my fingers through his hair.

Trajan's look of concern fades into something warmer. "Maybe."

"C'mon." I tip my head toward the house. "Time for a snack."

PART THREE: MO RÚIN

CHAPTER TEN

CONNOR

Too many balls in the air, MacPherson. I berate myself, aware of my own inconsistencies. I ask David for help, tease him with the offer of a partnership in my new project, then leave him with no real explanation.

But I have to find the princess, and if I'm going to be keeping secrets from Trajan, I might as well keep them from David, too. It's not fair to ask him to deal with my bullshit.

My first stop is Mr. Goldsmith's back yard, to make sure the damned revenant is staying dead. Everything looks calm, so I'm in and out before the dogs wake up to yell about it.

I'd learned more from Stone than just the name of that marginally cooperative guy in the bookstore. He'd connected me to an elf named Sam Kowalski. Sent the dude a text, even, so he's expecting me. I might have met Kowalski the last time I had this case, but I'd been more focused on finding a connection between Betancourt, Brendan Collins, and stolen magical materials. Now it's all-princess-all-the-time, and I need to make nice.

I'm later than I'd intended – damned murder screwed with my schedule – but Kowalski is still awake and willing to talk to me.

We meet at a twenty-four hour diner on Main Street in downtown LA. The awning in front advertises "kickin' hot fried chicken", and all of a sudden I'm hungry. I order food, but Kowalski just gets coffee. He watches me eat, his eyes following my hand to my mouth as if he regrets his decision.

We're at a table that's a couple inches too small for the pair of us. He's as tall as I am and wiry, with red hair and the kind of freckles that all blend into one. His aura stands out, too, a mellow bronze against the diner's black and white color scheme. I worked with a few elves on the Elites. They have kind of an attitude, but if I'm going into a fight, I want them on my side.

"So Stone says you're a private investigator." Kowalski sounds bored with the whole thing. Maybe he gets called to late-night meetings all the time. I don't know.

"I am now, yeah."

"Now? What were you yesterday?" He's got what David would call *resting smirk face*, which'll get under my skin if I let it.

"I was with the Elites until last June." *Huh.* Resting smirk face can be overcome by surprise. Good to know. I give him a moment to digest that information, then move on. "I'm also looking into the disappearance of Tatiana Ivanova." *The elven princess.*

His expression shuts down completely and for a moment I'm worried that he's pondering the best way of taking me out without causing a ruckus. I wish I were armed; that was another change from my days with the Elites. No toys, no weapons, and no backup.

"Lady Tatiana has been missing for over two years. Who hired you to find her at this late date?"

I suppress a snort of laughter. "You wouldn't believe me if I told you."

"Try me."

He's done playing around, and so am I. "Ananda Pendragon, the Morrigan."

Expression unchanged, he rests his right hand on the table.

His right hand and the pistol he's holding.

My muscles coil on instinct, ready to spring out of the way. Spikes of red disrupt his aura. Anger. We're sitting so close together, I'm unlikely to get far if he decides to shoot. The best I can hope for is avoiding a kill shot. I could shift, but the sudden appearance of a horse in a diner would be strange, even by LA's standards. A horse, or a dog, or…a shadowy thing I both fear and hate. I'd only made that shift once and vowed never to do it again.

Wishing I had something more concrete to defend myself with, a taser even, I feel my way through my next words.

"The thing I can't figure out, though, is why she cares."

His eyes narrow but he's otherwise still.

"Stone told me you're attached to the Princess's household, so I figure that gives you insights others might not have."

"I'm Lady Tatiana's cousin, and your Morrigan is the personification of evil." His hand still hasn't moved, though his glare is a tactile thing, a blast of heat against my skin. "If your intent is to find the Princess for that bitch Morrigan, I will not help you."

What the hell? "How about if I'm trying to find the Lady Tatiana because it's wrong when royalty goes missing?"

He tenses, and so do I.

"Why should I trust you?" His words land between us like darts.

I lean toward him, even though it's a risk. "Because your princess's disappearance has turned into a cold case and I'm willing to reopen it, and because finding her was on my radar two years ago and I really hate leaving a job undone, and because the idea that she's been missing all this time offends me."

I surprise myself with that blast of words, but they're all true. The idea that she's been missing for over two years makes me sick. "All I have to do is tell the Morrigan she's been found. Nowhere in our agreement did we specify that I'd be delivering the Princess anywhere to anyone."

Kowalski doesn't respond, but the wheels in his head are turning. I give him a minute, then continue. "The thing I can't figure out is why Ananda Pendragon cares about your Princess. It doesn't seem like they'd travel in the same circles."

Kowalski opens his mouth like he's going to answer, then closes it again. Opens. Closes. "The Lady Tatiana," he says finally, "has…unusual tastes. She crossed paths with the Morrigan in her search for…satisfaction."

I'm doing my best to keep my expression neutral, but it's hard. "So you think—"

"The Morrigan is a god, and what's normal for a god would be quite extreme for you or me. We have tapped every resource, human and supernatural, in our search for the Princess, and no one has found her. Our assumption was that the Morrigan had hidden her away, but your statement disproves that. Unless you're not telling me the truth."

He's still got that gun, and I'm still ready to dive out of the way, but his aura is calming down. "You've trusted me with information I didn't already have, and I have every intention of proving myself worthy of that trust."

Kowalski nods once, then pockets his pistol. He scoops up a messenger bag, one I hadn't noticed, and pulls out a folder. Handing it to me, he says, "This is what we've shared with the Securitas and the FBI. There's a few photos of Lady Tatiana, along with a listing of her last known activities, addresses, and contact information for her close friends. We want our Princess to come home, Connor MacPherson."

I take the packet, figuring a lot of it will duplicate what Poole's sending or what's already in my files, saved on a secure server. Still, there might be something new, and adding the Morrigan to the mix might refocus things.

Kowalski stands, so I do too. I've got some chicken to finish and the bill to clear. "I'll do whatever I can to find the Lady Tatiana. You have my word."

We shake hands and the elf with the bronze aura leaves. While I eat, I flip through the packet. The photos show a familiar figure, one with a delicately pretty face with golden-brown eyes. There's also a list of contacts, most of whom I've already talked to, two years ago, anyway.

I finish my dinner…or is it breakfast? Whatever meal it is, I finish and pay the bill. It's about one in the morning, still a while before sunrise, and I have a sudden need to see Trajan and David. The two of them mean more to me than anything else in my life.

The only thing stronger than my feelings for them is the fear that I'll ruin everything if Trajan finds out I'm working with the Securitas. I leave the diner, chased to my rental car by the hot, dry wind, the kind that makes your eyes burn and turns your spit to paste.

I'm in sight of the car with the keys in my hand when I notice something. There's a glow in the back seat, silver and green, an aura that really shouldn't be there. Someone's in my car. I slow my steps, narrowing my gaze.

Brodie. What the hell does he want?

I hit the keyfob and open the driver's side door. "You've got ten seconds to get out of my car or I'm going to start shooting." No, I don't have a gun, but he doesn't know that.

He believes me, though. He pops up from where he's been crouched in the rear seat. "Don't shoot, Mack. It's just me."

"I know it's you, Brodie. Now get out of my car. You're getting on my nerves."

His foolish grin broadens. "I just want to talk to you."

"About what? And this better be good because I can still shoot you." Not really, but…

"Remember that time in Paris?"

"What?"

"Paris, when we raided that guy who was trying to make zombies."

I slow blink. "Yes. I remember Paris." We'd come close to getting snuffed, and only the fact that we knew each other well enough hear the truth under the lies had saved us. "It was a tough one."

Something sincere crosses his eyes. "We're a good team."

"We *were*, yeah." The Elites didn't have formal partners. Poole paired guys up based on the skills they possessed and the job at hand. Even so, Brodie and I had worked together more than once.

"I was just thinking maybe you might want some help on this princess thing." Flickers of rose – vulnerability – flash through his aura and then disappear.

"Brodie, man." I don't know what else to say. Doing this job already has me twisted up. Adding a partner to the mix feels like a giant step too far.

Besides, the guy's part djinn. He'll probably drop by the house and introduce himself to Trajan just for kicks.

"Look, I appreciate the offer, but I gotta work this one on my own."

Brodie climbs out of the car. "Figured you'd say that, but I had to offer."

"Why?"

He knocks me in the shoulder with his fist. "You're a pain in the ass, Mack, but you're our pain in the ass. The guys and I decided one of us should volunteer to help, and I lost."

His aura says he's lying, but I jerk my thumb in the direction of the street. "Get outta here."

"Cowboy."

"Go!" Maybe I should start carrying a gun.

Brodie leaves, muttering various insults and threatening me with…I'm not even sure what. I let him go, hoping his number will get called and he'll have better things to do than harass me. Time to get home to my men.

CHAPTER ELEVEN

I rise to find David on his laptop, Connor holding a phone conference with Smith, an impatient voicemail from my real estate agent Glory, and a summons from Jacques.

A summons for me to appear at his home on Mulholland Drive no later than an hour after sunset. *Well, shit. What time is it?* My phone says seven o'clock, which means I have another hour or so before it's dark enough for me to leave the house. Jacques lives on Mulholland Drive, which is basically just a winding route uphill from the house we're staying in.

I leave my men to their work and get ready for my maker. With enough product, even my hair will lie flat, so I shower, dress, and slather on the hair dressing. Rather deliberately, I fish my gold nugget ring from the lock box I keep hidden in an old printer, a reminder to both me and Jacques that I've got resources of my own.

Pulling into a parking spot in front of Jacques' house, I check the time. It's just eight thirty, so I'm early. His house is hidden behind a profusion of green. Palms send their spiky branches up through the shrubbery, and trailing bougainvillea hangs heavy from a trellis along the front walk.

I knock, and while I wait I test the air for the scent of trouble. I catch Jacques' cold and familiar scent. Human, maybe more than one. And elf? No. *What is it?*

A young woman opens the door, distracting me. She's beautiful, her head shaved bald, her eyes accentuated with kohl and long, long lashes, and a dainty gold ring through her nasal septum. She's not wearing much else, and following her out to the patio, I can't help but admire the smoothness of her skin and the way the muscles in her buttocks flex.

Jacques is reclining on a lounge chair. He's dressed like an old-time Hollywood big wheel, in gabardine slacks, a silk shirt, and an ascot the color of plums. He's staring across the swimming pool where another young woman is doing laps. If she's got a bathing suit on, it's the same color as her skin.

The pool has lights embedded under the water and torches line the perimeter of the space. The combination gives the scene a flickering quality, as if everything is fluid, mobile.

And it makes the shadows darker.

Jacques raises a hand and points at the empty chair closest to him, but otherwise doesn't acknowledge my presence. I sit, and I wait.

It's hard, but I don't initiate a conversation. He called me here; he can explain why, or we can both watch naked women all night long. I don't care. They don't move me. They're more like watching mobile sculptures than anything that would set my dick on fire.

The woman who met me at the door is sitting on the edge of the pool, facing us, and the swimmer has come to a stop between her knees. Jacques' lips quirk, as if he's pleased with the performance, and soon even I can tell where the swimmer has her mouth.

I lied when I said the women don't move me. I find myself riveted in response to the intensity of the bald woman's expression and the way the light hits her throat when she tips her head back. In a surprisingly short amount of time, she cries out and her body shudders. She drops onto her elbows, her legs spread wide, and the swimmer ducks under the water.

When she comes up again, she pulls herself out of the pool and both women laugh. Jacques stirs and then coughs, holding a white linen handkerchief to his mouth.

A white linen handkerchief spotted with blood.

"You're harboring a snake," he says finally.

I have no idea what the hell he's talking about, but I don't give him the satisfaction of asking. "Guess I like living dangerously."

"You don't believe me, do you. Idiot." Jacques coughs again, and for the first time all night, his cold silver gaze meets mine. "I have a job for you."

I nod, waiting for him to continue, and after a measured moment, he does. "I put up with your deviance for all these years, but now you've found a new low."

I gape at him. Never once in all of 150 years has he given me any indication that my preferences bother him.

"And in my house, too."

"What are you talking about?"

"I don't mind the little wolf. He might turn out to be useful. It's the other one." He pauses for another cough. "I never liked him, you know. Never did, and when he pretended to be dead, I was relieved. Of course, then he magically reappears and you run right after him with your tongue out and your tail wagging."

I'd say something, but my jaw has dropped to the floor. This is Jacques talking, my maker, the person I've known longer than anyone else. He's impulsive, mercurial even, but rarely mean. I should be insulted but I'm too stunned.

He waves a pale hand at me. "You know I'm right. You can't even defend yourself. Now he's digging into something he should stay the hell away from, and so before you make an even bigger fool of yourself, I'm going to help you out."

"How?" I grind the word out.

"Kill him."

If I was stunned before, now I'm in shock.

He snorts, giving me another dismissive wave. "God's sake, Gall. Grow a pair. You've let that lying sonofabitch get close enough to take you down, so I'm doing you a favor. Kill him before he destroys you."

"No." The word is barely a whisper. I don't know what game Jacques is playing, but killing Connor is impossible.

Jacques pulls himself upright, his cold stare fixed on me. "You cannot refuse me in this. I am your maker and I'm telling you to kill Connor MacPherson."

His words land like blows. I close my eyes. "I'm sorry, my old friend, but I cannot do this."

"You will," he hisses. Another coughing fit takes him and he reclines in the chaise, his attention on the pool as if I've ceased to exist.

Toying with the gold nugget ring, I don't say anything that will remind him of my presence. A young vampire must obey his maker and I've always done so, out of habit more than anything else. Still, I am old enough to withstand his demand, if not indefinitely, at least long enough to devise an alternative solution.

I cannot kill Connor, yet something in Jacques' tone has kindled my own doubts. Mistrust is a bitter pill.

Jacques' two young ladies wander over. The swimmer sits down on the edge of his chaise, her hand coming to rest on his thigh. "What's up, darlin'?" she asks, her long damp hair trailing over her shoulders. Jacques takes hold of her hand and brings it to his lips. He kisses her palm and, catching my gaze, he nips at the pulse point in her wrist. He's gone sly, amused, as if I hadn't just openly defied him.

She moans and my own hunger rises. "Try the other one," he says, and then he licks the blood away.

The bald woman with the beautiful eyes straddles me, raising her chin to give me a clean view of her throat. She goes to work tugging my shirt free from my jeans but I stop her, grasping her wrists. I'm not so hungry that I can't turn her down.

Scooping her up with one arm, I stand and set her in the chair I vacated. "Nothing personal.

You're lovely, but I'm not into an orgy right now."

"He's got his own orgy at home, the freak." Jacques' nasty tone apparently brings on another coughing fit. The swimmer – she's now in his lap with his cock in her hands – pauses with her lips at the tip until the fit passes and he pushes her head lower.

"It's been nice catching up, but I'll be going now, unless there's anything else you need."

Jacques's scowl is so fierce I flinch.

Kill him. The words weigh down my gut like stones. Jacques is my maker, and though I've toyed with breaking things off with him – if that's even possible – the reality is something more serious. In time, refusing his command will make more trouble than I can easily handle.

But I'll walk into the sun before I'll kill Connor. I climb into the Range Rover and rev the engine. *Jesus, Mary, and Joseph. What next?*

Fueled by anger and frustration, I wind my way down the hill to the house where we're staying, the house Jacques owns. *Just like he owns me.*

I storm in, hoping Connor and David are home. Jacques' attempt at seduction-by-proxy has left me aroused and hungry.

They're home.

I find them poolside, in a weirdly similar setting. The underwater spotlights cast a kaleidoscope of shifting colors and light. David's in the water and Connor's sitting on the deck. Neither is wearing a swimsuit, although they appear to be talking.

Just talking.

I should just tell them, warn them, something. But I don't. Not yet. For now, I'll do what I can to keep them safe from Jacques. From me. Instead of talking, I tear off my shirt and lose my jeans. I've got my drawers off and my cock in hand before either of them knows what's going on. And I'm hard. Good god, I'm hard.

They're both so beautiful. One glowing gold in the moonlight, the other a warm copper I can almost taste.

"What did Jacques want?" Connor asks but I don't answer him. I dive into the water and come up between his knees. I reach out and pull David close. He starts to rut against my side and I pull him in for a kiss.

"What are you doing?" Connor's voice is breathy and his dick is filling. Dragging David with me, I pull myself up until I can get my mouth to the pulse point in his groin.

"Feeding," I say, and I bite.

His warm, salty lifeblood fills my mouth. I gulp and swallow more, then press my lips to his skin and heal the wound with a kiss. Sinking lower in the water, I lift David so they're sitting side-by-side on the edge of the pool, moving him like he's a doll. *A vampire's strength should be good for something.*

I drag myself out of the water and sit between them, pulling David in for another kiss. He's my sweet fountain of youth, and I cannot get enough.

Stretching us flat on the deck, I cover my body with Connor's and grab hold of both our cocks. I pull David close, resting his head on my shoulder. Connor reaches for David's dick and, alternating between one set of lips and the other, I start to thrust.

Connor's cock glides against mine, while David's already losing his rhythm. He lifts his chin as his back bows, and I nip the skin of his throat. He shouts and a thick strand of come shoots across his belly. He goes limp, and I gather him closer.

Thrusting harder, I plow into Connor's mouth, letting him taste the remains of David's blood. We're bound, the three of us, and I won't have it any other way.

Connor goes rigid and his dick spasms; his climax drives me further. Thrusting into his grip, now wet with his spend, I lose myself in pleasure. For one long moment, I forget everything except the visceral sense of these two men.

Mine.

Slowly, slowly I come back to earth. I'm on my back and they're mostly lying on me. The pool deck is rough but I welcome the pain. I'm going to have to tell them about Jacques' command, but I need time to find a loophole, a way out.

They're little more than warmth and weight in my arms, familiar, comforting, their scents weaving together like a blanket.

Abruptly, David sits. "What's that?" he asks, his gaze darting around the area.

"I don't—" A high-pitched whine interrupts me, and acting on instinct alone, I pull David close and drag them both to the water's edge. "Breathe," I yell, and we plunge in.

The explosion rocks us even through the watery buffer. When we surface, there's a crater in the pool deck exactly where we'd been lying.

We swim to the shallow end, but as we're climbing out, I hear another buzz, this one more like the whine of a mosquito. I turn, knocking Connor out of the way.

And catch the bullet with my heart.

CHAPTER TWELVE

When Trajan falls, I lose my mind. *Nonononono.* Not Trajan. Not him. Vampires might heal from just about any wound, but he'd been hit square in the center of his chest. If the bullet is silver, he might be dead.

Connor's yelling "Get down!" so I do. He runs into the house and I crouch next to Trajan, whose skin has gone alabaster white. The wound in his chest is oozing thick rivulets of dark blood over his ribs and down his belly, but oozing's better than spurting, right? I tell myself it is and look for something to put pressure on the wound.

He'd shucked his clothes on his way to the pool, and his jeans are just a few feet away from where we're lying. I get up, preparing to make a quick crawl-walk to grab them, but another bullet goes spinning right past my ear. *Fuck.*

Fucking fuck. I belly flop and press my bare palm to Trajan's chest. That'll have to do.

Connor steps through the sliding glass door onto the pool deck. He's carrying a big-ass gun, a black semi-automatic something something, and keeping to the shadows, he sidesteps to the opposite end of the pool. The end the bullets are coming from.

The bleeding from Trajan's chest wound seems to have stopped and I debate whether I should roll him over to see if there's an exit wound. I've seen his body heal over silver buckshot and had to cut it out. I've also seen his body force a silver slug out on its own. Since we don't know what hit him and whether it's still in there, I'm not sure I want it to heal over just yet.

Connor tosses something into the space between the end of the pool and the artfully arranged shrubbery that separates our yard from the one next door. It's some kind of explosive device, although all it does is send up a bright, white light.

There. Between a pair of spikey New Zealand flax, a silhouette with a metallic gleam from a snub-nosed pistol. With something to aim for, Connor comes out shooting. There's a muffled curse, then the sound of thrashing in the foliage.

And then silence.

The light grenade thing dims, but it's still bright enough to see that there's no more movement. From the street, the sound of a motorcycle's engine cuts through the silence. Connor darts into the house, although the place is big enough that it's unlikely he'll get to the driveway before the biker takes off.

Assuming our assailant isn't bleeding out under the flax.

I need Connor to help me move Trajan. He's still out and his chest wound truly has started to seal over. I want to check out the area across the pool, to see if the shooter's still there or if he left any scent, but the need to stay close to Trajan is greater than the desire to investigate.

I'm not a natural private eye. I'd rather dress pretty and act slutty, as long as my fellow sluts are Trajan and Connor. This getting shot shit is for the birds.

The motorcycle's long gone when Connor comes back. He's put on a pair of jeans and he throws me a pair of sweatpants.

"Let's get him in the house," I say, my hand still on Trajan's chest.

Connor glares across the pool, then nods. Whatever's over there will keep. He squats down at Trajan's head and I scoot over to hold his knees, and between the two of us we wrangle him into the house.

There's no way we're managing two flights of stairs to get to the vampire room. The media room on this level will have to do. As we're laying him down on one of the broad sofas, I tell Connor to check Trajan's back for an exit wound.

There isn't one.

The bullet's still in his chest and he hasn't regained consciousness. "Will a silver bullet to the heart kill a vampire?" I ask, and I'm not even ashamed about the quaver in my voice.

Connor's grimace is an answer on its own. "Hang on." He pulls a cellphone and a business card from somewhere and swipes across the phone's screen. He glances at the card and punches in a number. "This is Mack. I need Doctor Gray."

There's more conversation, though he's turned away from me as if he doesn't want me to hear. I decide I don't want to know what he's really up to and head outside. I poke through the foliage where the shooter had been hiding. There are dark splashes on the sword-like flax leaves, but the area smells wholly human with maybe a sprinkle of vampire dust.

Relieved that I didn't stumble over another dead body, I head back into the house. Connor's off the phone, kneeling by Trajan, murmuring in his ear. "The doctor will be here in a few minutes, Tray. Just hang on."

Calling in help seemed like the kind of thing a member of the Securitas could do. I have no reason for thinking that other than how Trajan responded when I asked him if he trusted Connor. When I find myself parsing whether a current member of the Elites would have a doctor on speed dial while a former member would have to look the number up, I drop it. The important thing is removing the bullet – silver or otherwise – from Trajan's chest.

Too close to Trajan's heart. Trajan's big heart, big enough to keep a punk werewolf alive, to forgive his not-really-dead ex, to go in on the purchase of a nightclub for his friend to practice her arts in safety.

Sheena.

Shit. My phone's in my room, so I gallop up the stairs.

Sheena answers on the first ring. "What?"

"It's Trajan." My voice cracks and for a second I can't say anything at all.

"What?" She's gone full Domme, commanding my answer, which is a good thing.

I inhale and spit the words out. "He's been shot, and I think you better come."

Now it's her turn to be speechless.

"I don't know who did it or why. We're at the house, and Connor's called for a doctor."

There's another beat of silence. "On my way."

She ends the call and I stumble down the stairs. Connor's still in the media room. "I called Sheena, and she'll be here soon."

He nods, propped against the wall as if he needs it to keep from falling over. "Doc's coming too. She's good. Pretty much only deals with supernatural stuff."

"If she can get the bullet out, it'll help us figure out who they were really aiming at."

He gives me a puzzled look.

"If it's silver, they were aiming at him. Otherwise it could have been any of us."

"Sure." He shakes his head as if disappointed by his own obtuseness. "You go outside?"

"Blood, 87% human with a touch of vampire, and no body." I kneel down next to Trajan. "You winged the guy, but that's all."

He slides down till his butt hits the floor. "Okay, so human with a touch of vampire makes me think we're going to find a silver bullet in there."

He's probably right. Still, I lean against the sofa's seat, as close to Trajan as I can get without sitting in his lap, and hope with everything I've got that he's not the target. "Seems pointless to mention that Tray met with Jacques tonight."

"And even more futile to bring up the fierce mood he was in when he came home."

Connor's grim tone weighs on me. Neither of us have a lot to say. We wait. For Trajan, for the doctor, for Sheena. Who's likely to land on us like a ton of…something heavier than bricks.

Regardless of whether any of this is our fault, Connor and I are going to catch high holy hell from Sheena for letting Trajan take that bullet.

The doctor gets here first, thank fuck. She's an odd little person who might well exist on more than one plane at a time. She reminds me of Edna from *The Incredibles*, but less substantial.

If it's possible for an animated character to be substantial in the first place.

The doctor is carrying a clichéd black leather bag, which she opens on the small table at the end of the sofa. I can't see what it contains – literally, the whole table turns blurry so I don't know what the fuck she's got in there – and she starts up the sort of tuneless humming that'll find my last nerve quicker than just about anything.

Under normal circumstances, anyway. If she wants to hum while she saves Trajan's life, I'm all for it.

She and Connor start up an intense, sotto voce conversation. They're either speaking a foreign language or the doctor can distort her words the way she blurs the table. I'm almost glad when I hear Sheena at the door. I'll be lucky if she doesn't beat the shit out of me before she comes down here, but the doctor is creepy af.

I meet Sheena at the top of the stairs. She's dressed for a night out with the gang, the toned-down version, which means she was probably playing bodyguard for some spoiled celebrity when I called. She gives me a quick once-over, taking in my swimming pool hair, bare and hairless chest, and sagging sweats. "You smell like sex. Tell me you weren't fucking when Trajan got shot."

I remind myself that he's her closest friend, and don't respond in kind. "There's a doctor with him now. Hopefully she'll be able to get the bullet out."

She pushes past me, heading down the stairs. "Is he in much pain?"

"I don't know."

She shoots a glare over her shoulder, a look so hot I should be cinders.

"He's been unresponsive since he got shot."

That slows her down. "Unresponsive? But you know he's alive, right?"

I don't have an answer for her, because I have no idea how to tell if an undead being is dead-dead instead of just unconscious. We get down the rest of the stairs in silence.

The door to the media room is locked.

I tap, politely, hoping Connor will stick his head out and tell us what's going on. Sheena literally counts to fifteen, then reaches over my head and gives the door a solid swat.

Still nothing.

She elbows me out of the way, making me growl. The look she gives me says plainly that I better come at her with some four-legged fur action or back the hell down. I yield, sick to my stomach that I couldn't shift now if I wanted to.

Trajan has to live, or whatever it is vampires do. He has to.

Sheena goes from smacking the door to hammering to slumping against the wall, sending a series of texts to someone, probably Connor. Whoever the recipient is, I can almost see the flames coming from her phone.

Just open the damn door.

I go from counting heartbeats to black speckles in the tile floor to how many ways I want to get fucked before I die. The door cracks open and I just about jump out of my skin. Sheena grabs it and tries to wrestle it the rest of the way open, but Connor holds firm. "He's going to be okay," he murmurs.

"Let. Me. In." Sheena's hiss has more threat than I'd care to face, but Connor doesn't back down.

"Chill out, will you? The doctor's still working with him. As soon as she says it's okay, I'll let you in."

"What doctor?" Sheena's slightly calmer, but not much. "Where did you dig someone up at this hour?"

"He called someone," I say, easing myself past her elbow so I can get to Connor. "If Trajan survives, it's thanks to him."

Sheena backs up a step and glares at us, her arms crossed. She doesn't say anything, but then she doesn't need to. I reach for Connor's wrist and give it a squeeze. "Thank you," I murmur, then step aside as he eases the door closed.

"That doctor must be someone from the Securitas."

I shrug because *Yes* but also *Let's not go there*. "He didn't say."

"Hmph."

The silence between us is only broken by the steady tap of her heel on the floor. She's wearing sleek black platform boots, and under other circumstances I would have coveted the hell out of them. As it was, I put them on the maybe list for whenever I shop for something more fun than groceries.

Finally – Lord have mercy *finally* – the door opens all the way. Connor's alone, and he steps aside so both of us can come in. The doctor's gone. Where? How? I don't even know. All I can see is Trajan, still fairly alabaster white, but sitting upright on the couch.

"He's going to need to feed," Connor murmurs, low enough that I'm the only one who hears. Sheena keeps going until she's sitting next to Trajan on the couch with her arms around him, hanging on like she's never ever going to let go.

"I can do that."

"I mean," he grabs my arm, "a lot."

We share a glance. "Like more than you and me together?"

His expression is grim. "Yeah, unless one of us wants a trip to the ER with hypovolemia."

Hy-po-vo-what…? "Okay, so what do we do?"

"We need to find a fourth, and maybe a fifth, and we need them fairly soon."

I glance at Sheena. "Maybe somebody from the club?"

"That's what I was thinking, to be honest." Connor plants his fists on his hips and arches his back. "We'll let her calm down, then come up with a plan. We don't need to make a whole scene out of it. If she just finds us a couple volunteers, we can take care of things."

I'm not at all sure what *taking care of things* means, but I nod in a close approximation of maturity.

And then, because I'm fucking twenty-three years old, my dick gets hard.

CHAPTER THIRTEEN

We need to get Trajan fed, and we need to do it asap, because in the midst of Doctor Gray's work, I get a text from Smith.

He's received the statements from the Pasadena PD and wants my help with follow-up interviews. Starting now.

First, though, we need to heal our partner, our lover, the tie that binds us all. I explain the situation to Sheena and without batting an eye she gets out her phone and makes a call. When she's done, she's got two volunteers waiting at the club for us.

Trajan's too weak to move very far, so we decide he'll feed from us here first. Sheena takes off in case things get messy, and David takes her place at Trajan's side. The wolf's eyes are huge and glassy; my internal distress is written clearly on his face.

"You need to eat, Tray." David strokes Trajan's cheek, but the vampire's head is resting against the back of the sofa and his eyes are half closed.

"'S okay, puppy. I'm okay."

"Come on, now, the doctor said you need to eat." David straddles Trajan's hips, his arms around his head, fingers threaded through his hair. Stretching his torso, David gently guides Trajan so his lips are against David's throat. "It's right there, baby."

Trajan gives a soft moan, and then he bites, a flash of violence in the otherwise peaceful scene. He grabs hold of David and drags his body closer, mouth locked on David's throat. This feed isn't a kind of foreplay and it's not likely to bring David to orgasm.

In fact, if it goes on much longer, I'm going to have to intervene, although fighting off a vampire in a bloodlust might do more harm than good.

Of course if the choice is David's life or mine, I know which way my decision will go.

David makes a half-hearted attempt to push himself away from Trajan and I poise, ready to dive in before he drains David. My gut is twisted, my muscles coiled, but with a jerk,

Trajan releases his hold on David's throat. The skin is already bruised, and with a sigh, Trajan kisses the wound closed.

Then it's my turn.

David's groggy and paler than usual, but he musters a focused expression. "Maybe I should shift. If he loses control on you, my wolf would be better able to fight him off."

"No, puppy, I'm okay. I won't lose control." At least his eyes are open, so maybe he's telling the truth.

I kneel in front of him, holding his hands in mine. "How do you want to do this?"

Trajan's smile is weak, but it holds more personality than I've seen since before he got shot. "How horny are you?" he asks, and I roll my eyes.

"You're hot, *mo shíoghrá*, but I'm not Superman. I just want you back to your full strength."

"True." He tightens his grip on my fingers. "But if I can make this pleasant, that's what I want to do."

I rise up, using his hands for leverage. "Here." I show him my throat. David's beside us, his silent presence both a comfort and an added layer of heat.

Trajan plants a kiss over my pulse, and then he bites.

I shift my hands to his shoulders so I can shove him away if I need to, but he's gentler, less desperate than when he fed from David. Low and behold, my dick does get hard, but before I can make much of it, he finishes. Pressing his lips to the wound, he lets me go.

"Okay." I'm smiling as I sit back on my heels. "You've got two more feeds, maybe three. Doctor's orders."

"I think you're making too big a deal out of this."

David grabs both of us by the arm. "Don't even," he says, expression stricken. "I thought you were dead for reals, Trajan Gall, and that is *not okay*. You will feed from two more men, and you'll enjoy it, and then we can get back to our regularly scheduled polyamory."

He gives us both a shake, for emphasis, then rakes a hand through his tangled hair. "And if we're going to the club, I need a shower. Last one there gets the cold water."

With that, he hops up and makes a run for it. I wonder if he's afraid we'll see him cry. But then, "I know how he feels," I say, brushing Trajan's lips with my own. "And I know better how you felt, *mo shíoghrà*, when you thought I was dead. I could not be sorrier I caused you that pain."

He grimaces, his gaze anywhere but at me. "We need to talk. Jacques said—"

"Later." I pull him in for another kiss. "Let's get you healed and then we can deal with whatever it is."

Because between Trajan and David, they're going to be able to connect the phone call I made to summon a doctor with the Securitas, and then things could get ugly.

Sheena meets us at the club door and hurries us past their guests, who are posing in various stages of undress. David once described the scene as a Gap ad, but bondage, and he's not wrong. She leads us to one of the private rooms in the back. There, two men are waiting. They're both young, somewhere in their twenties, dressed only in black athletic pants, and they're both vibrating with nervous tension. One has his hands bound behind his back and the other is cuffed to the wall with his back to us.

"They wanted it this way," Sheena says, and she and Trajan exchange a look.

He turns to David and me, his expression solemn. "I'm going to give them what they want. It's only fair."

David, dressed all in black with his hair starched high and a slick of red lipstick, gets right up close to Tray. "Just remember what's waiting for you at home," he says, and plants a kiss on Trajan's cheek, marking him with a bright red smear.

Trajan smiles at him, then turns to me. "Okay, *amore mio*?"

"Of course." It's not like I'm happy sharing Trajan, but these are exceptional circumstances.

I wrap an arm around David's shoulders and lead us over so we're leaning against the wall. Sheena stays with Trajan and the young men. "What are we doing here, gentlemen?" she asks, her voice snapping like the crack of a whip.

"Feeding," the man with his hands bound says. He's blond and blue-eyed, and his neatly trimmed beard is the only thing that makes him look older than eighteen.

"That's right." Sheena smacks the wall near the other man's head. He jumps, his gaze on the ground and she moves closer to him, her lips at his ear. "Is that what you're here for?"

"Yes, ma'am," he says, a fitting response given his buzz cut and the USMC tattoo on his shoulder.

"Good answer. My friend was badly injured this evening, and he needs to feed from both of you. Before we go any further, I want it out there. You both volunteered to be here, and you're aware there are witnesses. Right?"

Both of them nod. "Out loud," Sheena barks, and they both stumble over the words to agree with her.

"Have you ever fed a vampire before?"

"No ma'am," the Marine says. The blond nods his head in the affirmative, but he's not very convincing. Sheena pokes him in the arm.

"Answer the question."

"Yes, uh, no…no, I haven't."

She crosses her arms and grins at Trajan. "Take your pick."

"Is he going to fuck them?" David whispers the question, but Trajan answers before I do.

"No, puppy, but I will jerk them off."

I tighten my grip on David. "You know what it's like to get bit."

He doesn't respond, at least verbally. His gaze, though, stays locked on Trajan, his body tense, as if he's willing himself to stay still.

Sheena keeps up a running commentary, a combination of command and verbal abuse. Trajan starts with the blond, standing right behind him, running his hands up and down the man's torso. He whispers something and the guy smiles.

"Stop that." Sheena stalks over to them, her long blond hair swinging in rhythm with her stride. "No pleasure for you, punk, unless I say so."

Trajan murmurs something else and the guy presses his lips together as if it's all he can do not to grin. Trajan's hands drift lower till he reaches the waistband of the man's pants. He shoves the pants down to mid-thigh and grabs the man's cock, giving it a solid stroke.

The man's back arches and he bites his lower lip. Sheena watches, exhorting the guy to hold off until she says so. Trajan strokes him and he rocks his head on Trajan's shoulder, exposing his neck.

Trajan's smile is all fang.

When Sheena shouts, "Now," Trajan bites. David jumps and I hold him closer still, and the young man in Trajan's arm howls. Trajan holds him until the shuddering stops and he goes limp, then Trajan half-carries him to a long, low bench in the corner. After freeing his wrists, he settles the blond there and turns to the Marine.

This time there's less talk, more action. Sheena's approach is different; she positions herself at the guy's shoulder and starts murmuring in his ear, words I can't – and don't want to – hear. Whatever she says has him fighting the cuffs that are holding him to the wall while Trajan massages the guy's cock through his pants. They demonstrate a level of teamwork I'd never witnessed from them before, but they both know exactly what to do to drive the guy wild.

Then Trajan licks the side of the guy's neck and Sheena steps aside.

"You're going to make a mess of yourself, aren't you, corporal?" she says.

He shouts in protest, "No ma'am no I promise I won't make a mess," and Trajan bites.

The Marine climaxes, hard, still wearing his black pants. His jaw is locked so tight he can't even get any sound out and he stays that way, back bowed, chin in the air, for several long, pulsing seconds.

Trajan gets an arm around him and holds him upright when the guy's knees give way. Sheena unbuckles the cuffs, and the two of them maneuver the Marine to the bench in the back of the room.

And yeah, he's got dark patches where his spunk soaked through the fabric of his pants.

David's got his head on my shoulder and he's breathing deep. I sneak a glance at the telltale bulge in his crotch. "This turn you on?" I murmur and fumble for his fly. I didn't get hard watching Trajan and Sheena work over two strangers, but David's excitement is contagious.

I work my hand in to wrap around his cock, but he grabs my wrist. "Nah," he says. "Not now."

Shifting my weight, I slide my hand free. "No?"

The two men are cuddling each other on the cot. Trajan's got a hand on both of them, and Sheena's keeping watch over the whole thing.

"It's their show," David murmurs, and I guess I know what he means.

My phone vibrates against my hip. It's likely Smith again. I could Uber to wherever he is. Confirming that the text is from Smith, I debate how to approach this.

"You gotta go somewhere?" David asks.

"Smith."

"No."

"What?" The flatness of his refusal sets me back on my heels.

"Whatever it is can wait till tomorrow." He shoots a glance at Trajan. "I know you want to help, but not tonight."

His gaze is dark, defiant, and…frightened. "You're not in the Elites anymore, and you don't work for the LAPD. You can't tell me if you took off now that you'd be able to concentrate for worrying about Trajan."

The truth in his words hits home, making my shoulders sag. "How come the youngest is also the smartest?"

David gets a hand around my neck and pulls me to him till we're forehead to forehead. "The dead selkie will still be dead tomorrow, but we came damned close to saying the same about Trajan. Tonight, I want all of us in bed."

I pull out my phone and shoot Smith a text, promising to catch up with him by noon tomorrow. Then David and I wait, arm in arm, for Trajan to be ready to go home.

CHAPTER FOURTEEN

The doorbell rings, and I'm the only one who moves. Connor's gone and Trajan's unconscious.

But he's not dead-dead, so I'm okay.

The bell rings again, so I grab the nearest piece of fabric and head downstairs. I shake it out and realize I grabbed a towel – still damp and slightly musty – from someone's shower. *Whatever*. I wrap it around my hips and tuck the corner so it'll stay up.

There's a guy on the doorstep. At least, I think it's a guy. Pretty much all I can see is a ginormous bouquet of white flowers. I squint at them. Lilies?

"These are for Trajan Gall," the guy says, and I hold out my arms.

"He's not awake, but I'll take them."

"Who're you?"

"The Easter Bunny. Give me the effing flowers and let me get back to bed."

The guy huffs, and for a second I think he's going to argue, but then he shoves the blossoms at me. I catch the vase before the whole thing hits the stone steps – *go me* – but when he hands me an iPad and asks for my signature, I laugh. "I can sign, hold the flowers, or keep the towel up, but not all three."

Muttering about lazy ass perverts, the delivery guy turns on his heel and stalks down the front walkway. Still laughing, I kick the door shut and haul the load of lilies to the dining room table. We don't spend much time there, but the flowers are a little creepy so I don't really want to look at them.

"Now who sent these to my vampire?" I murmur, pawing through the greenery for the card.

It's clipped to one of those clear plastic fork-like holders. And yeah, Trajan's name is on the envelope, but I'm too curious to wait till he rises. I unstick the flap and tease the little card out of the envelope.

Hope you're feeling better. Remember what I said…

The only signature is a letter *J* signed with a flourish.

J? Jacques? Despite the sunshine, my gut turns cold. Trajan saw Jacques last evening, Trajan got shot last night, and now someone whose name starts with a J sent lilies. Maybe I'm wrong, but I'm pretty sure white lilies are funeral flowers.

Jacques had had Trajan shot, and damn near killed him.

I don't *know*-know this, but from the lump of ice in my belly to the heavy certainty in my bones, it's the truth.

I'm still processing the *why* of it all when Connor walks in.

"What's that all about?" He points at the flowers.

"My best guess is that Jacques heard about Trajan's little accident last night."

He squints at the flowers as if they're going to be able to explain the situation. "Vampires, man."

I force a laugh. "Right?"

"Not many are as independent as Trajan, though I've never been able to figure out why." He shrugs, his mind elsewhere. I tuck that idea away, because what I don't know about vampires and their relative independence could fill a library.

"What did you think about last night?"

Connor's question jerks me back to the present. "Which part? Because a whole lot of it could be filed under *Oh, shit*."

He circles the table, catching my shoulder in a warm grip. "Totally agree with you there. I guess I was thinking about the club. I mean, we've talked a little about what we're comfortable with, but that particular situation never came up."

"And I hope it never does again." I lean against him, glad for his strength. He and Trajan had stuck close to me after the scene at the club, and it occurred to me that Connor might be worried the situation had crossed a boundary for me. "I mean, I might not mind seeing Trajan jerk some guy off in principle, I just don't want him to have to suffer a near-death experience first."

Connor eases away and fiddles with his phone – because that's what he does when he's feeling awkward – but after a couple beats he meets my gaze. "You didn't mind? At the club?"

"In a way, it was fucking amazing." I catch my bottom lip in my teeth. "By the time they were done I mean, I was pretty fired up, or I would have been except for the bad parts."

He's looking at me carefully. "Do you want to play that way?"

Connor has never said much about the club, but now his reserve seems significant, so I throw the question back at him. "Do you?"

"Nah, I'm too old school for that. I like you and me and Trajan in the same bed, and that's about as exotic as I get."

"Did it bother you to see Trajan…like that?"

He leans against the table like he wants to dodge my question all together. "Not really. I mean, I understand why he needed more blood than we could provide."

I verbalize the "But?" he's leaving unsaid.

He scowls as if that one word cornered him. "Trajan had the club before he had me, you know? He asked me once if I wanted to go with him. I did, and it was….awkward. He's never asked me again, and last night was the first time I volunteered."

Okay, that's weird as fuck. "You two were soulmates for how many years? And the whole time he runs a BSDM club and you're not into it? How did that even work?"

"He didn't have much to do with the place, except to write checks and sign off on the occasional order, and I was busy with—"

"With a job that you lied about to keep him safe or whatever. You two." I give the towel a yank to keep it from sliding off my ass. "Here I've been freaking out over sticking myself in the middle of your true love sitch, and you two didn't know each other at all."

His expression shifts through several stages of surprise and anger and settles on something I can't read.

"You're not sticking yourself anywhere, David Collins. Right now you're the glue that's holding us together."

I don't know what the hell to do with that, so I leave it alone. I mean, I've known Trajan occasionally plays at his own club. Hell, he'd damned near jacked me off in public the first time we went there. I also sensed that it was sort of an unmentionable topic with Connor.

And…I slide a glance at Connor. Curious about how he'll react, I push him a little. "I might like to hang out there some."

He startles, like he's forgotten I'm there. "You want to get tied up?"

"Oh no." I let my grin turn feral. "I might want to be the one tying guys up, if you know what I mean. Sheena and Trajan were sexy as fuck."

Fortunately/unfortunately, his phone chirps with an incoming text. It's probably a good thing, because while teasing Connor is fun, I'm not sure what I'd do if he decided to tell Sheena I want to be a Dom when I grow up. I mean, never say never, but I'm pretty good with the deal we have now.

So I file Connor's unspoken disapproval and my own potential interest away in a place I can examine them later. For a guy who's always on us to discuss our relationship, Connor sure keeps a lot of secrets.

"It's Smith. They've found another victim, and he wants us to meet him there."

I check the time. "I want to be back before Trajan rises."

For a second I wonder if Connor's going to argue with me. He's giving his phone a tight frown, but after a moment he meets my gaze. "Sure. Cut out whenever you need to."

"Can we take an Uber?" If he's in a humor-David mood, I may as well work it. "I'm not riding in that cheap-ass Taurus rental."

Connor rolls his eyes. "Get dressed. I'll get us a ride."

I mock-glare at him, shaking my finger. "It better be something decent."

"It will be."

I head for the stairs, sniffing my pits as I go. I could probably stand a shower, but I'm not sure if there's time.

Besides, the murder victim won't care if I smell.

In less than an hour, our Uber – a late model Honda Accord saturated with the smell of cigarettes and fake pine air freshener – drops us on the campus of UCLA near the botanical garden. I'm basically wheezing by the time we get there, and Connor has the good sense not to point out how much better the Taurus smells.

We enter the garden through the main entrance and, according to Smith, it's a short hike to the pavilion.

All I know is that the Santa Ana winds are playing hell with my hair and there are way too many plants.

It's easy to find where the LAPD homicide squad has set up operations. Smith is on the periphery, as usual, and there's a small army of people. I don't really want to shift, and without Trajan, I probably shouldn't try. I do circle the area, catching as many scents as I can. Connor talks with the lead detective who grudgingly gives permission for me to come close to the victim.

About as eager as I'd be for a root canal, I follow the detective to where the body is lying. Her name is apparently Kitten Fletcher, and she's in a heap under the wing-shaped pergola extending from the main building, surrounded on all sides by folds of cloth.

Not cloth, I realize. Wings.

She's a fairy, or she was.

Fairies are rare, even in a city as crowded as LA. Supernatural creatures tend to travel to places where people believe in them, which is why there's always such a hodgepodge in a big city. There are never many true fairies, though, despite Disney's best efforts at making them seem real.

I squat down and wave in a hopeless effort to get people to back off, then do my best to sort through the scents they've left.

Human. Yeah, lots of human. Something smoky and strong, a scent I'm coming to associate with Smith. Fairy, which smells like talcum powder and roses.

I straighten, stretching out the kinks, and wave at Connor. He comes over and since I've been focusing on scent, I get caught in a wave of whisky and leather. It grabs me, and deep down I know something else is true. He's a good person, worthy of the affection Trajan and I have for him.

He might get lost sometimes on the way to the truth, but he's not evil.

With that little dose of maturity in hand, I relay the information I've gathered to him and to Smith. I'm ready to Uber back to the house, but Connor stops me.

"Smith asked if we could talk to the victim's wife."

"Why?" I'm sincerely confused. I mean, I'm here because of my nose, and even if I'd tried to dress up, these skinny black jeans are nowhere near professional.

"He's got a long list of people to contact for this one, and the victim and her wife were estranged. Her wife's living in a condo not far from where we're staying."

But still… I shrug, totally unconvinced this is a good idea. "Trajan'll be up in another hour or two."

"It won't take long. Smith already broke the news to her and he needs our help."

So now he's making me feel like an asshole. "Sure. Let's get it over with and get back home."

Connor gives me the address and I call an Uber. It's a strained ride, mostly because the last twenty-four hours have been a lot and I'm not sure what to say. When we get to the house, a neat stucco building a little bit west of Sunset Boulevard, I follow his lead and hope to hell he has a plan.

The victim's wife answers on the first knock, as if she's been waiting for us. Like the three victims, she's on the downhill side of middle age, and like the victims, she's a supe.

Succubus, unless my nose is lying like a rug.

Connor introduces us and we follow her into the house. The floor is tile and the walls are black and when we reach the living room, the windows look out over the city. The sunset is washing everything with amber, a fairly stunning and unexpected view. She invites us to sit, like this is a social call, and I perch on the edge of a swooping mid-century chair, keeping my mouth shut so Connor can do the heavy lifting.

"I'm sorry about your wife—" he begins.

"Ex-wife." She's made the correction before he can finish the word.

"I am sorry to be disturbing you in such a difficult time."

He's so composed, and so sincere, and so very, very handsome. My heart gives a poorly timed flip and *damn*. I must have exuded some kind of pheromone because the succubus looks over at me with an eyebrow raised.

"I didn't expect two of you," she says, her comment aimed at me. She clearly expects an answer, so I try to untangle my tongue.

"I work with Mr. MacPherson on certain cases where my, uh, skills would be useful."

"Ah..." She settles into an overstuffed chair, her loose silk gown draping gracefully around her. "You're a wolf. Did you smell anything funny when you saw my ex?"

"Actually no, I didn't."

Connor hushes me and I give an apologetic shrug. "We can't really speak to the investigation," he says, "as it's still in the early stages."

"Sure. They only called me a couple hours ago to share the unfortunate news." Again her gaze drifts toward me. "You're so young. Surely you've got better things to do than sniff around dead people."

Help me, Connor. I send up a mental SOS. I knew coming here was a shit idea. "I try and use my powers for good," I say a shade pompously, hoping she'll get the joke.

"Hmm…have you seen many dead bodies?"

Okay, that's enough. I give her my most polished, yes-I'm-an-alpha-wolf smile and nod in my associate's direction. "I think Connor has more important questions for you."

"That's right—"

"But I want to know." She speaks over him, her attention locked on me.

"Fine." I straighten, pretty sure there's no comfortable angle to be had in this thing that passes for a chair. "I'm fairly new to the game, but as you probably know from the news, your ex is the third in a recent string of murders. I've seen all of them."

"I don't watch the news," she says mildly. "What are their names?"

I glance at Connor and he shrugs. "I mean, you can google them if you want, but okay. They were Adaline Nosaka and Monica Johnson."

For the first time, the succubus looks flustered. "Adaline and Monica were two of Kitten's best friends from high school."

I blink and Connor sits up straighter.

"But they graduated from different schools." I can't remember the name of Monica's private school, but it wasn't the same as Adaline's.

Connor pulls out a note pad and starts jotting things down.

"I didn't know them then," the succubus says as if she couldn't believe we'd think she was *that* old. "I'm almost certain they were all freshmen at Beverly Hills High, however."

I can barely keep my ass on this funky old chair. If all three of our victims were friends, there has to be something in their shared past that would account for the killings.

Connor manages to get a couple questions in – how long she'd known Kitten and how long they'd been married. Whether she could think of anyone who might want to kill her ex. That sort of thing. I listen with half an ear, because really I'm planning the internet search that's going to tie the three homicides together.

Exhausting his supply of questions, Connor stands, so I do, too. "Thank you for your help. If you think of anything else, please let me know."

He hands her a business card, which she sets on an end table. She rises from her pillowy chair and offers her hand for Connor to shake. She just smiles at me. "You need to take this piece of Grade A beefcake home and roll him good, hon," she says, leaving me with my jaw hanging open.

I manage to garble something in the neighborhood of thanks and follow Connor to the street. "Succubus, man," I mumble, and he knocks into me with his elbow.

"Next time I'm getting on your nerves, you just remember I'm Grade A."

I laugh, probably too loudly for this neighborhood. I can't help myself, though. "You'd think the LAPD could find such an obvious link between Monica and Adaline."

Connor looks up from his phone. "You think they're even trying? The victims are supes. That's why Smith has such free reign, and you and I are allowed on the crime scenes in the first place. If we don't find the killer, no one will."

"Well, fuck." That takes me down a peg. Still… "But we've found the connection. It'll just be a matter of figuring out who they pissed off in high school. We can do this." I'm so excited it's hard to stand still. I'm not at all sure I want to be an investigator when I grow up, but if I decide to try, I want to be a good one.

Connor gives my arm an affectionate squeeze. "Let's get out of here." Before I can hit the Uber app, a big, black SUV pulls up.

The driver rolls down the window and shakes his finger at Connor with a grin that's on the wild side of human. "Well, look what the wolf dragged in," he says.

"Kerr," Connor says, his voice strangled. There's another man in the SUV, an older man. "Colonel Poole."

The Colonel rolls down his window. "Get in, Mack. We need to talk."

The back door pops open and Connor gestures at it as if he wants me to get in. I gesture right back because no way am I getting trapped in the middle of the seat. He gets in, leaving space for me by the window.

"What the hell is going on?" I hiss, climbing into the SUV only because I don't want to wear out my shoes walking all the way home.

"Hey, look at that little hot tamale," the driver says, giving me the creepiest once-over I've ever received.

"Fuck off, Kerr." Connor's uncharacteristic snarl freaks me out as bad as anything else. He sounds like he could take the driver outside and shoot him without breaking a sweat.

"Stop. Both of you," Poole says. He's clearly their commanding officer, and they both shut up. Kerr puts the car in gear, and Poole keeps talking. "I have new information for you, information regarding the missing princess."

"Wait a minute." He may be a military officer but my father is the American Alpha and hell yes I can shut people up when I want to. I turn on Connor, finger raised. "There's only one answer I want to hear. Are you back working for the Elites?"

"No," he says and flicks a glance at Poole.

The glance does it.

"Fuck the shoes, I'm out." I pop open the door, glad we're only rolling at about twenty-five miles an hour.

Kerr slams on the brakes, and Poole starts shouting. The only voice I hear is Connor's. "Please don't tell him, *mo mhuirnin*. I can explain, but you need to give me a chance."

"Give you a...?" I all but leap out of the car. "Aw, hell no. Fuck you, Connor MacPherson. Fuck you."

Why did he have to go and do the one thing he's promised not to do? I swear I don't get people sometimes. On one hand, he's upset by what happened at the club, but on the other, he's still mixing it up with the Elites.

Crudzilla, I really need a cigarette.

CHAPTER FIFTEEN

W hat the hell was that about?" Poole snaps, leaning over the seat so he can glare at me. I'm too busy staring at David's retreating back to answer him.

"Well?"

I tear myself away from David and face my former commanding officer. "It's personal, sir."

"Hey, like, I don't want to interrupt, but can we keep going?" Brodie's grin says he's actually quite happy to interrupt, that he's about two steps away from busting a gut laughing.

"Drive." Poole settles into his seat, facing the front window. "Elites don't let personal stuff interfere with their work."

I glare at the back of his head, biting back something sarcastic. "I'm no longer a member of the Elites." Even that's snottier than I'd intended. Well, I kept the words professional anyway.

Poole doesn't bother to reply, and we drive in silence for a good ten or fifteen minutes. I have no idea where we're going, except that we're on Santa Monica Boulevard heading in the direction of the 101. Rush hour's hanging on indefinitely, so instead of heavy traffic we're barely moving, making the tension in the car all the more unpleasant.

Brodie and Poole seem bent on the silent treatment, but I need to know what the hell's going on. "Do we have an actual destination, or is this a joyride?"

Brodie starts humming the *Ode to Joy* and I clasp my hands in my lap so I don't smack him.

"Your great-whatever grandmother is concerned that you're not paying enough attention to the problem of finding the missing elf princess. She thought if we had a little heart-to-heart, it might motivate you."

It takes me a moment to respond because my jaw has dropped. "And you went along with her nonsense?"

My head jerks as if I've been slapped. There's no one else in the car besides the three of us, and Brodie and Poole are facing front. I inhale a calming breath and allow my eyelids to slide nearly shut. Cutting out most of the visual input allows me to better see auras, and while I don't see her silhouette, there's an amorphous mass of darkness between me and the front seat of the car.

Apparently the Morrigan has come along for the ride.

That makes things more complicated. I don't want to share what I learned from Sam Kowalski, because Ananda Pendragon might throw me out of the vehicle for even hinting she might be a jilted lover. Plus, I want to keep my promise to Kowalski, that I'll let Ananda know the Princess Tatiana has been found, without divulging her location.

All that means I keep my mouth shut and ride along on this fool's errand, hoping like hell we turn up something useful.

In an odd way I'm grateful for the Morrigan's presence, because it gives me something to fret over rather than whatever the hell's going to be waiting for me at home. If David tells Trajan I'm working for the Elites, there's very little chance I'm going to be able to convince him otherwise.

And I'm not working for them. I'm working with them, helping out on one specific task and honoring my oath because Poole decided to be a dick about things. I don't quite understand David's anger, but I can only hope he calms down enough not to blow me out of the water.

Poole interrupts my navel-gazing with a stern, "So what were you doing at that house where we picked you up? Did that have something to do with the Princess?"

I reach for my wallet. "I'm a private investigator now, Colonel, and I'm working on a case with the supernatural liaison for the LAPD." I hold out one of my business cards, but before he can take it, the card bursts into flame.

"Damn." It burns my fingertips and I drop it.

"Hey now." Brodie swerves into the other lane, which is fortunately empty. "You behave back there. Don't bother the driver."

Poole shifts so he can glare at me. "Do you have any progress to report?"

"Yes." I'm just not going to tell him what I've learned.

The air temperature in the car increases until it's so hot sweat is beading up on my temples and above my upper lip. Brodie starts to whine because the windows won't roll down, and Poole's glare is almost as hot as the car.

I loosen my hold on those gifts I inherited from Mom and let the power fill my voice. "Stop, Ananda Pendragon. I said I would find the Princess Tatiana, and I will."

It's not like I'm going to win a war-of-the-powers with the Morrigan, but tapping into it reinforces my words as truth.

Maybe my coworkers had never heard that side of me, either. Brodie's shooting quick glances in the rearview, eyes so wide I can see the whites all the way around. Poole's not as dramatic, but even his gaze has turned wary.

"Is there anything else you all wanted? Because I need to get home." And god only knows what I'll have to face when I get there.

"Look, I'd rather be home in bed, too, and I don't appreciate being held hostage by a disembodied god." Poole's face pales, as if Great-whatever-Grandmother Ananda Pendragon has given him a private response.

"I said stop it, Ananda Pendragon. I can't find the princess from the back of this vehicle and these guys need to get home, too."

"You have three days, *meascach*. If you don't find her and bring her to me, the vampire will suffer, and so will that horrid little wolf."

The words are a hiss and given that neither Poole nor Brodie react, I must be the only one who can hear them. Brodie stops at a red light, and I swing open the door. "I'm sorry, Colonel. I'll retrieve the Princess as ordered and we can all be rid of my charming relative."

I've got one leg on the pavement when Brodie squawks. "What about me? Aren't you sorry that my night's been ruined, too?"

"Nah." I slam the door and, cutting between cars, make it to the sidewalk before the light changes.

I'm on the corner of Santa Monica and North Las Palmas Avenue, an area that's a mix of movie studios and strip malls. I could probably hike home, but it's uphill and I've had enough exertion for one night. It's dark enough that Trajan's risen, and if I'm going to be facing him for the final time, I don't want to do it covered in sweat.

The Uber driver covers the distance way too quickly. Maybe I should have walked. Staring at the graceful lines of this place that's starting to feel like home, I'm a jangle of nerves.

I'm not even at the front door when I hear it. Music. A loud, pompous orchestra and a shrieking soprano.

Wagner.

I am so fucked.

I'm debating whether I should come back after Trajan's down for the day when the door swings open. David glares at me from the threshold. "Get your ass in here. Now."

I can't make my feet move. "You told him."

His eye roll is one for the ages. "Hell no. I'm going to let you tell him."

"Then why Wagner?" David doesn't know Trajan as well as I do, but we've talked about his musical moods before.

"Maybe he hates lilies." He shakes his head, apparently disgusted. "Now get in here before I do tell him."

I do.

The soprano yields the floor to a brassy baritone, and I follow David into the house. He keeps going until we reach the swimming pool. Someone – probably David – has covered the crater left by the initial explosion with a piece of plywood and the deck is clean and wet. He must have hosed off all the blood, too.

David stands with his back to me, facing the pool. I'm not sure what to say, but after a couple moments he raises a hand, wiggling his fingers as if he's encouraging me to talk.

So I do. "I'm not working for the Elites."

He laughs, giving a half-hearted attempt to cover it with a cough. "Then what did Colonel Upchuck and his creeper sidekick want?"

"I'm going to tell you the truth."

This time he doesn't even try to cover his laugh.

I begin again, this time letting in some of the power I carry, power that I rarely ever use. "The truth is, several days ago Colonel Poole brought me to meet with a distant relative, my several-times great grandmother, who also happens to be one of the old ones, the Tuatha Dé Danann."

"Come on, pookie. You can do better than that."

His nickname for me sparks anger that I've done my best to quench. It flares and I raise my voice. "For the last time, I'm not a fucking phouka. My mother is descended from the Morrigan, and Ananda Pendragon has asked me to find a missing elven princess."

He stands frozen, hand still in the air. I move closer and interlace my fingers with his. "For whatever reason, the Morrigan used Poole as a go-between."

His fingers are stiff and he hasn't turned his head. "And you're going to tell Trajan this when?"

"Look, she's given me a deadline of three days to find the princess, and I'm hoping to beat that deadline. He's already having trouble trusting me. If I tell him now…"

He exhales, hard. "You're putting me in a shitty situation."

"I'm sorry. I didn't want either of you to find out. Please. If I haven't found her in three days, I'll tell him then."

A breeze kicks up driving wavelets across the pool. He doesn't say anything, but his fingers relax against mine.

"Thank you," I whisper. "Thank you for giving me another chance."

CHAPTER SIXTEEN

DAVID

Connor leaves right before the symphony of the damned – or whatever Tray's listening to – finally ends, almost as if he's afraid to face Trajan. *Whatever.* I kind of want to strangle him, so it's probably for the best.

I'm sprawled on the leather couch, counting tiny sparks of light in the inky blankness of the ocean. Boats…or mermaids. I'm not sure and I don't really care. Pouty David is pouty.

"What's that smell?" Trajan's standing in the doorway, scruffier than normal but upright, which I very much appreciate.

"Did you see the flowers?"

"What?"

"The lilies. Someone sent you a bouquet of white lilies. I" *—oops—* "read the card. The only signature was a fancy letter J."

Trajan stills, his cheeks turning an unnatural pale color and his eyes going dark. His snarl is full of fang. "Show me," he hisses.

His shift to full vampire has my wolf baring its teeth. I jump up, ready to run, both relieved that my wolf showed up and freaked out because the last time I saw Trajan lose his shit like this, he'd tried to drain Connor.

And the only way out of the room is past him. "They're in the dining room." I point in the general direction but don't move until he does.

The closer we get to the funeral arrangement, the more obnoxious the cloying and unpleasant sweetness becomes. Trajan pulls up in the doorway, so I slide past him into the dining room and pluck the card off its little stand. I hold the card out to him, but his attention is wholly on the lilies.

After an awkward moment, I toss the card onto the table. "It says he hopes you're feeling better and to remember what he told you."

Trajan doesn't respond, doesn't move.

"What'd he tell you, Tray?"

I might as well have been a fly on the wall.

"Did Connor say when he'd be back?"

I shrug, because I don't want to accidentally say something that I'll live to regret.

Palms together as if he's praying, Trajan presses his fingertips to his lips. There's something going on in his head but—

He spins and slams a fist into the wall.

I jump about three feet in the air and come down wishing he weren't blocking the room's only doorway. He stands there, fist embedded in the sheetrock. I can't see his face, but instinct tells me to keep very, very still.

It takes about three minutes for me to start feeling ridiculous. "Um, Tray?"

He doesn't move.

"Trajan? Are you okay, dude?"

"Go." He sounds like he's trapped in a sepulcher.

Part of me thinks going is a most excellent idea. Another part - *goddamn alpha tendencies* - sees a pack member who's hurting. I stay put, wondering whether my chance of survival would be better if I were on four paws.

Our confrontation lasts another couple minutes, until Trajan sighs, head tipped back, and shakes out his hand. I allow myself a slow breath. "You want to talk about it?"

His shoulders relax. "Nah," he says, giving me the least-convincing denial ever. He's flexing the fingers of his injured hand, and while there's no blood, his knuckles look pretty swollen.

"Are you…does it" —I take a tentative step in his direction, reaching for his hand—"did you break something?"

He snorts. "Doesn't matter. It'll heal."

Picking up the flowers, I nod toward the door. "Lemme toss these, and then we can..." My voice trails off, because I'm not sure what he's in the mood for.

"I've got to talk to Stone."

I blink at him over the death lilies. "O-kay."

He nods, as if he's agreeing with someone besides me. "I'll be back in an hour or so."

"You're not going to call him?"

"I'll be back." He pivots in full Terminator mode, and before I can track him, he's disappeared.

Standing there with my hands full of flowers, I address the place he had been. "Okay, that wasn't weird at all."

I'm dismantling the arrangement when I hear him leave. "Somehow," I tell one of the pristine white blossoms, "I don't think Connor's the only one with a secret." Whatever Jacques told Trajan had clearly rocked his world, and not in a good way.

Once I dump the flowers, I open some windows to clear the air of their lingering perfume. I drag my laptop into the living room and settle in, determined to find some kind of connection between the three murders.

If I keep my mind on Google, I might not start conjuring the perfect question to get Trajan to spit out what's got him all twisted, or planning ways to slip him Connor's secret without breaking my promise.

A promise that he extorted from me under extreme circumstances, I might add.

All right. Extorted might be too strong. Extracted maybe. Dragged out of me because, under certain circumstances, I'm better at conflict avoidance than anything else. Certain circumstances like this unexpected ménage relationship I've found myself in.

And what I'd do to keep it from ending.

Not just because then I'd be a lone wolf without a pack. And not just because I might have to choose between them. No, the real reason for my dread is that I've got as much invested in their relationship as either of them do. Their decisions affect me in a way I hadn't anticipated.

Opening my heart to more than one man has given both of them the tools to hurt me. I'll keep Connor's secret, but the words are clogging my throat and I'm worried they'll spill out before I can stop.

Google. Keep your mind on google.

In a couple of clicks I land on a website with an archive from the LA Times. I think my search terms are fairly narrow – events that occurred between 1978 and 1982 that are associated with

Beverly Hills High School – but once I click "enter" I've got almost fifty thousand hits.

Well damn.

It's going to take me some time to plow through all of them.

I click on the first link and learn that it's going to cost me eight dollars a month to actually see anything. *Oh ffs.*

I need some long-lived supe who might remember those days. Like, I don't know, Trajan maybe? I rub my temples where a headache is trying to settle in. Sheena's been in town as long as Trajan has, although I don't know if either of them were here in 1980.

Lydia? Yeah, she's old enough to remember those years. I shut down the laptop, figuring those fifty thousand newspaper mentions will still be there later. Lydia and I might not be friends, but I don't know many other people in this town. It's only eight or so. Worse case, she ignores me completely and I have to come up with another plan.

I send her a text and arrange a meeting. She asks me if I'm hungry and when I respond *I'm a twenty-three-year-old wolf,* she gives me a La Brea address. The street number suggests it's close to the place we've met before, so I aim for pseudo-grunge so I'll blend in with my surroundings.

As if. I put on a flouncy little dress that barely covers my butt and my favorite pair of semi-shredded jeans over fishnet tights, plus Doc Martens and a pearl necklace that Sheena was going to throw away. My coral lipstick clashes beautifully with my purple dress, and *Yes ma'am, baby is good to go.*

Turns out, I clash even harder with our destination, a treasure of a joint called Pinks. Lydia and a couple of her girls are on their bikes in the parking lot and they all grin when I hop out of the Uber.

"What in the world?" Lydia looks me up and down, chuckling to herself. "We're going to have to make you an honorary lesbian."

"Oh no." I match her tone, figuring if she's going to play nice, I can too. "I like dick far too much for that."

Lydia's two accomplices make appropriate gagging noises and we all head into Pinks, a real live, honest to goodness hot dog stand.

The two women with Lydia are butcher than me, even if I weren't wearing a dress. We make introductions and order from the eclectic menu. They're all appalled when I order something called a Tamale Sundae rather than a hot dog but I just shrug it off. "Sorry, ladies. I'm into adventure."

"We can tell," Lydia says, and that brings on another round of teasing. They like my dress but they're worried that I'm hot in both jeans and tights. They're not wrong.

Lydia must give her girls some unspoken sign, because they grab a table for two, leaving us with a booth to ourselves. We settle in; Lydia with her dog piled high with cheese and onions, and me with my sundae, which appears to be a tamale smothered in chili and cheese. We each have a soda to wash down all this mess, and once we're on our own, we're both surprisingly quiet.

I'm good with devouring my dinner, hungry enough to wonder if living on vampire time had me missing more meals than I realized. Of course, my recent blood donation might have something to do with it. If I dig too deeply into why I'm really here, though, it'll spoil my dinner, so I make a deliberate choice to worry about how my lipstick is holding up while I chow down.

"This food is really good," I manage between bites.

Lydia's poking at her dog. "Gotta keep a young wolf healthy. I am wondering what's up with you today, though."

I pause, fork in mid-air. "Welp, it's like this. Connor's doing this private investigator thing, and he's got me helping him."

"Private eye to the stars?"

"Nah." I laugh at the thought. "Private eye to the supes, more like it. He's working with Adam Smith, the supernatural liaison to the LAPD."

"I know Adam." She pauses for a swig of her coke. "He's a good dude."

"Seems to be, yeah."

Lydia's a good person, too. The lines on her face are honest, and I see both humor and caring in her gaze. Her wolves seem settled, secure, which makes me think she's the kind of alpha I would like to be.

"So Connor and Adam are investigating a string of murders. There are three victims, and they're all in their mid-fifties and they all attended Beverly Hills High School." I give her an apologetic smile. "I was just thinking if you were living here then, you might remember something that happened at that school, maybe around 1980."

She starts to laugh. "You say 1980 like you're afraid I'm going to be mad at you for guessing my age."

"Well, no, I didn't mean—"

"Sure you did. That's okay, too. I'm old enough to remember 1980, but sadly, off the top of my head, I don't remember anything that might help you."

I start to respond, but she interrupts me.

"Wait, now. Who might remember…"

She traces a fingertip through the sweat on the side of her soda, and I keep my mouth shut and let her think.

"One of my girls," she says finally, "her mother is about my age, and she's local, too. Let me talk to her and see if we can come up with something."

"Thank you. That would be awesome." More awesome than paying to dig through fifty thousand newspaper citations, anyway. We keep eating and I keep talking, and maybe it's because she's giving me older-sister vibes, I get into the thing with Trajan and Connor. Well, Connor's end of it, anyway. I'm not sure what's going on with Trajan. *Yet*.

"I don't want to lose either of them, you know?" The chili is sitting heavy in my gut. "But Trajan was pretty clear that he wanted Connor to leave the Elites, and Connor agreed."

"Why does Trajan get to say that?"

"I don't know." I smooth some hair that's starting to escape the product I applied.

"He try and dictate what you do like that?"

"No." The lie is kind of annoying because Trajan has been scheming for me to take over as his day rep for business. "I mean, he wants us to be happy and safe, and he was hurt pretty bad when Connor faked his own death."

She taps a French fry on her plate. "I agree that fake death was a shitty thing to do, but honestly, Connor could pull the same kind of bullshit even if he's not working for the Elites. The issue is trust, not what he's supposed to do with his life."

"That's true, and now he feels trapped in a situation where he's going to break Trajan's trust again."

"Seems like they need to work this out for themselves."

"But—"

"But you've got a stake in whatever they decide. I'm sorry, David. You're in a tight spot."

I smile in response, because even though she's right, it helps having someone get it. "Thank you for listening to me prattle. Worse comes to worst, I'll knock their heads together."

"And if that doesn't work, we can always make you an honorary lesbian if we need to."

No response is big enough for that honor, so I hope my smile is enough. I couldn't have said another word if I'd wanted to, not without crying anyway.

And if I cried it would ruin my mascara, so.

We finish dinner in a comfortable silence. Right before Lydia and her girls are ready to take off, I remember the Los Feliz alpha. "Did you ever hear back from that loser who thought he could grab your territory?"

Her grin takes on a dangerous edge. "Not yet, but when I do, I'm going to call you. If there's a rumble, I want you on my team."

I hold out my fist and she bumps it. "Any time, my friend. Any time."

CHAPTER SEVENTEEN

All that food has a sedative effect. I fall asleep before Trajan gets home and wake up right before he rises.

A text from Connor blinks at me from my phone. I need a moment, so I dive into the shower before reading it. Wrapped in the silky robe Trajan gave me on my birthday, I start a pot of coffee, then perch on one of the stools by the kitchen counter. With the pot burbling, I concede defeat and open the text.

Smith gave him the names of a dozen women who graduated the same year our victims did and he wants to decide to divide and conquer. *Should have waited till after I had some coffee.*

Making a mental list of all the ways this could go wrong, I respond with a vague *Sure.*

He responds quickly, as if he's afraid I'll change my mind, and before I've poured my coffee I'm reading through a list of names and contact information.

Then I get lucky.

Trajan strolls in, expression calm, hair slicked back, Micky Mouse tee shirt stretched tight over his biceps.

"Where'd you go?" I ask. He doesn't respond, but he doesn't stop moving until I'm wrapped in his embrace. He rests his cheek on the top of my head and some of the tension leaves the big body in my arms.

"Where'd you go?" He echoes my question.

I try to read the room. He's relaxed, no sign of impending doom. Good. "Grabbed a bite to eat with Lydia and a couple of her wolves."

He straightens, giving me a puzzled look. "Lydia Sanchez? The alpha?"

"Yeah. There was another murder." I tell him about my afternoon adventure with Connor, leaving out the side-trip with the Elites. "At any rate, when Kitten's ex said the murder victims were best friends in high school, I figured something must have happened back in the day that someone wants to kill for."

"That would be convenient."

"Yeah, it's a little murder-of-the-week, but it seemed like a good idea at the time."

"Did Lydia have any ideas?"

The coffee pot burbles and I hop up and give him a kiss. "Nope."

While pouring my coffee, I want to poke at him again, to try to figure out what really happened last night, but he distracts me with a question about Connor.

"Did he come home at all?"

The weight in his voice makes the identity of *he* obvious, but I don't have a good answer. "I didn't see him, but then I didn't check his toothbrush to see if it was damp." I shrug. "He just texted me, though. He asked me to interview a few women who might have been friends with the victims when they were in high school."

Trajan's look of interest takes me by surprise. "Let me see the list in case I know any of them."

I hold out my phone, half convinced that the thing we're best at is keeping secrets from each other.

"Laura Duran's a were from the Culver City pack. She's not Duran anymore, though, unless she's divorced and got rid of her husband's name." He scrolls down a bit more. "And Jennifer Maslow's a siren. She used to get singing gigs around town, but last I heard, she was living in San Francisco."

"Do you know every supernatural creature in town?"

He passes me the phone. "They say Hollywood's high school with money, and supes are just a different kind of celebrity."

"So if you're not busy, do you want to come with me to talk to any of these people?" Not that I couldn't do it alone but having Trajan along would make things more fun.

And I can keep an eye on him in case he turns back into a monster.

He agrees and I make a couple phone calls. There's no reason to expect any of them would be available for an interview after dark, but I do get three of them to agree. We plot their addresses on the map and I change out of my flirty little robe and into something a tick more professional. That means jeans with fewer holes and a University of Washington hoodie.

Our first interview is in West Hollywood, not far from the ex's house. The place Connor and I visited right before I caught him cavorting with the Elites. *Damn.* I keep my lip zipped while Trajan parks the car. We're looking for an apartment on the second floor of a three-story walk-up made of cinderblock and bougainvillea.

Trajan lets me take the lead, so I'm the one who knocks on the door. I'd be lying if I said I wasn't a little nervous about finding another dead body. Fortunately, someone living answers the door. He's tall – tall enough that I wonder if there's a touch of troll in his background – and his heavy brows give him a permanently suspicious expression.

"Hi," I say, trying to make myself look as benign as possible. "I'm looking for Janet Edmonds."

The guy's expression doesn't change, although his gaze drifts from me to Trajan. "Janet," he bellows, and without inviting us in, he steps away from the door.

A woman takes his place. She's tall and lanky, with at least some elven blood, judging by her scent. She doesn't look a whole lot older than me, but then supes don't age like ordinary humans.

"What do you want?" she asks, which is a little odd because I told her over the phone that I wanted to talk to her about high school.

"So I'm an investigator"—small white lie—"helping the LAPD with a series of murders. All the victims have been supes, and all of them went to Beverly Hills High School at the same time."

"So?"

"I'm wondering if you knew Adaline Nosaka, Monica Johnson, or Kitten Fletcher."

"Yeah. So?"

"Can you think of a reason someone would want to kill them?"

"Cuz they're stuck-up bitches and always have been?"

The venom in her tone takes me back a step. Literally. I bump into Trajan, and he puts a hand on my shoulder.

"When's the last time you talked to any of them?" he asks smoothly, and I take a minute to catch my breath. This investigator stuff is hard.

Janet plants her hands on her hips and snorts a laugh. "Never have spoken to any of them. Bitches like that don't hang with a low-class halfling like me."

"Shut it, Janet," her man-friend hollers from somewhere in the apartment. "You're worth two of any of them."

"So you say," she responds, but her expression softens some.

An idea occurs to me, one that I hadn't entertained before. "Were they all, like, cheerleaders or something?"

Her lips press together in something like exasperation. "You're going to make me dredge it all up." She rubs her forehead with the palm of her hand. "Monica and Adaline were cheerleaders and Kitten was homecoming queen. Can you believe that? A fucking fairy for a homecoming queen. There were a couple other bitches in their posse. Uh…what the fuck were their names?"

I keep my mouth shut and let her think.

"One of them was Amanda. She was another cheerleader. The other was…shit…Donna.

Donna Del-something. They ruled the school. I kid you not."

We talk for a while longer, but other than that she still carries a grudge because the murder victims always wore the cutest designer clothes, we don't learn much. We say goodnight and head back to the Range Rover.

"Good job," Trajan says and hits the switch to start the engine.

I give a half-hearted laugh, because *what the hell is he talking about?*

"I mean it. You managed to keep her talking. She even smiled a little bit when we left."

"Smiled because she was happy to get rid of us, you mean."

"No, you come off as cute and a little goofy, and people like talking to you."

"So I should be an investigator when I grow up?"

"Only if you get bored being my daytime business manager."

I roll my eyes and plug the next address into the map app. "I mean, I can see why she'd hate them. I have a hard time with anyone who consistently dresses better than I do."

Trajan raises one eyebrow but otherwise keeps his mouth shut. We make our second stop, a lovely home in Beverly Hills where the couple were both petite and perfect and clearly had pixie blood in them. They were brother and sister, and they both remember the murder victims from school. Other than to confirm Janet Edmond's assessment – that the victims were school royalty and potentially not very nice – we didn't learn anything new.

Our third visit, however… "Hey, this is interesting. The name Smith gave us is Bobby DelMarco. Wonder if she's any relation to Donna, the one Janet mentioned."

"Bobby DelMarco…I know him, too." Trajan backs the Range Rover out of the driveway, his expression showing a hint of fang. "Did you talk to Bobby himself?"

"I talked to an older guy, but I assumed Bobby was the one who attended school with the victims and the old guy was Bobby's father."

"Nah, I bet you talked to Bobby. He's a biscione, and oh for fuck's sake…"

"What?"

"So biscione are rare. They're Italian, and they can take the form of a snake. They only breed every seven years, and they stay true to their race."

"What does that mean?"

"There are no half-bisciones floating around. Their women can only conceive with a male biscione, and only once every seven years."

"Which is why they're so rare."

"More or less. As a race, they seem destined to die out."

"Sounds like."

"So when a young biscione dies, it's a big fucking deal."

I shift in my seat so I can stare at him. "What?"

"So." He bumps the heel of his hand against the steering wheel. "Bobby DelMarco had a daughter who died before she turned twenty-one."

"A daughter named Donna?"

"Not sure, but maybe."

"Huh." I settle back in my seat, pondering this new information. I'd been searching for something that tied the victims together, something that would give someone a motive for murder. "Wonder how Bobby DelMarco's daughter died."

We're headed into East LA, to the town of Montebello. It's maybe nine-thirty at night and traffic is heavy on the–Ten, which gives me plenty of time to think. My mind skips from Trajan's comment about my investigation skills to his reminder about the daytime business manager idea to wondering why I'd assumed there had to be an event that tied all the murders together.

"I mean, there could be another bitter Janet like the one we just talked to, taking revenge against all the girls she hated in high school."

"Maybe?" Trajan shoots me a glance, then curses because some idiot in an overlarge truck moves into our lane with no notice and barely enough space.

Things calm down, which is why I decide to throw a verbal hand-grenade. "Who do you think shot you?"

Trajan goes awfully quiet, even turning a little pale. I count to ten, hoping the fact that he's driving will keep him from turning full vamp. He finally answers, but the words come at some cost.

"If I had to guess, I'd say Jacques."

"I mean, the J on the card gave me a clue, but he's had 150 years to get rid of you. Why now?"

Trajan shrugs, slow, like his shoulders are weary. "We had a difference of opinion."

I let the intensity of my stare be my only answer, and after a minute, he keeps talking.

"I asked him if he'd sell me the house we're living in, and when he refused me flat, I said I'd buy someplace else. He didn't like that and well," he shrugs again, "if I die, he inherits all my possessions. I think he just wanted to remind me of that."

"Jesus." I drag the word out, because there's a tightness around his eyes that makes me wonder if he's telling me the truth.

"Yeah. It was a strange night all the way around. For the first time ever, he complained about my deviant lifestyle."

The tightness fades, or maybe my weird-ass alpha upbringing has me seeing trouble where there is none. I mean, I have no reason to think he might lie – other than the hole in our dining room wall, which seems like an excessive reaction for an argument over a house.

He navigates around another asshole driver, then puts his blinker on. The map app is warning us to take the next exit. We do, and it doesn't take long to get from there to Bobby DelMarco's house.

The Montebello neighborhood is more suburban than the places we've been in LA. The lots are bigger, and while the houses all have a hacienda influence, they're larger, newer, and they sprawl over their lots like piles of tumbled bricks. I let Trajan take the lead, since he's met Bobby before. My investigator skills might have impressed him, but I don't want to push my luck.

The door is opened by a man. He's not much taller than I am and while there's a sprinkle of grey in his dark hair, his face isn't lined and his body is firm. He might be forty. Maybe.

"Are you Bobby's son?" Trajan asks, and the guy nods without speaking. "We're here to talk to your dad."

He steps aside and motions us to follow him. We do, down a long hallway with a tile floor and into a huge room with a ceiling that has to be two stories high. There's a kitchen at one end, separated from the rest by a large, faux-antique island. At the end closest to us, a couch and two overstuffed chairs are pulled up close to a fireplace. Two people are side by side on the couch, and they stand up when we walk in.

The man is an older version of the guy who answered the door, and weirdly, the woman is an older slightly-more-feminine version. They all share thick, curly dark hair, dark eyes, and the skin tone that the southern California sun keeps permanently tanned.

Trajan introduces us, and the old guy, Bobby, asks us to sit down. We do, though I'm so nervous I'm twitching like a cat in a rainstorm.

"We're working with Adam Smith, the supernatural liaison to the LAPD. He's looking into a series of murders where all the victims were supes," Trajan says.

"I heard about Addy Nosaka," the woman says, her voice the kind of well-modulated purr that fits the palatial setting. "Have there been others?"

"Unfortunately, yes," I say. Bobby and his wife share a glance. The younger guy sits at the long dining table. It's in between us and the kitchen and could easily seat twelve or fourteen.

The current mood in the place doesn't fit a large, boisterous gathering.

Trajan gets them talking about mutual friends, and I take stock of all the scents. The two most prominent are old roasted meat and a light, unfamiliar fragrance that is likely biscione. I've never met one before – hell, I'd never heard of one until Trajan mentioned them half an hour ago – so I make a mental note and stick a pin in it for later.

"I understand you have a daughter." I wait for a pause in the conversation and float the comment out there.

"We did, yes." Mrs. DelMarco's tone deepens, as if sadness is weighing her down.

"She died about forty years ago, actually," Bobby DelMarco says. "She drowned out at the Santa Monica pier right after graduation."

"What school did she go to?" I ask.

"Beverly Hills High." Mrs. DelMarco has picked up the baton. "We moved out here after Donna...." She makes a weak wave and I fill in the blanks.

"Joey went to Montebello High," she finishes sadly.

Okay, so the younger guy is Joey DelMarco. I make another mental note.

"Do you remember who her friends were?" I'm hoping against hope that some of the victims come up.

Bobby DelMarco reaches over to his wife and takes hold of her hand. "Addy Nosaka was her best friend," she says. "I got to be pretty good friends with Akira, Addy's mother. That's how we knew about her death."

"There was that Monica girl," Bobby mumbles, and his wife nods.

"Yes. Monica Johnson and Kitten Fletcher. The four of them were very close." Mrs. DelMarco smiles but even that is weighed down with sadness. "We used to call them the brat pack after the kids who were in all those movies."

I'm not sure if I should tell the DelMarcos about Monica and Kitten or not. Trajan's expression is carefully neutral. No help there. I decide not to – the evening news can do the job for me – but then Bobby sits up straighter.

"You said Smith is looking into a series of murders. Is Addy one of those?" he asks.

Trajan nods calmly. "Yes."

The color rises in Bobby's cheeks. "And who else?"

"Monica and Kitten." Trajan sounds calm, but his posture firms, as if he's ready to wrestle a snake if necessary.

"All of Donna's best friends." Mrs. DelMarco finds a new depth of sadness.

"So why didn't you lead with that, tell us right up front?" Bobby's *s*'s have taken on an extra hiss.

"Because we didn't know they were your daughter's best friends." I hold my hands out, palms up. "We didn't know until you told us."

"Joey." Bobby snaps his son's name. "See these two hoodlums out."

The younger DelMarco reaches my chair so fast I blink. I stand and so does Trajan.

"Can you think of a reason someone would kill those women?" Trajan sounds reasonable, but the air crackles in response to his question.

"Good night," is all Bobby will say, and his wife stays silent.

"Well, if you think of anything, call my associate Connor MacPherson." Trajan offers a business card to Bobby, who ignores him.

The young DelMarco grabs my shoulder, just this side of rude, and I shake free. "All right, we'll go. Thank you for your time." *And for tying things up so neatly.* Trajan sets the business card on the small table in the foyer, and we leave.

We make it out to the car without any inadvertent snake-wrestling, and Trajan has us on the road to home a helluva lot faster than we got here.

"Okay, that was weird, right?" I finally manage.

"Yup," he says grimly. "That was weird."

"Do you think DelMarco killed them?"

"But why? What happened in the last month to prompt him to take action now, after forty years?"

"Good question."

Trajan wrangles his big rig through traffic on the Ten and I text Connor, asking where we can meet.

Because he and Smith need to know what we've learned, and it's not the kind of info I want to share over the phone.

CHAPTER EIGHTEEN

David texts me to say he's learned something important but wants to tell me in person. That's a good thing, but I'm in the car with Smith and we have an appointment.

The kind of appointment I can't miss.

We're meeting a necromancer at the Hollywood Forever cemetery, and unless I want to piss off a fairly powerful supernatural being, I'll be there. Trajan's always warned me about messing around with necromancers, but I need answers, and sometimes the fastest way is to pose those questions to the dead.

Smith was weirdly reluctant to come along, but once he was in, he took charge and insisted on driving. Cruising down Santa Monica Boulevard, we don't talk much. He's wearing the kind of jacket and pants an aging hippie might drag out to prove he's respectable. Except for the flipflops. Must be a shark shifter thing.

The police radio under the dash of his Jeep Cherokee chatters away – the LAPD never sits around bored – while I try to compose the kind of text that will get David to tell me what he's discovered without actually asking him.

David shuts me down at about the same time Smith pulls into a parking lot, right past a sign that says Hollywood Forever Cemetery.

Hollywood Forever.

The cemetery is closed for the night, and I wonder whether the LAPD will charge us with trespassing if we get busted. Being designated Supernatural Liaison might have enough cred to keep us from a citation, but I'm pretty sure a PI's license does not.

"The necromancer's name is Sunbeam and she says we're meeting at the mausoleum by Chris Cornell." I pull up a map of the cemetery on my phone.

"I know it," he says, and there's a grim note to his tone that catches my attention. I don't know. Maybe the guy just doesn't like dead things.

We climb out of the Cherokee and Smith takes off as if he does know exactly where he's going. I follow him on the paved drive through the manicured grounds. I'm telling myself I'm more curious than nervous, until a flash of movement makes me jump.

A cat leaps from the top of one of the mausoleums and lands on the ground, tail switching.

"What is it?" Smith asks.

I point at the cat and he laughs softly. Now that I know to look for them, there are cats everywhere. Cats and white marble statuary and tall palm trees casting distorted shadows in the moonlight.

We've walked maybe five minutes when the silhouette of a man catches my attention. I reach for the weapon I shouldn't be carrying, and all my muscles tense.

Smith doesn't even ask, this time. He just laughs as we pass the statue of Chris Cornell, grunge god.

Okay, that's enough. "We must be close."

"Right here." Smith points behind Mr. Cornell, where a large pool lies glassy and still under the moonlight.

There's a mausoleum on an island in the center of the pool, a larger version of the chest high temples of the dead that are scattered around the cemetery. White marble steps lead from the mausoleum to the water, and a young woman sits on the lowest step.

Her feet are submerged and she has a cigarette in one hand. Periodically flicking the ash and kicking up swirls of water, she watches us approach.

Smith stops, fists notched on his hips. "Sunbeam?"

"Aye aye, Captain." She kicks harder, splashing water in our general direction. Her aura, if you can call it that, is a thin outline that's not so much black as it is the total absence of light around her.

"Should I roll up my pants?" I ask.

Smith ignores the question. He walks along the perimeter of the pool, and it doesn't take long before we come to a little bridge to the center island. Another statue startles me, and without breaking stride, Smith says, "It's one of the Ramones."

Laughing at myself, I keep walking.

The bridge is blocked with a sawhorse and a "Closed" sign. Ignoring it, we walk around and come up on Sunbeam from behind. She's still splashing her feet in the water, and if it makes her nervous to have two guys creeping up on her, it doesn't show.

"You can stop now."

Something in her tone of voice locks my feet in place on the top step so sharply I almost lose my balance. Smith is at my elbow and just as stuck.

"Oh, sorry," she says, with just a hint of a snicker. "Wait. Hang on. What's *he* doing here?"

Smith twitches like he's been stabbed with a pin.

I put a hand on his arm. "I told you I'd be bringing the guy I'm working with."

Whatever is gripping my feet tightens its hold. "Wait. Which of you is the guy from the Securitas?"

"I am. Connor MacPherson, but I'm not with them anymore."

"You didn't tell me you were also one of *those*."

Smith glances at me and I give him my best clueless shrug. "Should I go back to the car?" I'd hoped she could help me find the princess, but if she kicks me out, Smith can ask her questions about the murders.

"As long as you promise to keep it in your metaphysical pants, we're good." Sunbeam the necromancer laughs at her own joke, and I ignore Smith's raised eyebrows.

"Your message said you wanted to hear from a couple of our recent dearly departed." All of a sudden her voice is too close, too intimate, and it sends goosebumps down my neck. "This town's full of 'em, you know? You might need to be more specific."

"Three women," Smith says tightly. "All of them in their late fifties."

"Hmm…" Her feet still. "They're all together. Are they sorority sisters or something?"

"They all went to the same high school," I say.

She tosses the smoke into the water and raises her arms. Three figures rise from the pool. One is Asian and the other two are white, closely resembling the photos of the victims. They appear to be solid, although I cannot see their auras, which is unnerving. There's either something dark wrapped around their feet or they're standing a few inches deep in the water.

"Ask them if they know who killed them," Smith says, his voice barely above a whisper.

Sunbeam literally wiggles her fingers like she's some kind of Scooby Doo cartoon villain. When her fingers still, the darkness surrounding them rises and then consolidates.

The head of a snake takes shape, its tongue a gold flash flickering in and out.

"Well, that's weird," Sunbeam says. "Guess someone doesn't want them to tell you anything."

The snake's head rises above the spirits' heads, glaring eyes gone red. Smith mutters something that begins and ends in *damn*.

"They can't tell you anything?" I ask, although the snake is threatening in a way a spirit shouldn't be able to manage.

Sunbeam shakes her head no, and the figures fade.

"Can you look for someone else? There's an elven princess who's been missing for a while. Does anyone there know if she's still alive?"

Smith gives a frustrated huff and I ignore him. Sunbeam wiggles her fingers again, the least-frightening necromancer move ever. A figure takes shape, but this time it's no one I recognize.

Not an elf, either.

"Connor MacPherson. *Meascach*." The voice comes from a patch of grey blotting out the moon's reflection on the water. "Tread carefully. The Morrigan is no one's friend. The vampire's desires are evil, but so are hers, and she'll start a war if she can."

The words and the grey fade away, to be replaced by a much more intrusive voice. "Cryptic much," Sunbeam says, so close it's as if she has her chin on my shoulder. "If you need me to take care of a vamp for you, it's a g-note per attempt. I usually get it done in one."

A puff of air hits my neck, making me jump. Smith still looks a little constipated, unhappy with my question. The figure disintegrates into a cloud of fluttering insects and Sunbeam's knees give way. She lands hard on the steps, the darkness of her aura almost obscuring her.

Smith gets to her first. He helps her sit and waves at a leather satchel near the mausoleum.

I grab the bag and bring it to him. He pulls out a bottle of Jack Daniels, then helps Sunbeam hold onto the bottle and bring it to her lips. A healthy swig brings on a coughing fit, but when she calms, she's sitting straighter and holding the bottle on her own.

"I should charge you extra for bringing up one of the fucking old ones."

"Who was it?" Smith asks.

"Sorry. I didn't ask."

She didn't, but my gut said we'd been visited by Dian Cecht, the one they call the healer. Dian Cecht, son of the Morrigan's husband Dagda by a different goddess. *If this is all some kind of metaphysical marital spat, I'm going to be so pissed.*

"…start a war if she can," I mumble, earning a glare from Smith.

"Send me the bill and I'll have the department pay it."

That makes her laugh. "Oh yeah, I'm just sure the business office of the LAPD is going to be good with an invoice from a fucking necromancer."

She takes another hit off the bottle, caps it, and shoves herself to her feet. "As much fun as that was, I've got another gig. You two take care and, uh, *meascach,* be careful. I don't chat up many living gods, but the force of his concern about made me gag."

Looping the satchel over her arm, she's got the bottle in her hand as she heads for the bridge. We follow more slowly, and by the time we reach the lawn, she's disappeared.

"Well that was…" I can't think of what to call it. Disappointing? Frustrating? Minimally helpful? I have no idea what to make of the stuff about the Morrigan. Which vampire did the spirit mean? Not Trajan. He's not up to anything evil.

"You going to explain that?" Smith sounds testy, and to be honest, I can't blame him. Still, he's been willing to share, so I give him the bullet points – without mentioning my family connections to the story.

"So…" Smith drags out the word. "One of the oldest of the Celtic living gods hooked up with an elven princess, who broke up with her and then disappeared, and now this Morrigan may or may not be trying to start a war between the vampires and the elves."

"More or less, yes."

"Why does she care what the vampires and the elves do?"

"I don't know." Frustration leaks out in a sigh. "And to be honest, I'm not even sure it's possible. I mean, the vampires don't have any kind of central organization the way the weres do. At least the elves have royalty who can bring their subjects together. Vampires owe loyalty to their makers, but that's about as far as it goes. A war between the vampires and the elves would be a quick one, because the elves would coordinate their efforts and stake them all while the vampires were still deciding whether or not to trust each other."

Still combing the facts to find the Morrigan's angle, I follow Smith to his car. He takes me to the park-n-ride where I left the Taurus, and we make a plan to regroup in the morning.

"Before we split up, I have a question." I'm halfway out of the car and my eyes are gritty with fatigue. Murder investigations don't run on vampire time. They're more of a 24/7 operation. "Besides Jacques Betancourt and that vampire sire in Pasadena, are there any other pods in the greater LA area?"

Smith pulls an irritated face. "I've got that in a file somewhere. I'll shoot you a copy."

"Thanks," I say, climbing the rest of the way out of his Cherokee. He drives off and I stare at my Taurus, wishing I'd had the cojones to rent something a little more comfortable.

"Don't need a Mercedes-Maybach, but damn." The engine starts, so I count it as a win and head for home.

I've got a bottle of cold brew in the car so by the time I pull in behind Trajan's Range Rover, caffeine has my motor running. Still, I pause for a minute to sort through my priorities.

The Morrigan has made it clear the princess is being held by a vampire, and that finding her should be my top priority. After combing through my old files, the packet from the elf Kowalski, and the cartoonishly thin file Poole sent me, I hadn't found anything to dispute that. Everything pointed to a vampire, most likely Jacques Betancourt.

Per my old files, the last time the Princess Tatiana was seen, she was with Betancourt.

And although Betancourt has more money than god, he's rumored to be linked to a series of petty thefts of magical materials he could easily have bought. He's also been in league with David's late uncle Brendan, on some level, a relationship I can't easily explain.

And – *surprise!* – Poole had actually sent a guy into Betancourt's house, and while he hadn't found the princess, he reported a weirdly blank space, a closet his sensors couldn't penetrate.

So, Princess Tatiana might have decided that powerful vampires were her thing and moved on to another after Betancourt, but nothing in the files hints at that.

I figure I must be down to about sixty hours before hitting the Morrigan's deadline, and the message tonight was pretty much preaching to the choir. I don't trust the Morrigan, and other than Trajan, I don't trust any vampires.

Due diligence would have me contact other vampire pods in the city in a way that doesn't involve Trajan. Hopefully, Smith will follow through and send me some names. LA is a big place, but there can't be more than one or two other pods or there wouldn't be any humans with enough blood left to clog the freeways the way they do.

Next on my list is the high school murders. The snake tonight was interesting, although I couldn't tell if it was a threat or not. Hard to threaten a dead woman, right?

With any luck, the news David didn't want to share by text will push at least one of my priorities along.

The house is quiet when I let myself in. I find David on his laptop in the living room.

"Trajan was getting twitchy so I sent him downstairs to the weight room," he says. "He might not be able to bulk up, but at least he's not getting on my nerves anymore."

He sets aside his computer and hops up. Coming so close I'm fluttering his hair when I exhale, he wraps his arms around my waist. "I won't tell him, Connor. I promise. You have to, though."

I tip my head to press a kiss against his hair. "I will, *mo mhuirnin.*" He sighs and I pull him closer. "Now spill." I squeeze him like I can force the information out of him. "What did you not want to put in a text message?"

He plants his hands on my chest and shoves, forcing me to give him a little more space. He's smiling, which is about the prettiest thing in my world. "Well," he says. "First we learned that those old friends were high school royalty, and the have-nots don't remember them fondly at all." He goes back to his laptop, opening a new browser page and typing something in.

"And, they had a fourth, a girl named Donna DelMarco." He holds up his laptop to show me the image of an old LA Times article. The picture that goes with the article shows a beautiful girl with long, straight hair that curled back from her face starting at about her cheekbones.

"Apparently they were close enough their parents called them the brat pack."

"Cute."

"And Donna died right after high school graduation."

"What'd she die of?" I ask, turning because I hear Trajan's footsteps on the stairs.

Trajan reaches the main floor in time to answer. "She drowned off the Santa Monica pier." He joins us in the living room. "The LA Times article implies the kids were partying, and the cops at the time ruled out foul play."

"So a drunken accident, then?"

"Something like that," David says. "Although that doesn't seem to be much motivation for murder, especially forty years later."

"Hmph." I reach around to give Trajan a kiss, because it's been too long. Have I seen him since the night he got shot? Maybe. Even with the caffeine, my brain is next to mush. "So I did something weird tonight."

Both of them ask what, so I continue. "Smith and I consulted a necromancer, and—"

"You have got to be joking." Trajan's calm is gone in a second. "Necromancers are the worst. What if they find out where you live?"

I pat his arm. "I didn't even give her my name, let alone our address, so calm down."

"What did you give her? They don't come cheap."

"Smith told her to invoice the LAPD, but that's beside the point. The necromancer raised the spirits of Adaline, Monica, and Jasmine, and you know what?"

Another chorus of "What?" and "Tell us already!"

"They were surrounded by the body of an enormous serpent, and when the necromancer asked who'd murdered them, the snake threatened us." I shake my head. "One of the top ten freakiest things I've ever seen."

"Well, hold on to your sunbonnet, sweet pea." David's tone is jocular but his expression is dead serious. "Because tonight we talked to the dead girl's parents. They're biscione, an Italian shifter that can turn themselves into a snake."

The room gets very quiet.

"Well, shit," I finally say. "Looks like we might have our killer."

PART FOUR: MO CHONTÚIRT

CHAPTER NINETEEN

TRAJAN

necromancer. Why the hell not? If things are going to fall apart, they may as well go all the way.

This is the first time I've seen Connor since my meeting with Jacques, and the exhaustion in his expression distracts me from my ugliest impulse. "When's the last time you slept?" I ask, and he rakes a hand through his hair.

"Don't remember. All the days are running into one."

Jacques' command is a slow drumbeat in the back of my mind. So far, I'm not having trouble resisting, but I'll do better if I remind myself why I need to.

I catch David's eye. He's parked against Connor's side, his arm around Connor's waist. I gesture to the stairs and David's grin says he catches my meaning. Pivoting on his heel, he aims Connor upstairs.

"What are you doing? I've got to check—"

"Hush." David covers Connor's mouth with his hand. "You need some sleep before you do one more damned thing."

We start up the stairs, David tugging on Connor's arm and me pushing from behind. "His room," I mutter. Jacques' demand is like a stone in my shoe; persistent, annoying, but possible to ignore. If I yield, it won't matter where Connor sleeps, but giving us both space seems prudent.

But I will not yield. There is a way for me to circumvent Jacques. I just need to put the pieces in place. Stone will help, Sheena will help, and although he doesn't realize it, David is helping, too. I ground myself in the here and now: Connor's familiar scent, David's warmth, the soft hum of traffic rising over the city.

No, Jacques Betancourt, I will not kill Connor MacPherson, even if that means I must kill you.

Connor's room is as spare as mine. Dark wood furniture and very little clutter, but his has linen drapes over the windows. David had picked him out a deep purple velvet bedspread and coordinating throw pillows, along with a small bedside lamp that turns on with a touch to the base.

David flicks on the lamp. I close the door and, bracing myself against the door frame, I shut off my mind and simply watch.

Connor's sitting on the edge of the bed, shoulders slumped and eyes closed. David's busily unbuttoning everything with buttons and dragging the clothing off his body. Connor doesn't help, but he doesn't resist him, either.

I love to see the care David's showing Connor. For such a powerful wolf, he can be amazingly gentle. Connor has to scoot up for David to get his pants down over his hips, and when he sits down again, David gives him a push so he's lying flat on the bed.

Quickly, David sheds his jeans and his hoodie. He's naked except for a pair of fishnet tights. And damn, even Connor's dick perks up at that sight. David crawls up the bed over Connor, settling his hips to capture Connor's dick in his crack.

And then he starts to rock.

I'm still watching but so turned on I've got a hand on my own cock. David lifts himself and scatters kisses over Connor's forehead and each of his eyes. He works his way down over

Connor's cheekbones, stopping to nip the end of Connor's nose. He kisses around Connor's lips, then licks across the seam of his mouth. Connor opens, but rather than kiss him fully, David catches Connor's lower lip in his teeth.

He worries Connor's lip, then moves lower, licking and kissing Connor's throat, leaving soft bite marks in his wake. Connor's still got his eyes shut, and though his cock is at half-mast, he's not nearly as hard as that good loving should get him.

David reaches Connor's chest, working on one nipple and then the other. He nips, which makes Connor twitch but doesn't interrupt his deep, regular breathing. When David reaches Connor's belly he glances up at me, a grin in his eyes. He slides off the bed, bending over to plant a soft kiss on Connor's cock.

Connor's flaccid cock.

Connor responds to the kiss with something that sounds suspiciously like a snore.

"Nighty night, *amore mio*," I murmur. David's attention is locked on my cock, now in my hand. He stalks toward me, his own erection doing its best to bust out of those tights.

David and I couldn't be less alike. He's slight and feisty. I'm tall and forbidding. I don't bother with haircuts or manscaping, because I'd have to do the same thing every day when I rise. His hair is styled to play up his exquisite bone structure and his body is clean-shaven, those fishnets tracing lines over his smooth golden skin.

He reaches me and sinks to his knees. I'm so hard I could cut something.

In our situation, opposites very definitely attract.

He grasps the base of my shaft in a firm, no-bullshit grip. Just the way I like it. With no more preamble than that, he sucks me down. The sudden shift to warm, wet heat makes my head spin.

"I want," I gasp, "to come all over your pretty face, puppy."

He nods without breaking his rhythm, sucking me all the way down, then stroking me with his tongue on the way out. I time a thrust with his suck, going deep enough to make him gag. Even that doesn't stop him. He takes me that deep again, fighting his own gag reflex, tears leaking from the corners of his eyes.

Between the way he rocked Connor to sleep and those damned tights, I'm ready to blow like a teenager in a porn store. My hips move faster, apparently taking matters out of my conscious thought. The pleasure builds until I'm skating along the crest of my release.

I yank my cock away from him and start stroking fast. My nuts are so tight they almost hurt and then I'm gone, falling, shooting hot come all over David's face and his beautifully smooth chest.

My knees soften and I brace myself against the wall. Connor's snoring steadily, and David's got his eyes shut, an image of debauched beauty. "Don't move," I whisper and even though my legs aren't completely steady, I stagger to the bathroom for a wet rag.

When I return, he's where I left him, still on his knees, eyes still shut. I crouch next to him and carefully wipe the spunk from his face. "Now," I say, moving the rag to his chest. "What would you like?"

"I want you to jerk me off, then bite me so I come."

"I can do that." I move the rag lower, covering his dick where it's trapped against his thigh. He hisses when the rag hits him and I tease him with it for a while. "Want to go to another room so we don't wake our sleeping beauty?"

Connor answers me with a stertorous snore.

"Pretty sure we could set off a bomb and it won't wake him." David covers my hand with his. "More please."

Pondering the logistics of stroking him off through a pair of tights, I shift us so I'm leaning against the wall and he's sitting between my legs. Now I can reach around and slide my hands under the waistband of his tights.

I get hold of his balls and tease him, leaving his cock where it is. He starts to writhe in my arms, and when I finally take his dick in hand and drag it out into the air, he groans loud and long.

Connor snores in response. It crosses my mind that I'm going to need to give our lover shit for sleeping through our orgasms. That's followed by a burst of relief that I hadn't thought of *the command* first. I smile and curl over David, kissing my way from his ear to the pulse point in his throat.

"Yeah," he gasps, his voice cracked and raw. "Right there."

I tease him with lips and tongue, slowly tightening the grip I've got on his cock. He's so damn gorgeous and when he's all laid out and vulnerable like this, I want to give him everything in the world.

He tries to spread his legs, but he can't unless he takes off his tights. He tries to shove them off but I catch hold of his wrist, leaving him trapped.

Giving up, he grabs hold of my arms to give himself leverage. He starts rocking his hips, growling with each thrust, and his head tilts to show me more of his throat. So exposed, but never weak.

His hips work fast, then faster, and his growl turns into a high-pitched whine. I wait until the first, tell-tale throb in his cock, and then I bite.

David cries out, going rigid in my arms. He explodes over my hands and across his belly. His whine turns to whimpers, and his body slowly relaxes. He loosens his grip on my arms, and I'm pretty sure I'm going to have crescent-shaped marks where his nails dug into me.

I use the wet rag to wipe the come off my hands, but it's cold. "Do you want me to wipe you down with this, or leave for a minute so I can warm it up?"

He scoots closer to me, resting his head against my shoulder. "Just use that." Of course, as soon as the rag touches his belly he yelps. Curling up like a pill bug, he tells me to "warm that thing up."

Chuckling, I crawl out from under him. When I've got the washcloth suitably warmed up, I come back and clean him up, then squat down and scoop him up in my arms.

What's the good of being a vampire if you can't carry your lover from one room to the next when you want to?

We end up in the living room, wrapped up in each other on the big couch. David's kicked his way out of the fishnet tights, so he's naked in my arms. He's dozing and I'm watching the city lights flicker and trying not to think.

At least I think he's dozing until he surprises me with a question. "So which one of the DelMarcos seemed like a murderer to you?"

"Dunno." I weigh my memories of each of the people we met. Connor's snores have faded to deep and heavy breathing, still faintly audible in the quiet house. "I can make a case for any of them."

"Me too." David starts tracing circles on my thigh, lightly, teasing. "I mean, the fact that the spirits of the murdered women were surrounded by a snake does point to a member of the family. Although..."

I stay quiet, giving him a chance to sort out what he wants to say.

"One thing bothers me."

"What's that?"

David shifts from tracing circles to tapping me as if he's trying to knock the right answer out of thin air. "When we first learned that all three victims had gone to high school together, I immediately jumped to the conclusion that they must have been involved in something that would motivate someone to kill them.

"I never really considered that there'd be someone with a grudge against all of them, or someone who's trying to get some long-delayed revenge. I always figured they'd seen something or done something specific that made them targets."

I nuzzle behind his ear, distracted by the herbal scent of the product he'd used. "Sounds like you're splitting hairs to me."

"I don't know. If I'd only searched the newspaper archives for an incident that would fit, I'd have missed all the people we ended up talking to, the ones who pointed us in the right direction."

"But you did talk to those people, and I think we are moving in the right direction."

"Yeah, but what if I'm jumping to conclusions again? What if the snake was there because Donna's protecting her friends?"

"Protecting them from who?"

"I don't know!" He sits up fast, swinging his legs to the floor and standing over me. "I don't know the answer, but I don't want to miss anything by asking the wrong questions."

He heads for the stairs, giving me a glimpse of his cute little ass on the way by. I settle against the leather upholstery and return to pondering the view. David's taking this investigation thing seriously, and as much as I'd like to sign over my business stuff to him, I have to respect the effort he's putting into helping Connor.

Connor. The man asleep upstairs. *Amore mio.*

The man I'm supposed to kill.

Alone with those cold and glittering lights, I can admit that I have no idea how long I can hold out. Whether it's my age or the strength of the bond Connor and I share, I'd been able to refuse a direct command from my maker.

But if I don't find a way to cut ties to Jacques, obedience is only a matter of time.

CHAPTER TWENTY

I'm awake. I think. My eyes are still glued shut, but I'm conscious of lying in bed. I move a hand and run into something warm and solid. Okay, not dreaming either. I'm in bed, and – I touch my own chest – I'm naked and there's someone in bed with me.

And I'm supposed to meet Smith at noon. *Shit.* I pry one eyelid open. The blond blur to my left must be David. The red flashing light to my right must be from my phone. I reach for it, pretty sure I've missed my appointment with Smith.

Two thirty. Yup. I'm late.

I manage to peel open my second eyelid. There are two text messages. One from Smith, the other from David. Odd. I check David's message first.

I'm in bed with you to keep you from leaving before we can talk.

Smith's message is shorter.

Call me.

I close my eyes and set my phone back on the nightstand. I'm still exhausted, but the connection between Betancourt and the princess has crawled into my subconscious like a tick. My proximity to him is the reason the investigation got dumped on me in the first place and it sure fits with the Morrigan's threat against Trajan.

I shoot Smith a text, telling him there's something I need to look into and that I'll call him when I can. We have another three hours before Trajan – and Betancourt – will rise. As much as I want to wrap myself in David's body, I want to look into that mystery closet at Betancourt's house more.

I stifle a groan and slide to the edge of the bed. David's breathing is quiet, his body relaxed. Pretty sure I can make it out of the room without—

"Don't even." His voice freezes me with my feet a couple inches off the floor. "I saw you check your text messages. You can't leave until we talk."

I sag back against the mattress. "What is there to say? I can't tell him yet and I can't tell you where I'm going. I have a little over twenty-four hours to find the princess, and I don't see the point in wasting time telling you I can't tell you anything."

He sniffs, obviously not happy with my attitude. "What happens if you miss the deadline?"

Willing my feet to the floor, I stand, trailing one hand along his shoulder. "Can't tell you that either, but trust me, you won't like it."

"This is bullshit, and the more I think about it, the angrier I get."

I look at him, really *look* at him. His hair is a bird's nest and he's got heavy circles under his eyes. An alpha wolf needs control; it's in his nature. But I can't give him that, not now.

"I'm sorry, *mo mhuirnin*." I squeeze his shoulder, grateful he hasn't moved out of my grasp. "We'll get through this and then things'll be different."

He snorts a laugh. "I need a cigarette."

Stretching makes my joints pop and gives me time to think. I've put him in a bad position, so it's up to me to figure out how to fix it. "If the investigation into the whereabouts of the missing princess comes up, you know *nothing* about it. Nothing."

"Pookie." He shakes his head.

"Listen to me." I grab for his arm, but this time he does jerk out of my grasp.

"No, you listen," he says, as angry as I've ever seen him. "You didn't tell him the truth – *again* – and it's going to be a clusterfuck when he finds out."

"I can't."

"Why not?"

"Please trust me when I say—"

"You should have told him already." He jumps up and heads for the door. "I'm going to go do some yoga."

The door doesn't slam behind him, but it comes close.

"Nice job, MacPherson." And yeah, I'm talking to myself, but that's only because no one else wants to listen to me. David's right to be angry.

Fucking Poole and his fucking oath.

I need to finish this today. Betancourt won't be up for a while yet. I glance at my phone. Brodie could go in with me as back-up, and if we find anything that can be linked to the Princess, then I've got something to bargain with.

I hope.

I shoot Brodie a text. It's only one forty-five, so if he can meet me at Betancourt's house in an hour, that'll give us a good four hours before sunset. Betancourt is old enough that he might rise early, so this caper is not without risk, but it's a chance I've got to take.

Brodie is in San Francisco helping out another agent. He suggests I get in line.

I guess I'm on my own. It's probably better that way. If Brodie had managed to get damaged in some way, it would have been my fault and Poole would take it out of my hide.

With that in mind, I shower quickly and dress. Black jeans, black shirt, two pistols, one loaded with silver bullets, and a hunting knife. Connor-the-PI might not carry weapons, but the Elite team member sure does. Of course, the Elite team member wishes he still had all the toys, but whatever. Choices have consequences.

Downstairs, I make a quick circuit, looking for David. I spy him from the living room windows; he's on a yoga mat by the side of the swimming pool bent in an unnatural position. I leave a note on the kitchen island.

I'll be home soon.

Assuming I'm still alive.

I haven't been to Betancourt's house since Trajan and I first got together. I plug the address into my GPS and follow the instructions further up into the hills. I park a good block away and with the sun sending shadows in front of me, I slip into the mass of foliage concealing the house from the street.

The landscaping might have been designed for privacy, but it works really well for subterfuge, too. I circle the house, looking for an easy way in. As a member of the Elites, I could have requested a sensor which would have told me which doors and windows were being monitored by a security system. As it is, I'll have to take my chances.

Then I get lucky. The back yard is equal parts swimming pool, patio, and jungle, and two young women are catching a few late-afternoon rays. I settle in behind a mass of shrubbery, prepared to wait. For a little while, at least. This'll all be a waste of time if I can't get into the house somehow.

One of them has a shaved head and what looks to be yesterday's make-up smeared around her eyes. The other woman has long hair twisted into a tangled mass on top of her head. Neither is wearing a top, and both have the telltale bruises on their throat that mark them as a vampire's supper.

They don't talk much, or at least not the kind of chatter that might provide me with a clue. Both lie with their eyes closed, apparently dozing. I shift my position and although a branch snaps under my weight, neither of them move.

Five minutes pass. Then ten. I shift again. The women doze, undisturbed. There's about twenty feet between me and the back door. I move forward, finding space between two spreading clumps of pampas grass. The bald woman shifts so she's propped up on her elbows, phone in her hand.

I freeze.

"Almost three," she says. The other woman hums in response. "You wanna go in soon?"

The other woman raises her arms over her head, giving herself a full body stretch. "I need a dip first."

Pushing herself off the chair, she takes a couple steps then dives gracefully into the water. She's wearing a thong which puts even more of her skin on display, and she's all over a beautiful bronze color.

The bald woman follows, though rather than dive, she goes to the end of the pool where there's a set of steps going down into the water. She keeps walking until the water is up to her chin, and I ready myself to move.

The two women paddle closer together, and then I get a break. The bald woman pulls the other one in for a kiss, and while they're distracted, I make a move for the door.

As an Elite, I'd have had access to a screen that would cast me into shadow at the push of a button. Now, I'm stuck moving quickly and carefully, hoping I won't be seen.

I make it through the door and into a room that must double as a terrarium. Windows fill the wall facing the swimming pool and the air is humid enough to form a beaded mist on the glass. The space is filled with plants: small trees in knee-high pots, smaller pots on tables, and shelves covered with tinier specimens. The air smells rich and fertile, and there are a pair of grow lights set over one of the shelves, casting a bright fluorescent light over the far end of the room.

There's also a spot behind a pair of shrubs in the opposite corner where a man could hide if he needed to.

I keep moving. The terrarium room opens into a short hallway with a door on either side and one straight ahead. Poole's notes said the mystery closet was in a main floor powder room. There's a wide staircase to the right, so I head up.

The stairs open into a tiled foyer. Must be the main entrance. The lights are dim and I stand for a moment, holding my breath to see if I hear any evidence that I've got company on this floor.

Nothing.

I make a circuit, checking out the area. One large room encompasses the kitchen, dining room, and a casual seating area. The windows overlook the pool, or they would if the drapes were open. The kitchen has fancy equipment but little evidence it has ever been used. One wall has a fireplace open on both sides, visible from both the great room and a bedroom, with only an unburned firelog on the grate.

A single hall comes off the foyer. The closest door opens into the fireplace bedroom, and the room next to it is a bathroom.

The door next to that is locked.

I come back to the bathroom. It's large enough for a soaking tub next to the window and a separate shower. The closet between them, though, won't open.

The closet door has a simple porcelain handle with no evidence of a locking mechanism. I tug on it a couple times, then lay my palms flat on the wood. Something is in there. Something cold and watchful. I quiet myself, trying to reach through the wood with my senses.

No luck.

This has to be the mystery closet, the one the Securitas sensors couldn't penetrate. A vampire's daylight refuge? I doubt it. Jacques Betancourt doesn't seem the *bathroom closet* type. But the closet shares a wall with the locked bedroom, so maybe?

Or maybe the mystery closet is a special accommodation for an elven captive.

Poole's report doesn't say anything unusual about the room next to the mystery closet, the one with the locked door. Frustrated, I finish my inspection of the rest of the floor. One room appears to be occupied and judging by the scraps of silky fabric draped around the place, it's probably by the two women in the pool. That's as close as I come to finding something interesting.

The last door opens to a staircase. I jog up, but the door at the top won't budge. My gut tells me this is the vampire's lair, so I leave without really trying to get in.

Sneaking around Betancourt's house is one thing, but penetrating his fortress is another level of stupid.

Back on the bottom floor, I crack open the closest door. It's a security closet with half a dozen monitors showing different angles on the property. Plainly there's supposed to be someone in there watching those monitors, but the room is empty.

I take a moment to check the place out. Someone's left their laptop on, and a tap of the touch screen shows the log-in for Netflix. "For a master vampire who might be at the center of an interspecies war, you sure have shitty security."

"And for a wanna-be cat burglar, you sure have shitty timing."

A gruff voice speaks right in my ear and there's a point of pressure between my shoulder blades consistent with the barrel of a gun. "I want your weapons on the floor and your hands on top of your head."

"It's good to want things," I say, then drop and spin, catching the security guard behind the knee with the hunting knife. The bullet he'd intended for me strikes the office chair and sends it rolling.

I come up in a crouch, the knife in one hand and the pistol with silver bullets in the other. The security guard is an elf, and he's not bothering with any sort of glamour. He's got a few inches on me, though he's slender verging on skinny so I probably outweigh him. His eyes are gold with the long narrow pupils of a cat, and his ears form elegant curves on either side of his head.

He's crouched, too, with a bloodstained tear in the right leg of his trousers. Our gazes clash, each taking the other's measure. I decide to probe, to see how he'll respond. There's something going on. The shape of his aura doesn't quite match his physical appearance.

"There's no good reason I can think of for an elf to be running security for a vampire."

He grins, giving me a good look at a row of long, pointed teeth, like somebody's Halloween dream come to life. "What can I say? The pay is good."

I stand and so does he. Despite his injury, he's light on his feet. We're so close a bullet from one of us will likely hit both. I should have found some back-up. There's no way out of this short of killing him, and a dead security guard will raise all kinds of alarms. "Nah, I don't buy it. I bet you're some kind of undercover agent."

He laughs, putting those vicious teeth on display. "And what are you? A member of the Elites on a secret mission."

I raise my pistol. He's still laughing when I shoot.

"Damn it." He clutches his shoulder, expression torn between laughter and rage. "You fucking shot me, motherfucker."

I pocket my pistol. Shooting him with silver dispelled the glamour. He's not an elf, he's a phouka, and to an uncomfortable degree, it's like staring in a mirror.

"That elf suit must have cost you some bucks."

He shrugs, laughter filling his green eyes – the same green eyes that stare at me from the mirror. "The boss pays for it."

"The boss? Jacques Betancourt?"

"Ah oui, le mort-vivant."

Oh for Christ's sake. "So you're a French phouka?"

"No." His smile is turning into a grimace. "I'm just a simple boy from Illinois who came to LaLa Land and instead of fame and fortune I found a vampire who's willing to pay beaucoup bucks for me to keep the bad guys out. Are you a bad guy?"

"If I said no, would you believe me?"

"No."

"Then why ask the question?"

He lets go of his shoulder, hissing as he moves it up and down. "Because there's only so long I can be entertained by naked chicks eating each other out. We maybe got off on the wrong foot, but I think you and me can be friends."

I'm blinking at him like he's rambling on in a foreign language. Maybe French, since I don't speak it. *Why would he think we could be friends?*

"Names Balderdash Dolivo, but you can call me Dash." He extends his hand like he really thinks I'm going to shake it.

What the hell? I grasp his hand and it immediately turns into a wrestling match. I'm able to extract myself from his grip by the application of the pointy end of my hunting knife to his chin.

"Aw man, we coulda been friends." He scoots away from me and I stand there stunned, shaking out my hand where he squeezed it.

"I'm guessing that since you didn't knock, you didn't come through the front door."

"Correct," I say, wondering how the hell I'm going to get out of here before either the women come inside or Betancourt rises. I decide to roll the dice and let him know why I'm really here. "I'm looking for an elvish princess...a *real* elf, not some overpriced glamour."

"Ahh...unfortunately, you missed her."

"She's dead?"

"No, but she's gone beyond our everyday existence."

I parse that, trying to decide if I can trust this guy or not. Just because we look like cousins doesn't mean he's not selling me a load of garbage. "How do I get to where she is?"

"You need to be a good boy and say your prayers."

I spin around, reaching for my pistol. Betancourt is standing between me and the doorway out. His eyes are frosty silver and he's aiming a classic Colt Python revolver at my head. "You halfbreed piece of shit." The words are hard and deadly. "What are you doing in my home?"

Since I'm likely to die, I might as well try the truth. "Looking for the Princess Tatiana."

Apparently, that was the right answer, because instead of shooting, he narrows his gaze. "What makes you think she's here?" He coughs weakly, wiping away some spit with the back of his hand. He's not nearly as physically impressive as Trajan. He's short and wiry, with grey eyes that shine silver when he's angry.

And right now his eyes shine like chrome.

I ease my pistol from its holster. If I can get a good shot at him, I'll put an end to more than one problem. Of course, if I miss, I'm a dead man.

My first priority is to keep Trajan and David safe. Then I want to keep Trajan from finding out I'm working with the Elites. Then I want to find the Princess. And then, I want to get out of here alive.

Yeah, I've got my priorities in order.

"I don't *think* she's here, I know she's here," I lie. "And so, Jacques Betancourt, I'm going to do you a favor."

"What makes you think I want one from you?"

"Because there's a price on your head and I figure you might appreciate a warning so you can beat it."

Not as bold a lie as the first one. More of a useful exaggeration. I force myself to stand calm. Dash, the security guy, has come around next to Betancourt. "I don't know, Mr. Betancourt. Can you trust a guy who was dumb enough to get busted sneaking into your house?"

Excellent question. I really should have waited for back-up.

"That's true, Monsieur Balderdash, except that he's got the kind of connections that make me think he could be telling the truth." He's still aiming the pistol at me, but his hand is wavering.

I meet Betancourt's gaze head on, aware of the tell-tale vibrations in my aura that say he's trying to manipulate my thinking.

"Won't work," I say.

Betancourt shrugs, relaxing his arm so the pistol is aimed at the floor. "So tell me what you think I want to hear."

"Oh, I know you're going to want to hear it, but I have a favor to ask, first."

He scoffs at me, his sidekick Dash laughing out loud.

I raise my hands, showing them my palms. "Okay, don't believe me, and when the person who hired me to find the princess unleashes Armageddon on you, don't say I didn't warn you."

"Who is this Armageddon person?" Jacques asks.

I smile and reach for my knife. "Here," I say, making a shallow slice across my palm. "I swear on my own blood that I'll tell you who wants you dead, but only after you tell me where the princess is."

Betancourt is staring at my palm like he wants to drain me dry. "I don't know where she is."

"Liar." I curl my palm into a fist. "So I guess you'll figure out who's going to unleash Armageddon when it happens."

"You're bluffing," he says.

"Try me."

With that, I shove between them, heading for the back door. I almost make it, too, when he calls my name.

"You're a dead man, Connor MacPherson. If I were you, I'd start running now."

"That's why you're you and I'm me."

I don't breathe until I hit sunshine. The women must have gone inside, because the pool is empty. I fight my way through the foliage at a jog and don't stop moving till I'm safe in the Taurus. "Mission accomplished," I whisper. I might not have found the princess, but now I know where to look. *She's gone beyond our everyday existence*, Dash said, but at the same time, she's not someplace a necromancer could find her.

Which means she's in the netherworld between life and death, the place Catholics would call Purgatory. It'll take some work to reach her, and probably some help from the Securitas. Difficult, but not impossible.

As long as I'm around to try.

CHAPTER TWENTY-ONE

I should probably have gone directly to Smith, but after my misadventure at Betancourt's house, I'd wanted to see my men.

Needed to see them.

And yet as I sit in one of the living room chairs, I know in my bones coming here was a mistake.

We're testy, all of us. Trajan looks like the reincarnation of Zeus, his dark hair slicked back to highlight his bone structure. The button down he's wearing makes his shoulders even broader than normal and the tension in his body has me worried he might start throwing thunderbolts. He's taken a position by the living room window, facing away from me.

David comes down the stairs wearing a simple black suit with no shirt and perfect make-up. A large, ornate gold cross hangs from a chain around his neck, hitting the level of his heart. The look he gives me could frost a beach ball, and I don't blame him. I'd tried to talk to him earlier, to let him know what I'd learned, but he didn't want to hear it.

Trajan crosses his arms, squaring off with me. "So you went over to Jacques' house today?"

"Tell him." David's words are close to a hiss. Clearly, I've exceeded his tolerance for secrets.

I set down the smoothie I'm unable to stomach. "Okay, yes, I did go over to Jacques' house this afternoon."

Trajan waits a couple beats, but when I don't volunteer any other information, he prompts me with "And why was that?"

A vampire's aura is hard to read, but I swear there are as many spikes of fear as there are anger. I meet his gaze straight on. I've got to tell him why, and that'll lead to a conversation about Poole and that'll lead to anger and the kind of words you can't always take back. *Shit.* Still, I've gotta say something before David implodes.

"Okay, so you've heard me talk about the missing elven princess, right?"

Trajan tilts his head, his gaze never leaving mine. "Maybe."

"Yeah, well—"

My words are cut off by the sound of breaking glass. The noise is coming from somewhere near the front door. We're still standing frozen when the teargas canister explodes.

The clouds of burning gas fill the foyer. I sprint for the kitchen and start throwing drawers open, looking for hand towels. David's in the doorway, holding a forearm in front of his nose and mouth, his eyes red and watering. The vampire's coughing. Something to note for the future.

Teargas affects all manner of supernatural creature.

I shove a towel in David's hands and keep going. Trajan's still in the living room. The white clouds are spilling out of the foyer, infiltrating every room on this level. Handing a towel to Trajan, I say, "Cover your nose and mouth with this and get David outside by the pool."

He grabs my arm, hard. "What are you going to do?"

I shake free and tie a towel around my face. "I'm going out front and see if our attackers left any evidence." Reaching under my leather jacket, I pull out my handgun. "When you get to a place where you can breathe, call Smith."

David comes stumbling into the living room, the towel I gave him tied over his nose and mouth. I shove him toward the stairs and motion at Trajan to go. Once they're both headed down, I squint into the smoke. The foyer has begun to clear, and while I can't take a deep breath, I'm able to maneuver by panting through the towel. My eyes are streaming with tears, though, so odds are I'm stepping right past A Clue on my way by.

The front door is flanked by a pair of narrow windows. The one nearest the handle has shattered and a black canister sits in the midst of broken glass. I jerk the front door open and stop, frozen with surprise.

There's a body on the walkway, and even with my impaired vision, I can tell there's no aura. The body is either a figment of my imagination, or they're dead.

My eyes are too watery for me to operate my phone. Hoping Trajan has called Smith, I squat down, the heels of my hands pressed into my eyes. Somewhere along the way I'd learned that milk could cool the burning from teargas, but none of us are milk drinkers. It's not worth the exposure for me to fight my way back into the kitchen to find something that likely isn't there.

I'm still letting the gusty Santa Ana winds cool my burning skin when a car pulls up. It's a couple of uniformed patrolmen, swaggering in my direction like they're going to show the rich kids how it's done.

"Careful," I say when they're still several feet from the body. "I think this is a homicide."

The lead cop crosses his arms and sneers at me through the dusk. "You kill someone?"

"No."

"Then how do you know he's dead?"

"Pretty sure the victim was female and I can't see her aura."

The second cop, a slighter version of the first one, shines a high-beam flashlight at the victim. "Should we check her pulse?" he asks without any enthusiasm. His light shows a pool of blood and the ugly wound where her throat used to be.

"Wait," the lead cop barks.

"Did someone call Detective Smith?" I ask.

"He's on his way," the second cop says. "He called us to check things out first."

"Will you shut up? He could be the murderer." The first cop elbows his partner.

"He's not," a third voice says. Smith strides up, stopping when he reaches the uniforms. "You want to tell me what happened?"

I stand, the fire in my eyes down to an unpleasant burn. "We were in the living room when someone threw a teargas canister through the window." I point to the broken pane of glass. "David and Trajan are around the other side of the house, and I came out here to see if I could catch who did this. The body was here when I got here."

Smith nods like he's composing a list of questions to ask me later. Instead, he turns to the policemen. "I want one of you to call homicide and the other to secure the scene. No one has touched the body, have they?"

"Nah." I squeeze my eyes closed. "I stopped here when I saw it and these two haven't come any closer."

"Good." Smith reels off a stream of instructions. When both uniforms are occupied, he tips his head in my direction. "Any thoughts?"

"Tear gas fucking hurts."

Smith snorts. "Go back inside. As soon as the incident team gets here, I'll find you."

I don't really want to go back inside, but the clouds of white gas are dissipating. It's still hard to breathe, so I head directly downstairs where Trajan and David are waiting by the pool. This whole thing is spiraling out of control in a way I don't like. I might have attributed the teargas to Jacques – after all, Trajan blamed him for the bullet to the heart – but the old vampire would have no reason to leave a dead body on our doorstep.

David's leaning over the pool squirting water from a plastic bottle into his eyes. He's taken his jacket off so he's bare chested, and his hair and the cross are wet. Trajan's stretched out in a chaise, his eyes closed.

"You guys okay?" I ask.

Trajan tips his head in what I take to be an affirmative. I perch on the edge of a chair. One knee starts to bounce, bleeding off the tension that's twisting me up inside. "There's a body on our front walkway."

David wipes his face with a towel, eyes ringed with smudged kohl. "What kind of body?"

"Elf, or half-elven." Smith comes around the corner of the house. His eyes are red enough that I guess he must have gone inside at one point. "Her name was Janet Edmonds."

"Fucking fuck," David says. "We talked with her."

Trajan sits up and scoots to the end of the chaise. "She's the one who told us the murder victims were high school friends."

Smith swipes the screen of the iPad he's holding, mouth tight. "Yeah, I have the notes from your interview here."

"You're positive about the ID?" I ask.

"She had her wallet on her."

David's gone pale except for the bright red skin around his eyes. "I…got a text from her."

My knee stops vibrating, the tension in my gut ratcheting up even higher. "When? That didn't seem like something you'd keep secret."

"About an hour ago, while I was getting dressed." He grimaces, clearly beating himself up harder than any of us could.

"What'd she say, puppy?"

Trajan's concern only makes David scowl harder. "Said she'd heard a rumor about who might have killed the women. She wanted to tell me in person, so I made a tentative plan to go by her apartment later tonight."

"Instead, she came here and someone killed her." I spring up from my seat and pace along the pool deck. It's either that or I'm going to start hitting something.

"She didn't get killed here," Smith says. "There's not enough blood. Also, there was a note on the body."

"What'd it say?" Trajan sounds like he'd like all of this to go away.

Smith's smile holds as much sympathy as his half-stoned professional demeanor will allow. "Back off or you're next."

"Awesome." David rubs the towel across his chest. "Was that offer a three-fer? Or are they planning to hit us one at a time?"

"David…" I go to him, but Trajan gets there before me. He puts an arm around the young were's shoulders. I ease off, debating what to say next. "I think we need back-up."

"What do you mean?" Smith asks. Trajan's expression closes down and he goes vampire still.

I give him what I hope is an apologetic smile. "We could ask the Elites to help us keep an eye on things here."

"No." Trajan's flat refusal doesn't surprise me. David turns so he's nestling his face against Trajan's chest, leaving me on my own.

"Look, I know you're not a fan, but—"

"No, I don't want them lurking around. We can take care of ourselves."

Pick your battles, MacPherson. "Okay, scratch that idea. We just need to figure out who else knew Janet Edmonds had more information for us."

"She had a boyfriend or husband or something." David's voice is muffled.

"That's where I'm headed next." Smith flicks a finger at me. "Let's catch up later."

"Sure. I'll call you when I'm on the road." I need to do some damage control first.

Smith takes off the way he came in and I focus my attention on Trajan. "I need to tell you something, but this isn't the time or the place."

If I thought his expression was closed down before, now it's icy, more of a mask than an actual expression. "This is regarding…"

"It's not as bad as you think." I grab the back of my neck where the muscles are twanging. "I know I'm asking a lot, but trust me, Trajan. I'll explain everything when there aren't cops crawling all over the place and a dead body out front."

My heart stops and restarts more than once before he finally gives me an answer.

"I hate secrets, Connor. This is the last one."

"Thank you," I whisper. I desperately want to close the distance between us and give both him and David a hug, but I doubt that gesture would be welcome. Instead I follow Smith around the side of the house, wondering if there's any way I'll be able to patch things up between the three of us.

CHAPTER TWENTY-TWO

DAVID

Oh my fucking god. I got a text from someone an hour before they end up dead on my doorstep. *How does this even happen?*

Connor's footsteps fade. He's gone after Smith to do some actual work, while I'm hiding under my favorite vampire's batwing. I press a kiss to his smooth cotton shirt and ease out of his grasp. "This is fucked up."

"Yeah." His response makes it obvious his mind is far away.

I don't blame him. Hearing Connor say "Trust me" made my heart hurt for both of them; Connor, because I understand exactly why he doesn't want to tell Trajan the truth, and Trajan because Connor's last lie had Trajan pondering suicide.

He's only admitted to that last part once, but that was enough.

"The cops are going to be a while," I say, more to fill in the silence than anything else.

"Yeah." Trajan's slightly less distant this time and he actually looks at me. "I'll call the cleaning service before I retire in the morning."

"Would it help if you fed?"

He claps a hand on my shoulder. "Thank you, but no. I just want this over."

I wrap my fingers around his wrist. "Me too." There might be slight differences in how we define "this" but I'm not the one to point that out. Instead, I reach for my jacket, now damp and crumpled from its time on the pool deck. "Do you think it's okay if I go inside and change? The smoke must have dissipated by now."

"They can't keep us out forever. We may as well give it a go."

I take the lead and while the place still smells like chemicals and there's literally police tape barring our way to the foyer and front door, we do have access to the stairs. A nasty white powder covers everything the smoke touched. "You better tell your housecleaner to bring the industrial strength gear and some extra help."

Trajan gives my observation the little attention it deserves and heads for his office. "If you want, later on I can show you the draft proposal for the restaurant concept."

"Sure, I can take a look and give you feedback."

"That'd be swell, because I'm still hoping you'll want to take it on."

I stop with my hand on my bedroom door. "Take it on?"

"Running the place."

"Uh…"

"You said you'd think about it."

"Sure. I'll take a look and I'll keep thinking about it." Because maybe I did. The problem is that I've been spending a lot more time thinking about Connor's various investigations. I'm not sure I'm ready to be a junior detective, but I'd never seen myself as a restaurant manager, either.

"You two," I whisper and strip off my soggy trousers. I'm going to need to send this suit to the dry cleaners. Do people even do that anymore? I find my softest pair of jeans and a hoodie, and I'm about to text Connor to see if he needs help when I get a text from him.

Smith wants me to talk to the DelMarcos again, and if you're willing, I'd love your input.

That made sense. If there was a change in their behavior or the way things smelled, I might pick up on it before he would. Yes, I'm angry at him and yes, I'd told Trajan about his trip to Jacques', but he was still one of my men.

Simple as that.

I send him a message saying I'll meet him at the Whisky a Go Go on the Sunset Strip because I've been in LA for something like six months and have only driven by. I'm not planning on spending time there tonight, but at least I'll be able to say I'd seen the place.

That, and Google tells me it's literally a mile from here, so I won't have to call an Uber.

"Hey." I tap on the door of Trajan's office. He's sitting in profile to me, two large monitor screens showing layers of spreadsheets. "How did you get all that open so fast?"

"Never closed it. Come take a look."

Hoping that he's not too bummed that I'm sidestepping spreadsheets, I stay put. "Connor asked if I could go with him to interview the DelMarcos again and I said I would."

"Oh." He manages to hide any and all emotion behind a mask of vampire calm. *Neat.*

"I'll be back in an hour or two and I'll take a look at it then." It's not even midnight yet. I've got all night – and potentially the rest of my life – to evaluate his restaurant plans.

Before he can mount more of an argument, I head for the stairs. I leave by the back door and circle around the house to the street.

A couple of cops notice me attempting to sneak through the side yard. They holler and then a woman in street clothes jogs over to intercept me. "Are you one of the residents in the house?"

Shit. "Yeah, I've been living there for the last couple months."

"I'm Detective Lawrence, and we'll need you to give us a statement before you go anywhere." She's wearing the kind of slacks that never lose their crease in the front, a blazer that came from a different suit, and a couple weeks grow-out of silver at her hairline.

"I'll give you a statement before morning, but right now Connor MacPherson has asked me to go with him to interview a suspect." Might be a slight exaggeration, but I was pretty sure Connor would back me up.

Her skeptical look gives the impression that Connor's going to need to get involved. "I don't know who that person is and I'm not sure why someone who looks like he's just out of diapers would be much help with a suspect."

Aw, man, to be able to shift just my hand right now. I poke at my wolf, who side-eyes me and sends out a burst of heat. It's not enough to do more than give me hope, so I straighten to my full five-foot-whatever inches and give her as much alpha attitude as I can muster. "Because when the suspects are supernatural, it helps to have a werewolf there for the interview."

She blinks, real quick, the only tell that I've made an impression.

"Connor's working with Detective Smith. Let me text them both and they'll vouch for me."

"Text Smith. I don't know or care about the other guy."

I do, shooting off a quick variation of *Will you tell this person I'll give a statement in the morning*. I think about adding *please*, but skip it. Smith responds by asking for the detective's name and within a minute of my answer, she reaches for the phone in her pocket.

"All right." Her expression has warmed up about zero percent. "Smith says he'll be able to find you in case you skip out."

Not exactly the reinforcement I'd hoped for, but if it gets me on the road to the Whisky a Go Go, I'd take it. Giving her a semi-serious salute – that might be interpreted as mocking if you look at it from the right perspective – I head for the street. Moving at either a very fast walk or a light jog, I wind down the hill, aiming for the Sunset Strip.

The Whisky sits on the corner of a block, the neon sign and reader-board making it impossible to miss. I don't recognize any of the bands they're advertising, but I gotta love the thudding bass and the smell of sweat rolling through the open front door. A parade of sweet rides cruises past: a pretty little convertible Mercedes, a vintage Camaro tricked out with neon running lights, a black Escalade that makes me think of Trajan.

And a beige Ford Taurus.

There's too much traffic and too little curb space for Connor to stop, but he slows to a crawl. The car behind him honks its displeasure, but I manage to get the door open and my butt in the seat while the Taurus is still moving.

"I have got to get you a proper set of wheels," I say, scrambling to get the seat belt buckled so the thing will stop beeping.

"I've been thinking about that." Connor's glance is shy, as if he's not sure what to expect from me. I can't blame him. I went from sucking him to sleep to screaming at him without a whole lot of explanation.

"Tell me your thoughts," I say, making an effort to be Normal David instead of Freaking-Out David.

"What about a Mini Cooper?"

"What about one?"

"Well, they're small and easy on the fuel costs, and I'm pretty sure they make an electric model."

I make a sour apple face, but between the circles under his eyes and the fact that his beard's almost as long as that hipster thing he had when we met, I keep my snark to myself.

"You can come with me and pick out the ballsiest one in the showroom."

I slide into a grin that might resemble the Grinch when he has a terrible, awful idea. "I'd be happy to."

Connor shakes his head and fights our way through the late evening traffic, and I exhale. Things aren't altogether normal, but they're close. It takes us twenty minutes to get from Sunset to the freeway, but once we're there, traffic eases up and we make decent time. We don't talk much. Connor periodically spits out bits of information and I try to help him connect the dots. Other than that I drift along, supported by the road noise and his whiskey and leather scent.

No matter how I redirect my brain, I keep coming back to the same thought: If Connor and Trajan break up, I'm going to be so fucked. It feels selfish to admit that, although I don't mean the pretend pack thing. I care about both of them, probably more than I should, and if either of them leave our little triad, it's going to hurt. Bad.

We hit the quiet streets of Montebello. "Smith said he'd go talk to Janet Edmond's boyfriend and see if he knows what she wanted to tell us."

Connor says. "We just need to see if the elder DelMarcos remember her in any way."

"If there are rumors floating around, I wonder if Stone or Lydia might have heard them." I fish out my phone, looking for an errant text. "Lydia did promise she'd let me know."

"I have a couple contacts out there too, and they're not pinging."

We pull to a stop in front of the DelMarco house. The porch light is burning, but the rest of the windows are dark. "You talked to Mr. DelMarco?" I ask doubtfully. "The place looks shut down for the night. I know it's late, but they wouldn't have gone to bed before we got here."

"Yeah." Connor reaches into his jacket and brings out his handgun. "Come on."

Not at all sure I want to see any more dead bodies, I follow him out of the car. The front walkway is lined with the kind of low lights that run on solar power. Things are still, quiet; too still and too quiet for me. We reach the door and Connor raises his hand to knock.

The door swings open before he hits it and the younger DelMarco, Joey, stands there staring at us. "Shh." He holds a finger to his lips, his face very pale and his eyes gold with a horizontal black line down the center.

Snake eyes.

"Mom and Dad went to bed already, but I'm happy to answer your questions."

He didn't look happy. He looked creepy af, and I say that as someone who can run on four paws when he wants to.

"Should we stay outside?" Connor asks. He's hiding the gun behind his back.

"Probably."

We stand aside and he leads us down the walkway in the direction of the Taurus. Connor holsters the gun and I hope we don't live to regret that decision. When we get to the sidewalk, Joey stops. "Now what did you all want to talk about?"

"You'd be what, seven years younger than Donna?"

Connor takes the lead in questions and I stand there sniffing things. Snakes smell weird.

"Fourteen, actually."

I can't look at Joey's eyes for more than a couple seconds at a time because when I do, it's like he wants to hypnotize me and freeze me in place.

Connor's either not bothered by him or too focused to notice. "So you probably don't remember her very well."

His answering laugh is equal parts pathos and frustration. "There's a shrine in our living room. I might not have physical memories, but my spirit knows her well."

Huh. File that bit away for future reference.

"You ever hear of someone named Janet Edmonds?"

A shiver passes through Joey's body, as if he's fighting the impulse to shift. "Yes, the evil elf bitch. She hated Donna, even years after my sister was gone."

"She's dead." Connor speaks somberly and Joey gives off a burst of pheromones. I narrow my gaze, trying to tease out the threads of exultation and fear and…something else.

"Good," Joey says, and I realize that whatever else I'm sensing from Joey DelMarco, surprise hasn't made the list.

I'd intended to let Connor do the talking but can't keep my big mouth shut. "Who killed her?"

Joey turns his snakes eyes on me and I wish to hell I'd stayed quiet. "I'm not sure," he says, and his tongue flicks out like David Tennant playing Barty Crouch.

Yeah, he's lying.

"Seems odd that Donna's best friends and her worst enemy are all dead." Connor speaks slowly, as if he's tying the ideas together as he goes. "Can you tell us more about how Donna died?"

Another burst of pheromones, this time anger, no, rage.

"She and her supposed friends were down at the Santa Monica pier. They'd been partying there all day, and to hear Adaline tell it, Donna took some pills that she thought were quaaludes but they weren't. Donna wanted to fly, they said, and went running off the pier." He stops, his eyes closed, jaw tight.

"You two know nothing of biscione, do you?" He glares at us, his eyes even less human. "When you can only breed every seven years, every life is critical. Those girls let my sister drown. None of them tried to save her. There were no lifeguards. They didn't even call for help."

Another shiver shuts him up and for a flash, his skin shows the mottled gold and green markings of a snake's skin.

"So why now?" Connor asks. "Why did you wait forty years to kill them?"

Joey laughs, a caustic, bitter sound. "You really do know nothing about biscione. We cannot kill. Never. Even when it means somebody gets away with murder."

CHAPTER TWENTY-THREE

TRAJAN

Do I want to know what David and Connor learned from the biscione? Not particularly. I care even less about whatever it is Connor is up to – although I have a pretty good guess. And I'm even less thrilled about David working with Connor.

Being a private investigator is not a game, at least not how Connor plays it.

Do I think it's odd that Jacques ordered me to kill Connor and then Connor snuck over to Jacques' house? *Odd* is the wrong word for it, and every time I try to find the right word, my mind shies away. I might have had a better sense of humor about the whole thing, but the damned police department still has my front yard and foyer blocked off with crime scene tape.

By the time I rise in the evening, the cleaning service has done their best. The cops are gone but so are Connor and David. I'd swear on my mother's Bible that the feeling in my gut isn't jealousy.

Or not only jealousy.

I put on Verdi and turn it up loud enough to scare away any visitors. Even wet and slicked with product my hair refuses to cooperate, so I let it hang. I dress in black because it suits my mood and I buckle a holster with a small six shooter around my lower leg.

Not because of Jacques' command.

I'm doing my best to reconcile the month's end inventory for one of my retail projects when someone knocks at the door. I check my phone to make sure I haven't missed any texts and go downstairs to see who my visitor might be.

"Sheena." I grab for her and drag her through the open door. "I'm so glad to see you."

We embrace, my throat so choked with gratitude I can't speak. She eases away first, keeping hold of my hands and giving me a thorough once-over.

"David said you might need some company, and I'm not working tonight so here I am." She flashes me a grin. "Company."

"Thank you. For a young pup, David's pretty wise."

We move in the direction of the living room, though half a dozen steps in, Sheena stops. "This place smells like someone's tried to cover up a meth lab with Pine-Sol."

"True." I tug on her hand. There's a remote on the coffee table that'll bring Verdi down to a conversational level, so that's where I go first. "You should have seen it last night."

The music fades to background levels and Sheena sprawls out over the couch. "You want to talk about it? I'm happy to listen."

I sit in the chair across from her, even though it puts my back to the window. "All right, here's the skinny."

"The skinny? What decade are we in, again?"

I wave her teasing aside. "When I rose yesterday, David told me he had reason to believe Connor had gone to Jacques' house."

"Wait. Connor saw Jacques on his own?"

She has a knack for hitting the sore spots. "Yeah." I make an attempt to rake the hair out of my face, but it's only partly successful. "At any rate, we're all standing here with our thumbs up our butts—"

"Yuck."

"Not literally." She smirks at me and I scowl back. "We're standing here staring at each other and someone throws a teargas canister through the side window. The whole place fills with smoke. Connor grabs us dishtowels to give us something to breathe through and I hustle David down to the pool. That stuff is awful, really bad."

"It's been years since I had the pleasure, but you're right."

"Connor tries to go out front to see if anyone's lurking but he runs into the body."

"That's the pits, man."

"Yeah, Seventies Mama, it was a major bummer."

She laughs, which is a good distraction. Then she asks who I think is responsible, a subject I've been doing my best to avoid.

"I can think of a couple possibilities." I pause and collect my thoughts. "Connor's been working with the LAPD on a series of murders, and the victim seems to be tied to that."

Apparently my next pause goes on too long, so she prompts me with an, "Or…"

"Jacques."

"Jacques," she echoes.

"I need to break his hold over me." Sheena is my oldest friend, my closest friend. We'd discussed this before, but never with this urgency. "It's not easy, but it's not impossible."

She mutters "JFC" under her breath and I give a rueful laugh.

"It's been done before."

She gives me a sympathetic smile. "Once."

"Maybe."

She flicks an imaginary piece of lint off the leather seat. "The only way you can break away from Jacques is with the help of someone more powerful."

I give her a palms-up shrug. "Yes. A more powerful vampire."

She shakes her head. "Which means you'll owe someone else allegiance."

"True." I cross my arms, not sure I should say this out loud, but then I go for it. "But this time he's gone too far. I don't have a choice."

She leans forward, elbows on her knees. "You sure?" Her smile turns sad, but then her attention shifts sharply. "What was that?"

I follow where she's pointing. It's the pool, the deck empty and the wind kicking up little ripples in the water.

"What?"

"I saw someone move out there."

I get up and walk closer to the window. "Let's go check it out."

We jog down the stairs to the big slider that opens onto the deck. Sheena's not wearing black, but her jeans and hoodie are dark enough to blend in with the night. She slides the door open ten inches or so and slips through. I follow and take a position to one side of the door, gathering the shadows around me.

At first the night is quiet, but as I let the stillness fill me, I hear sounds. The distant bark of a dog. Small creatures scuttling through the shrubbery. Sheena moves to the opposite end of the pool and squats down between two palms. She's not vampire-still, but I have to work to find her.

The air is carrying a scent, strong enough for me to catch it, a masculine mix of citrus and sweat. Someone is here, or they've been here recently. I wait, the seconds ticking in time with the slow beat of my heart. I'm about to call Sheena off when I hear a very definite footstep to my right.

I freeze, wondering if Sheena heard it too. She doesn't move, so it's possible.

I haven't yet begun to breathe normally when a second footstep follows the first, a crisp click and then the scratch of leather on cement. A soft chime tests my ability to stay still when something startles me, followed by the soft murmur of a man's voice.

"You have a visual?" he says, followed by another step. "Let me know."

Whoever he is, he has friends. Another step and I catch sight of movement. A man stands on the deck near the corner of the house. If it weren't for the sound and the movement, I'd never be able to pick his silhouette out of the darkness. He must be wearing gloves and a mask in addition to his dark clothing.

Slowly, as if I've got nothing but time, I crouch so I can take the pistol out of its holster. Shooting him will be a last resort, if for no other reason than his friends would hear the gun's report. No, I want him to walk right up to me so I can grab him and knock him out without making any noise.

He seems to be down with that plan, making slow, steady progress in my direction. He gets close enough for me to smell the richness of his blood under the citrus notes I'd noticed earlier. Finally, after what feels like hours, he's right in front of me. I reach out, one hand over his mouth, the other around his chest. He starts to thrash, and I bite.

I don't intend to feed. It's about control, distraction, and, suckling at the wound, I drag him into the house. I turn him so I can look into his eyes and give him a simple command.

"Sleep."

He does. I find the toybox I keep down here for more entertaining circumstances and use zip ties to cuff his hands and his feet. His phone gives another chime, and a man's voice says sternly, "Dillon, report in."

I don't answer until I can hear the man outside as well as through the phone.

"Dillon?"

"He's having a little nap," I say, kneeling so my mouth is right above the pocket where he keeps his phone. "I think you should join us. Come inside."

The guy laughs. "If you think your vampire juju can work through a cell—"

His voice is cut off, and a minute or so later, Sheena hauls him through the door. "There might be one more," she says, and dumps her catch next to mine. I cuff him the same way I did the first one, then sit back on my heels.

"Yup."

"These guys look like pros."

"So professional one walked right into my arms?"

"You know what I mean."

I shrug, because yeah, I do know what she means. Anger echoes in my heartbeat. "Connor asked if I wanted the Elites to place guards around the place."

"Oh shit."

"Yeah."

"They can call it a training drill and their fearless leader will reprimand his subordinates."

"Or not." A man steps through the open sliding glass door, some kind of automatic weapon pointed in our general direction. "Get away from both of them."

"Why?" I ask, lifting my hand so he can see the pistol pointed at his friend's head.

He glares at me. I return the favor, with interest. Jacques had ordered me to kill Connor, and the man underneath me was very close to becoming a substitute.

"I'll shoot to kill," he says, and Sheena laughs. "You wish."

I bring my pistol closer to the sleeping man. I hate that I might have to kill him when he's so vulnerable, but I will if his asshole friend doesn't back off. "Unless that thing's loaded with silver and you empty the whole thing into my chest, you'll be dead long before I will."

"Asshole." Sheena launches herself in a standing swan dive. She hits him in the gut before he has time to react and knocks the weapon out of his hand. The spray of bullets he manages to get off hit the wall or the ceiling, except for a couple that tag me in the shoulder.

Now he's pissed me off.

While I don't like the idea that I might have to kill a sleeping man, I have no trouble at all with planting my fist in the face of a guy Sheena's got pinned to the floor. Knocks him right out, too, which is good because he'd eventually have said something that made him dead.

I toss her a pair of zip ties and survey our accomplishments, keeping one ear out for a possible fourth visitor. The sleeping dude will be out for a while, and the other two for longer. We lay them side-by-side, working in tandem with very little discussion.

"Let's go sit out by the pool," she says.

I push the sliding door open the whole way and follow her out. I check my phone. David's sent a text saying they're on their way home. I tell him to look for us by the pool. "That way they'll stumble over Connor's friends before they see us."

Sheena opens her mouth like she's going to say something, then closes it and shakes her head.

"What?"

"You think Connor's working for the Elites again?"

"Pretty sure of it." *But he asked you to trust him,* a small voice in my head says, nearly drowned out by the memory of Jacques. "Shut up."

"Excuse me."

"Arguing with myself."

"Let me know who wins and I'll take them on."

My confusion must have shown on my face because she laughs.

"Back when you all first moved in here, did Connor announce he was going to quit the Elites or did you ask him to?"

"One of those things. I believe it was a mutual, shared decision." Even I flinch at how pompous I sound.

Sheena just laughs some more. "Sure, and there's no possible way Connor gave you what you wanted out of a sense of guilt or responsibility or something."

"No, he wouldn't…"

If she laughs any harder, she'll pull a muscle, so I shut my mouth and wait for Connor and David to get home.

I hear them before I see them. Footsteps on the stairs. A choked exclamation. Connor coming through the door with his eyes shooting daggers. "What in the hell did you do?"

"Subdued a trio of intruders." Gazing up at him, I'm aware of little besides the gulf between us.

"God damn it."

His raw anger sets me back a step. I've seen Connor worked up before, but not like this. David puts a hand on his arm, but Connor shakes free of him.

"Those are my friends. They were doing me a favor."

I huff, holding on to a self-righteousness that's my paltry defense. "You might have said something."

"I did, but you said no."

"So you did it anyway."

"Look, Tray, maybe you don't care that you took what could have been a kill shot and then someone lobbed a teargas canister into the house, but I do. I want to keep you safe."

His pain tears something inside of me, and I don't know what to do. If there's a way back, I can't find it.

"It never occurred to you that if I found someone lurking on my property that I would do whatever it took to make them stop?"

"They were keeping it on the down low."

"So low that we corralled them all, unless there were a dozen or so we missed."

"No." He's got his eyes shut and he's shaking his head. This time when David puts his arm around him, Connor leans into his embrace. "Only three. My friends. Doing me a favor."

There's so much sorrow in his voice I want to apologize, except this isn't my fault. "Your friends or your coworkers?"

He straightens, pulling away from David. "It's not like you're thinking. Colonel Poole asked for help with a certain project, and I'm in the best position to give that help. I'm not working for him anymore. I promised you I wouldn't, but I'm working with him and his team for this job."

This job. This job? "Wait." My hands are fisted so tightly my knuckles all but crack. "You said something earlier about a missing princess."

"Yeah." Connor looks around desperately. "But if I tell you why, you have to swear to keep it a secret."

David shudders. "Of course he swears."

Instead of pointing out the irony in his request, I meet Connor's gaze dead on. "I swear." Again Connor looks around, and I'm shocked to see the tears in his eyes.

"When I joined the Elites, I swore an oath of loyalty, a promise I was happy to keep until recently." He glances in the direction of his friends with an expression I can't read.

"Colonel Poole asked me to find a missing elven princess, and he made me swear on my oath I wouldn't tell you because we have reason to believe she was abducted by Jacques Betancourt."

"Jacques?" Sheena's voice is muffled, almost inaudible over the roaring in my ears. The roaring gets so loud I can't hear anything else.

And then I start laughing.

"Trajan." David comes at me at a run, his expression stricken. I bend over, bracing myself with my hands on my knees, laughing in great, gulping, sobs.

"That…" I choke out a word. "Fucking…" Another one, forced out between gales. "Bastard."

Connor's frozen in place, his green eyes gone huge. David's got a hand on my shoulder and Sheena's right behind him.

"What is it, Tray?" David asks.

I bite my lower lip hard, a jolt of pain that calms me. For a moment, all I can do is breathe, but then I straighten, meeting Connor's gaze. "He ordered me to kill you." The silence is broken only by the scuttle of some small creature through the shrubbery. "You start looking for a princess and Jacques decides he wants you dead. Sounds like he's guilty to me."

"Oh, he's guilty," Connor says coldly. "Are you going to kill me?"

David gasps loud enough for all of us.

"Of course not," I say.

"I thought a vampire must obey a direct charge from their maker."

"That's why…" Sheena murmurs, and I nod in agreement.

"I refused his command, which means I'll have to break from him," I say, with more confidence than I feel.

Connor nods, a flicker of uncertainty in his eyes. "I need to make a phone call to have someone come pick up the guys." He shoots a look to where the three men are still unconscious. "And then I think I should take off. I do believe you"—he takes a step in my direction, his face a mask of conflicting emotions—"I do, *mo shíorghrá*, but if your maker finds out I'm here and you haven't killed me, he'll take it out on you."

"No one will tell him. He won't find out." The claim sounds false even to me, and Connor's grimace says he doesn't buy it either.

"Look, for now, Smith needs my help. I'll take off and you can come up with a plan, because when Jacques hits us, it's going to be hard, and I'm not sure we're ready – that *you're* ready – for that fight."

David murmurs a protest, but I stay silent, and when Connor goes into the house, I stay by the pool. I don't want to see him leave.

CHAPTER TWENTY-FOUR

rajan won't kill Connor. He just won't. Though now that fist through the wall makes sense. I should be relieved that both he and Connor have been honest with each other. Instead, I pretty much want to puke.

"He's not wrong," I murmur. Trajan doesn't answer, except to drop into one of the deck chairs and rest his head in his hands.

"I mean, he comes at stuff sideways, but in his head, he's protecting us." I rest a hand on Trajan's shoulder. "He's protecting you."

"You should go help Connor. If you see Sheena, tell her I'll talk to her tomorrow." He's muffled, but the underlying suggestion is that I should go find Sheena or just plain go.

So I do. I hide in my room, not interested in dealing with anyone. And although it's a stupid idea, I reach for my wolf. I used to be able to shift without the physical presence of my pack. Trying it now, when Trajan and Connor have never been further apart, might be a huge mistake.

My wolf waits, testing the bonds between the three of us. They're thin, fragile as a spider's web. I hold my breath. The shift starts slow, but when the bonds hold, it gathers speed. I give over to the wracking pain of bones and muscles changing form. After a long, agonizing stretch of minutes, my wolf stands on the shredded remains of my jeans.

I test the air and immediately sneeze from the traces of teargas. I have no plan, no agenda. This form is its own comfort. The wolf has what he needs and he buys the man some time.

Because bringing Connor and Trajan together again is my priority.

I trot out through the foyer. Sheena has left the door ajar and I push through. She can't have gone far. I huff along the ground, attempting to sort through the myriad of scents. The wind has cleared away the teargas, at least, so I'm not sneezing. Still, there's Connor and Sheena and too many other people for me to make sense of what happened.

The scent trail doesn't begin to make sense till I'm on the sidewalk down the street from our house. I'm following Sheena, who's following

Connor. Even though I don't smell him, I keep going. There are other human scents, old and faded, and the smokey scent I've connected with Smith.

My wolf pauses, huffing a particularly strong spot. The scent raises my hackles. Not sure why. I file the scent in my memory under what-was-Smith-doing-here-? and keep moving.

Another block, another stretch with the same mix of scents. Sheena's up ahead, walking in my direction with a scowl that I could see from the moon. I trot forward, and I can tell when she sees me. She freezes, muscles coiled to spring.

"David?"

The tension in her voice matches the threat in her posture. I slow my pace. My wolf has never tried an Amazon before. There's a first time for everything.

"David?" She crouches, as if she's going to launch herself at me.

My wolf stops about six feet from her. It'd be nice if we had a code worked out – one nod for yes, two for no – but we don't. Instead I wait for her to make a move. Neither of us is likely to take a submissive posture, so this could take a while. Still, she's seen my wolf before, at the *beurteilung* if nothing else, and I'm ready for whatever she does next.

"Okay, it must be you." She crosses her arms in front of her chest. "No one else would be stupid enough to try to play Dom with an Amazon."

I can't use a snarky comeback, so I take a few steps closer to her.

"Yeah, all right. It's you. You and your boyfriends are in a tough spot." She puts her hands on her lower back and stretches. A gust of wind whips through her long blond hair. "Connor wouldn't stop that piece of shit rental car he's driving and talk to me, and Trajan's decided to do the impossible."

My wolf yips once.

"No choice. I get it." She's relaxed, resting her fists on her hips. "I don't blame you for taking off. I mean, you must be about out of patience." She smiles at me, as warm as I've ever seen her. "When we first met, if anyone had tried to bet me Mr. Sparkles-and-Pigtails would be the common sense in the relationship, I would have taken them up on it.

She reaches over and ruffles my fur. "And I would have lost a lot of money."

I snap my teeth at her, play fighting, and she laughs.

"I guess you can't tell me where you're headed but somebody's got a hurt-on for you three, so be careful."

I tip my head down in the briefest show of submission I can manage, and trot past her.

"If you need me," she calls, "I'll be up the street trying to help a certain vampire figure out his next move."

Good luck with that. I sigh and keep moving.

The odds of me tripping over Connor somewhere in the greater LA area are pretty low, and if I wanted to talk sense into Trajan, I'd be back at the house with Sheena. Somehow I'd managed to live in this place six whole months without making any friends.

Except Lydia.

Are we friends? Close enough. Her name gives me a destination. I pick up my pace, heading for La Brea. Moving by instinct rather than any memorized map, I go looking for the lesbian biker alpha.

It takes a while, but I find the dark little pub on La Brea where the lesbians hang out. Three or four motorcycles are parked out front and the scent of wolf fills me with longing.

Pack. Home. Alone.

The door swings open and a couple of women come out, arms around each other. The acrid scent of elf has me ducking into the shadows. I manage to catch the door before it closes, conscious of the risk my wolf is taking by walking alone into another pack's territory.

But I'm David Collins, son of the goddamn American Alpha, and there ain't nobody in the place who can take me.

With that thought girding my loins, I enter the bar.

To say *The place went silent* is an exaggeration. I mean, the stereo keeps playing. Conversations lag, though, as one by one, the dozen or so women in the place catch sight of me.

Unfortunately, Lydia isn't one of them.

The bartender sets down the cocktail she's shaking and comes out from around the bar. "Nope. Not welcome. Get out of here before I chase you out."

She's a vampire and she pulls a gun out of somewhere. Awesome. I scan the room for someone I might recognize. *There.* The two women who were with Lydia when we went to the hot dog stand. I nod at them, hoping they'll connect the dots.

"Hang on, Candy." One of them raises a quelling hand at the bartender and gets out of her chair. "You're David Collins, aren't you?"

I yip, exhaling with relief.

"He's a friend of Lydia's, and…" she gives me a closer look, "I'm going to say that since he's here in wolf form, he needs to talk to her."

I go for a noble nod of the head, letting her know I appreciate her help but that hell yes I'm still the alpha here. Her friend gets out a cell phone and, after a minute, she addresses the bartender.

"Lydia's on her way. She says to let him stay and if he wants to shift back, lend him some clothes."

"Well alrighty then." Oozing with sarcasm, the bartender tucks the pistol away. "Our stash of clothes for those who've shifted skews toward the female, so maybe you want to wait."

"Nah," my rescuer says. "That boy's worn more dresses than anyone in this bar."

There's a round of nervous laughter and the bartender waves me toward a doorway in the corner. I follow her into a dank little room that pretty much convinces me to drink only straight alcohol in this place and to pay attention to how clean the glass is.

"That's our donation box. Help yourself, and keep in mind the dress code here."

I tilt my head in a nonverbal question.

"Tits and ass covered, spunky. Tits and ass covered."

She leaves me alone. I push the door shut then inhale deeply. I'm either unexcited about shifting in a strange place or I'm just plain scared to do it at all. I sink inside my wolf, searching for the bonds holding me, Trajan, and Connor together.

They're whisper-thin, but present. Filling my heart with gratitude that my wolf managed to appear at all, I shift back.

"Ow. Fuck. Damn. Damn. That fucking hurts." I'm bouncing on my toes, shaking out my hands. My five-fingered hands. *Oh lordy* that freaked me out, and I'll add it to the list of things a lone wolf is not supposed to be able to do.

The donation box is full and my wolf is still present enough to flinch at the bouquet of odors rising from the pile of clothes. I dig through, and my first find is a gorgeous tie-dye sarong in sunset colors. It's too windy to wear it around my waist without anything to cover my bits, so I set it aside.

Most of the stuff is black and there's an unsurprising amount of leather. At the bottom, though, I find a red-and-white checkered blouse and a pair of cut-offs that are almost my size. I tie the blouse in front instead of buttoning it and dig out a rope-like belt to keep the shorts up. There are even shoes, although the only ones in my size are ballet slippers.

I'll just have to intimidate them with attitude, because I'm too short to do otherwise.

By the time I'm presentable, Lydia has arrived. She sends her wolves to the bar and takes over their table, waving me over to join her. Her hair is tied up in a scarf and her eyes are sleepy, as if I've just dragged her out of bed.

"Thank you for coming here." The gratitude in my heart extends from my wolf to hers.

Her smile acknowledges my gesture. "Figured you wouldn't parade in here on all fours if shit wasn't getting weird."

"You could say that." I pause, sorting through what I want to say. Might as well lead with the big one. "Trajan and Connor got into it tonight and Connor left, maybe for good."

Leaning forward on her elbows, she stares at me, hard. "I'm sorry, because that shit sucks, but you're telling me your pack might be falling apart and you were still able to shift?"

I shrug, momentarily shy in the face of her intensity. "They are my pack, and if I'm going to hold us together, I needed to know I could shift even when one of them is supposed to kill the other."

"Ballsy move." Then she blinks, as if the last phrase just caught up with her. "Do I wanna…?"

"It's a vampire thing."

"Ahh." She doesn't ask for more, and I add that to the list of things I'm grateful for.

The bartender brings her a cup of coffee and asks me what I'm having. "Bring him a shot of tequila," Lydia says. "He's had a rough night."

Tequila reminds me of Trajan, which makes me sad. The bartender doesn't rush. When she sets the glass in front of me, there's a lipstick mark on the rim.

Whatever doesn't kill you makes you stronger, right?

I wipe it off and take a sip. It warms me all the way down. "Thanks for this."

"Strange that you should turn up like this. I meant to text you tonight but I got sidetracked."

"Yeah?"

She stirs her coffee. "Been hearing chatter about those dead women, you know? There's this weird dude with snake eyes who's been saying he knows who the killer is."

"Joey DelMarco?"

"That's his name, yeah."

"Last night he claimed he didn't know who murdered them."

Lydia set her spoon on the table, leaving a small puddle of milky brown. "Then last night he lied, because I've heard from a couple of people that he's offering the name to the highest bidder."

I toss off the whole shot of tequila and gasp as it burns its way down. "That's fucked up."

"Yeah it is. I heard the bidding's up to twenty grand but between the kitsunes, the selkies, and the fairies, it's only going to go up."

"Shit. I guess he lied to us because he knew we wouldn't pay him for the info."

"Right."

"To be honest, even though he denied it, I'd pegged him for the murderer. He says biscione can't kill, but maybe he plans to pay the hitman with money from the auction."

She takes a sip of coffee. "Or maybe he figures the money will give him enough of a head start that the hitman can't find him."

That makes me laugh. "The LAPD isn't involved in this one at all, are they."

"Nope."

"And now there's been another murder." I tell her about the teargas and the body, in all its gory detail.

"Janet Edmonds...Janet Edmonds..." She stares into her coffee. "I did hear something about her, but I think what I heard was that her boyfriend Tommy got killed."

That has me flopping back into my seat. "When did that happen?"

She shakes her head. "Last night or maybe the night before. I'll ask around and see if I can come up with any more details."

"Thank you." It feels weird that Smith didn't mention her boyfriend's death, and I'm wondering if Connor knows. And then I start wondering if I'm just making shit up so I'll have a reason to call Connor and talk to him.

We sit for a while longer. Lydia tells me about the time her pack nearly split up and how she managed to keep them together. There's a lesson in there for me, something about the combination of strength and sympathy that might be very useful. In return, I offer to back her up, anytime, anyplace, anywhere.

"Don't you worry about that," she says, her grin broadening. "If we get into any trouble at all, I'm going to call on the biggest gun I know."

She holds her hand out on the tabletop and I take it. "Whatever you need, boss lady."

"Back atcha," she says and squeezes my fingers.

CHAPTER TWENTY-FIVE

My phone rings and when I see it's David, I almost hit the button to ignore the call. I've mishandled just about everything, and David's the one with the most to lose.

He doesn't deserve having his de facto pack blown up by my stupidity.

I should have refused Poole's request, said I couldn't keep the investigation a secret from Trajan.

Told my great-whatever grandmother to go back to hell.

On the third ring, I do answer. I'm at a house that's apparently some kind of group home for disaffected shifters. Smith had an appointment with one of them, so I'm waiting outside till he's done.

"Hey. Thanks for taking my call," he says, like he can sense my ambivalence from wherever he is.

Where is he? I hear traffic sounds, louder than if he were at the house. "What's up? Do you need a ride somewhere?"

"I'm waiting on an Uber, thanks." He pauses and says, "See you later" to someone. "Sorry," he continues. "I just talked with Lydia and there's a couple things you should know."

He's very matter-of-fact and professional, which helps me be the same. "Should I take notes?"

"Hang on. I can text you."

"It's okay. I'll remember. Just tell me what she said."

He cuts off a sigh. "She said Joey DelMarco is spreading the word that he'll sell the name of the murderer to the highest bidder."

Smith comes up the front walkway, so I repeat what David has said. His eyes widen but he doesn't otherwise respond. I go back to my phone call.

"Smith is here," I say for David's benefit. "That's pretty crazy, especially since we just talked to the guy."

David laughs. "Must be neither of us look like we've got an extra twenty grand hanging around."

"True."

"She said something else, too. She's heard that Janet Edmond's boyfriend, Tommy, was killed the other night, too."

Janet Edmond's boyfriend Tommy…the guy Smith went to talk to last night. "Yeah, that's crazy too."

"What?" Smith asks, but I put up my hand. Smith hadn't mentioned the guy was dead, and all of a sudden I have a really bad feeling. "I'll tell you later," I murmur, and then, to David, "Stay safe, okay? I'm going to come by the house after sunrise and pick up my stuff."

There's a long enough pause that I'm not sure David will answer me at all.

"Not all of your stuff."

"David." It's more of a sigh than an actual word. I want nothing more than to talk to him, but not with Smith breathing down my neck.

"Don't you *David* me, drama queen. You don't get to cut and run. You're going to come back here and the three of us will sit down like fucking grown-ups and come up with a brilliant plan."

And a little child shall lead them. That bit of religiosity has me stifling a laugh. "Okay, I'll call you when I'm headed your way." I mean, there's no chance in hell Trajan will be able to cut his ties to Jacques, and as long as his maker's around, I'm on very thin ice.

We end the call and I meet Smith's gaze. He's got an eyebrow raised, as if he's expecting me to spill more information. I'm already unhappy that I told him about Joey DelMarco. "You talk to Janet Edmond's boyfriend last night?"

"Yeah, he's a dirt bag. Didn't have anything worthwhile to say."

If Smith is lying, it's one of the coldest displays I've ever seen. His aura doesn't even flicker. "Cool, well, do we have anyone else on the list for tonight?"

"I think we about covered it. Why don't you head home and we can touch base around noon tomorrow."

"That'll work."

He heads for his car, and I hit the key fob to unlock the Taurus's door. I want to tail him, because if the next person to turn up missing is Joey DelMarco, I'm going to feel like shit.

I turn the engine on and my phone vibrates with a new text. *"Call me."* It's Brodie. I don't want to deal with him, but I've just about hit the Morrigan's seventy-two hour deadline, so I probably should. I swipe the screen and place a call.

"What?"

"We need to talk," he says, all business, no bullshit.

I exhale hard. "Where and when?"

"Look behind you, asshole."

A large, black SUV is parked behind me on the street, with a familiar silhouette in the driver's seat. "Coming, mother," I say, and shut the Taurus down.

When I try to open the SUV's passenger door, it's locked. I knock, once. Hard. The lock pops and I try again. The door opens. "I mean, I can stand out here all night," I say, and climb in.

"Just keeping you honest," Brodie says.

"Honest?" I have no clue what he's talking about. His aura is a deeper green than normal, which sobers me.

"Why do you think I'm here?"

"At a guess I'd say it has something to do with the Morrigan's friendly request that I track down the Princess."

"You always were a rocket scientist."

Dia á sábháil! I have no time for his idiocy. "Look, are we just here shooting the shit, or what?"

"You got somewhere to be?"

My jaw gets tight enough to crack. "So here's a hypothetical situation. A certain police detective told me he was going to go interview someone close to a murder victim, and then, a day or so later, you find out the victim's friend was murdered too."

"Must have been a short interview."

Irritation explodes in my chest. "Jesus, Brodie, this is serious."

He waves me down. "Chill already. You're always spun so tight."

I open the car door.

"Fuck. Sit down," he says, grabbing hold of my sleeve. I jerk out of his grasp but keep my seat.

"So," he says, "does your hypothetical police detective tell you he had trouble interviewing the vic's friend?"

"Nope."

"Well that's pretty damned sketchy."

"I think so too."

Brodie's expression matches mine in intensity. "And did your hypothetical police detective file a report about the interview that wasn't?"

"Now, that I don't know. There's an additional complication, though."

Brodie twirls his index finger in a 'keep going' gesture.

"I may have just told the hypothetical police detective that another person I interviewed is auctioning off the name of the murderer."

"O-kay." Brodie drags out the word. "Does that person have a death wish? Because it seems like he or she must."

"Hell if I know. I am inclined to track this person down before the hypothetical detective gets to him. I mean, I don't know that the hypothetical detective is our murderer, but if he's not involved somehow, why lie about interviewing a murder victim?"

"It kinda does place him at the scene of the crime."

"Anyway." I scan the area. Smith is long gone. "I might need you to pull that police report, since I don't have the same level of access anymore."

"Sure."

"Thanks." Mind on how I'm going to find Joey DelMarco, I pop the door open again.

"Hey." Brodie punctuates his exclamation with a honk on the horn.

"Yes?"

"You got another problem, son."

Shit. The Morrigan. "I'm out of time, aren't I."

"Yes, and that freaky hag is breathing down Poole's neck. I hope you have an answer that'll send her on her way."

I flop back in the seat, fists knocking against my forehead.

"I'm going to take that as a no."

My laugh is somewhere between cynical and bitter. "I haven't found the princess, no, but I'm pretty sure I know where she is."

"And…?"

"I think her spirit's in the netherworld and her body's in a bathroom closet at Jacques Betancourt's residence."

"Let's get a search warrant and look."

My answering laugh holds actual mirth. "Yeah, private investigator, dude. It's not that easy. And, lest you forget, but my significant other is a scion of Betancourt's, and the fallout from a full-on inquisition would be grim."

Brodie gives me a wtf shrug. "So…tell the Morrigan that Betancourt has her and walk away."

"Yeah, can't do that, either."

"Because? Also, things are *never* easy with you, I swear to god."

I ignore his sarcasm. "Because I spoke with an elven flunky, a guy named Sam Kowalski. I wanted to know why the Morrigan's so hot to find Princess Tatiana. According to him, they had something of an *affaire du cœur*, and the elves didn't immediately notice the princess was missing because they assumed she was hiding from an angry god-adjacent creature."

Brodie stares over the steering wheel, with an uncharacteristically thoughtful expression. "That actually makes things easier," he finally says.

"How?"

"Call Kowalski right now and tell him he's got twenty-four hours to get the princess's body away from Betancourt's house."

I open my mouth to argue with him, then close it when the beauty in his idea hits me. "That could actually work."

"Sure. Tell Kowalski to get her, then tell the Morrigan that Betancourt's to blame. The princess is more or less safe and the Morrigan has a punching bag."

"And I have time to find Joey DelMarco."

"Is that the genius who's looking for a payout?"

"That's my boy."

"Well get on it, skippy. I'll have Poole try to convince the Morrigan you need an extra twenty-hour hours."

"Thanks, man." I climb out and he takes off, and I realize I'm feeling a sense of loss. Being one of the Elites meant being part of the team. Flying solo is a much different experience.

I pop the lock on the Taurus and as I'm climbing in, my cell phone rings. The name on the display sends chills down the back of my neck.

Bobby DelMacro.

I can't think of a reason for him to call me, either good or bad. Only one way to find out.

"MacPherson."

"Yeah, detective, it's Bobby DelMarco."

He's whispering, which makes me even more unsettled.

"There's some cop here, asking to talk to Joey. He says he has more questions, and that if we don't tell him where Joey is, he's going to bring all of us in."

Shit. Fuck. Damn. "Where is Joey?"

"I don't know," he holler-whispers. "But something about this guy doesn't feel right, and since your vampire friend gave me your card, I'm hoping you can help."

Smith must be acting pretty desperate if a vampire scores higher on the trustworthiness scale. "Keep him talking. I'm on my way."

I pull up their address. The GPS says it's going to take about forty-five minutes to get to them, which is a long time to keep a jittery cop occupied. Gritting my teeth, I start to drive as fast as the LA traffic will let me.

Managing to beat Google's predicted arrival time without getting a ticket makes me feel a little bit better. Smith's car is still parked in front of the house. I check my gun to make sure it's loaded and tuck it back in my shoulder holster. Jesus, I wish I had back-up right now.

But I don't, and by the time I get in there, Smith could have offed the whole damn family.

That lights a fire under my cockles. I take the front steps at a jog and knock on the door with the kind of determination that says *Let me in or else.*

An older woman opens it. Her eyes are open wide, the pupils long oval slits. Snake eyes. "Go away," she says, but she tilts her head like she's inviting me in. Her aura is full of static. *Fear.*

"I'd like to talk to you for a minute." I take a careful step through the door and she nods her approval.

"I'm sorry, but it's the middle of the night. Go away. We don't want company right now." She slams the door and I press myself against the wall, barely breathing.

"Can you shift?" I whisper and she nods. Given the state of her eyes, she's halfway there already.

Smith starts barking threats at someone, probably the guy who called me. "Tell me where your son is before I make things even worse for you." His voice is deeper, gruffer, like he's on the verge of losing control. *Shark shifter.* Might not be able to do much out of the water, but those teeth. Damn.

Which means I might need to shift to fight him. The thought curdles the tension in my belly. A horse wouldn't help me, so maybe a dog?

I can also take the form of the Bodach, a portent of death. I'd only done that once, and it damn near destroyed both me and the one I valued the most.

Mother has never told me who my father is, and I've never had the balls to ask. Whoever he is, the combination of his genes and hers turned me into a hybrid; never truly accepted by the Tuatha Dé Danann, but in my own way, more powerful than any but the oldest of them.

The Morrigan can take me in a fight, and so can others of her generation. The rest of them hate me because they cannot.

Mrs. DelMarco – I assume that's who she is – heads down the hall in the direction of Smith's voice. I follow, slowly and silently, trying to figure out where to go from here.

"So your son is going to stay hidden while his parents die? Sounds like he needs a lesson in family loyalty."

I'm close enough to see Smith. He's in the middle of a large room, his service revolver pointed at someone outside my field of vision. His aura is black, a deep, non-color void. A man mumbles something about different kinds of loyalty, and Smith laughs.

He's enjoying this.

"Put the gun down, Adam." I step through the doorway, my own pistol leading the way.

He glances in my directly. "Really? You think you've got the balls to shoot me?"

"Drop the gun." I'm aiming at his legs, not a kill shot, not yet.

"You're an asshole." He swings his gun in my direction and takes a shot. It's not well-aimed and easy to duck but by the time I regain my footing he's gone.

I run into the room where the DelMarcos are huddled together on a couch. They're to my right and a large kitchen is to my left. Bobby DelMarco points in the direction of the kitchen. I take off, heading through a pantry area and into what the real estate agents would call a mud room. There's a back door and it's open.

I keep running, through the door and around the house. By the time I get to the street, I've got a stitch in my side and Smith is nothing but a pair of taillights traveling fast.

"Damn it." I grab my side. "How'd he move so fast in flipflops?

Frustrated, I head back into the house.

There are now three DelMarcos by the couch; the older couple and their son Joey. He does a little tongue-flick thing that looks way too snakelike for a human and his aura matches his eyes; green with yellow spikes.

The three of them stare at me. The woman's way too hopeful, the older man's just tired. The younger man, Joey? He's pissed as hell.

"So let's start with introductions." I put my gun away and return their stares. "I'm Connor MacPherson."

Mrs. DelMarco's name is Sheila. The men introduce themselves, and we return to our stare-down.

"Okay, so you called me, and I guess I successfully chased Smith off. I'm afraid he'll be back, though, so we should come up with a plan."

"Thank you," Sheila says. "We need your help."

"No we don't, Ma. He'll just bring more trouble." Joey flicks his tongue again and I fight the urge to smack him.

"That attitude is going to get you killed," I say. "That's if the game you're playing doesn't."

Bobby sits up straighter. "What game?"

"It's nothing, Dad."

I talk over him. "Rumor is, Joey's running an auction for the name of the murderer. What's the bidding up to now? You hit fifty K yet?"

"What?" "No!" Both parents start yelling and I keep out of their way.

When the family calms, I try again. "Is it safe to assume that Smith is the name you've come up with?"

Joey's grin is more serpentine than the tongue flick. "If you've got the cash, we can talk."

"God, you're an idiot," Bobby says, and I have to agree.

"Look, do you have a safe place to go when you shift?"

The parents share a glance. "Yes," Sheila says.

"Then I suggest you go there."

Joey starts to argue, but I stop him with a raised hand and a glare. "Not you, cowboy. You're coming with me."

There's another spate of yelling, but this time I'm pretty sure the parents are taking my side.

"Because, you idiot," Bobby says, "I don't want to die because you're stupid enough to poke a shark shifter."

"Wait." I raise my hand again. "You all know what Smith's supernatural form is?"

Sheila gives me a perplexed look. "Of course. He went to high school with Donna."

Of course he did. "And do you know why he might want to kill Adaline and the others?"

It's Joey DelMarco who answers me. "Because he sold them the drugs and he tried to have sex with Donna while she was high. He freaked her out so bad she ran off a dock to get away from him."

"You don't know that, Joey," his mother says.

"Yes I do. Adaline told me that much. That night on the pier, they were all drunk and stoned and whatever. When Donna fell in, the girls told Smith to run to the nearest pay phone. He was the football player, you know? The fastest runner. Monica dove in after Donna, but between the drugs and the current, she couldn't get there fast enough."

He sighs like he's exhausted by the story. "None of them were at fault, but they all were. They were all high, wasted, stupid kids."

"So why start killing them now?"

"The job. He relocated to San Diego until he got that supernatural liaison thing. I guess Adaline and Kitten ran into him at some fundraiser and he threatened them if they told anyone what had happened that night."

"But they told you he'd threatened them."

He nods, his eyes fading into something more human. "Kitten did, after Monica died. She figured if something happened to her, I'd have the strongest motivation to get to Smith."

Feeling like all kinds of jackass, I do my best to revamp my plan. "Are you sure he won't know where your hiding place is?" I ask the parents.

They share another glance. "Yes," Bobby says. His confidence almost convinces me.

"All right. Joey and I will find a hotel room where Smith won't think to look, and you two go to ground. Give me a couple days to solve this thing before you come out."

Joey sputters a string of protests, but I ignore him. Bobby and Sheila stand, their arms around each other. I grab Joey's elbow hard enough to get his attention.

"Fuck off." He tries to jerk away but my grip is too tight.

"Say good-bye to your parents, junior. We've got a shark shifter to fight."

"I want to stay here."

"Should have thought of that before you offered to trade Smith's name for twenty thousand."

He starts to laugh. "What?" I ask.

"It worked. If I hadn't done something to get his attention, you'd still be flailing."

"Good point." I steer him out of the house and aim him at the Taurus. "And in return for that, I'll do my best to keep you alive."

"You couldn't even let me get an overnight bag?"

I sigh. "And give you the chance to shift and disappear? I don't think so." Swinging the passenger door wide, I shove him toward the seat.

"I could just shift right now," he snarls.

"You could." I grab his elbow again and reach across him to the glove box. There's a set of silver cuffs, real silver, not one of Trajan's toys. Before he can mount a defense, I have them clapped on his wrists. "But now you can't."

He starts to thrash, describing in detail all the ways reasons he wants to see me dead. I pull out my gun. "Look, here's the deal. You made a stupid decision and now you have to pay the price. You can come with me and I'll do my best to keep you safe, or you can keep carrying on and I'll save Smith the effort and kill you myself."

"You won't."

I squeeze the trigger. "Try me."

My sincerity must have convinced him, because he settles back in his seat, tongue flicking. Taking advantage of his momentary calm, I slam the door and make a run for the driver's seat. He's still muttering as I buckle myself in. "Now, I'm going to start the engine, and we'll find someplace safe for tonight."

He doesn't respond, so I take that as a yes and put the car in gear.

PART FIVE: MO CHATH

CHAPTER TWENTY-SIX

DAVID

I've got the tune to "Sunrise, Sunset," the song from *Fiddler on the Roof*, running through my head. Little did I know, back in high school when I scratched a very brief musical theater itch, that someday my life would be governed by those two points on the daily calendar.

Although I guess in this case it'd be "Sunset, Sunrise."

I stifle a yawn. Goddamn I'm tired. The sun is high enough in the east to turn the western horizon light blue, and Trajan headed for the vamp room about thirty minutes ago. I'm waiting up, though, because I sent Connor a text and I'm pretty sure I won't be able to sleep until he answers it.

Another half an hour passes. *Screw it.* I pick up my phone and call him. Then I nearly drop it when he answers.

"David?"

"Where the hell are you?"

"I…can't tell you that."

Fear sends all my blood from my brain to other parts of my anatomy so fast my head swims. "What do you mean?"

There's a long pause before he answers. "I've figured out who the murderer is."

"Yes…?"

"I can't tell you who, and I can't tell you where I am, because he could turn up asking questions that I'd rather you didn't know the answer to."

"O-kay." Someone who could turn up here asking questions? I want to start guessing names, but I'm afraid I'll be right. "So you're in hiding?"

He sighs. "Basically."

"You're on your own, hiding somewhere."

"Not…alone."

My earlier fear starts to shift toward anger. "Let's make sure we're on the same page, here. You and another person know who the murderer is and now you're hiding from him or her. On your own. With no one to help you. Is that about it, or do you have a cadre of Elites backing you up?"

His laugh sounds broken. "Nope, no Elites. Trajan put an end to their willingness to cooperate."

"But you're still working with them?"

He gives an exasperated sigh. "Poole and Brodie, the guys you met, are my only contacts at this point."

Matching his exasperation with some irritation of my own, I poke at him again. "So…would you like some help?"

"I don't…I just…"

"Oh for crying out the upstairs window. Your need to play solo is getting really fucking old. Grab your friend and come here."

He's silent for a long minute. "I don't want to put you in any more danger than I have already."

My eyes roll so hard it makes my ears ring. "Which of us hobbled around on a broken knee to take the kill shot when my former pack cut me loose?"

He doesn't respond.

"And like, which one of us stepped up to help me create a new pack, one I should never have been able to create on my own?"

Silence.

"That's what pack is for, pookie. You've risked your life for me, and now I'm going to return the favor."

"You are?"

"Hell yes. Come home. We've got you."

He hangs up without answering. "Well, fuck." I have no idea if he'll show up or not, and if he does show up, I don't know who he's bringing with him. Uncertain when or if I'll get more sleep, I stretch out on the couch. The city lights blink off as the sky turns brighter and an early wind is speckling the water with whitecaps.

I shut my eyes and doze, but part of my brain is lining up who I'm going to call when it's not such an indecent hour. Sheena, for sure. Lydia and her girls. Stone'll show up too. My gut's telling me that things are coming to a head and I want an effing army around us when it does.

And yeah, part of my motivation has to do with fucking Jacques and his fucking command. If Connor does show up, I want bodies between him and Trajan.

I wake up shortly after noon and start making calls. I'm the only one conscious – technically the only living person in the house, if you buy the idea that vampires die during the day. Although I've joined Trajan during his day sleep, and he's definitely not a corpse. A little cold and impossible to wake, but he doesn't do that rigor mortis thing, so.

Sheena gets here in less than an hour, and Lydia's on her heels. Lydia's got about half a dozen pack members. *Yeah baby*. Now we just need Connor and his sidekick.

"What time did you talk to him?" Sheena asks. She's dressed in black, with her blonde hair a braided rope between her shoulder blades. She's at our dining table with the biker weres.

"Early, like before seven." I've got a mug of coffee – not my first – which makes me twitchier than normal.

Lydia's in the living room with her girls. "Someone's coming," she calls and I hold up my hand to mute the family reunion.

A car door slams, close to the house. I head for the foyer and peer through the window by the door – the one that's not covered with a sheet of plywood. My breath catches under my sternum.

Connor's frog-stepping some dark-haired guy up the front walkway. It takes me a minute but I recognize him before he gets to the door. It's Joey DelMarco, the twenty-thousand-dollar man.

I open the door slowly so Connor'll see it's me. Our gazes click and I fight the urge to smile. He looks fried. Done in. I want to drag him off to the shower and soap him up and make him come till he collapses. "Which'll probably take around three minutes," I murmur.

"What?" He's close enough to have heard me.

I shake my head, relaxed enough to grin. "Get in here. I've rallied the troops."

He tugs Joey to a stop in the foyer. The biscione's hands are locked in a pair of silver cuffs and his human eyes are shooting sparks. Sheena and the other Amazons stare at him from the dining room, and Lydia's leaning on the doorframe between us and the living room.

"Wow." Connor's expression blanks out.

"Maybe I'm crazy, but I have a feeling…" I say, coming closer to him. His pal Joey does that weird little tongue thing and I kinda wish he'd turn into a snake so we could put him in a box.

"You wanna tell us what's going on?" Lydia asks. She and Connor have met before, but they're not like bosom buddies or anything.

"This is Joey DelMarco." I point to the newcomer.

"The idiot who promised to name the murderer for cash money?"

Joey twitches like he wants to break free of Connor's grasp. "You all know about that?"

Lydia's expression doesn't change. She's dressed for battle, too, in black leather with a heavy chain belt. "You all but took an ad in the LA Times, dumbass. What did you think would happen?"

"Yeah," I echo, "what did you think would happen?"

"I thought one of the kitsune brethren would find me, or maybe a bad ass fairy; anybody with enough strength to take Smith out before he kills anyone else."

The house goes silent.

"Smith?" one of Lydia's weres asks. "You mean Adam Smith?"

"The LAPD supernatural liaison, that Adam Smith?" I can't even believe it but one look at Connor's face tells me it's true. I close my eyes and think back over the events of the last couple weeks. I can't come up with a smoking gun, but on the other hand, I can't think of a reason he *couldn't* have killed all those women, either.

Wait. Smoke. "I picked up his scent at each of the murder scenes, but just figured it was because he'd been doing his job."

Connor clears his throat. "Yeah, so Smith told me he'd interviewed Janet Edmond's boyfriend the night before last. Unfortunately, the man was already dead. Whoever killed Janet killed him, too."

"And since Smith lied about talking to him, he's guilty of all the murders?" There's a leap of logic I can't quite make, and disbelief shows in my voice. Smith is one of the good guys. *I think.*

"Sorry, no, sunshine." Joey's grin is infused with anger. "If Smith had called the cops like they asked him to, Donna might still be alive, and when he got his fancy police gig, he decided to kill Donna's friends so they wouldn't tell everyone what a chickenshit he was back in the day."

Sheena's now standing in the dining room doorway. "Seriously? I've known Adam a while. He's not a bad guy."

Connor shrugs like lifting his shoulders is almost more than he can do. "Last time I saw him, he had a gun drawn on Joey's parents, threatening to kill them if they wouldn't give up Joey's location."

The silence in the room deepens. A couple of Lydia's wolves have joined her in the doorway, arms around each other, expressions concerned if not fearful.

"I guess not many of us would like to be judged by our behavior in high school." My words draw a small smile from Connor.

"You really are the smartest of all of us," he says.

Our mini-moment ends when Joey raises his arms, trying to yank apart the cuffs. "Take these off me."

"Sorry, but you're our closest link to Smith. If you shift and disappear, it's my word against his that he committed the murders." Connor meets my gaze, then Sheena's, then Lydia's. "Trajan won't rise for three or four more hours, so it's just us until then."

"Stone should be here by three," I offer. I'd called him earlier in the morning but he had a job that would keep him tied up until then. "He said he'd bring friends." Other trolls, I hope, although I don't know how many are around.

"Good. I asked Brodie to pull the police reports that'll show the inconsistency in Smith's story and in the meantime, we wait. At this point he's got the whole LAPD behind him, so it's possible this whole house will be surrounded by the SWAT before very much longer."

On cue, a disembodied voice from out front calls out, "Connor MacPherson, we know you're in there. Drop your weapons and step out of the house."

CHAPTER TWENTY-SEVEN

We are so fucked. I run from window to window, and the house is surrounded by black-suited robocops. I swear, norms get so spun up about supes. Their presence is really overkill.

Connor, Lydia, and Sheena have converged around the dining room table. Lydia's girls are spread out through the house, keeping watch through the windows, and since I have trouble keeping still on a good day, my job is to make a circuit, asking for updates.

Stone messaged me and he can't get through the police blockade. Says he'll hang around, though, in case the line breaks and we need back-up.

Every so often the cop on the loudspeaker commands Connor to come out. So far we've ignored him. Smith is behind all this, though. They've set up a command post at the end of the driveway. He's there, along with the detective who came the night Janet Edmond's body was found and a couple more, older guys in SWAT-lite attire.

The rest are faceless behind black masks, genderless under thick layers of body armor. I'd never really considered becoming a cop before, but now I'm sure I'd suck at it. These assholes are following orders, and they'll all go home and sleep fine tonight, whether or not any of us survive.

Not that I think they're going to firebomb the place or anything. I settle into my chair at the dining table. "Nothing new," I say. Connor looks up from his phone.

"Brodie's working on the police report."

That seems to be our best hope, the false report Smith filed and Joey's story. That's if Smith hasn't destroyed the original report or otherwise disrupted things somehow.

Joey's sitting in a chair in the corner, periodically rattling the chain between the cuffs on his wrists. One of Lydia's girls is with him, murmuring consolation like Joey's a kid at church. His behavior fills me with a sense of responsibility.

Because if Connor's arrested, there's no way Smith won't come after Joey as soon as they zip up Connor's orange jumpsuit.

Meanwhile, Trajan's going to rise at any moment. I need to get to him before he trips over one of our houseguests. I spring up, mumble something about making another lap, and leave them to their plotting and scheming.

I make another lap of the upstairs rooms. No changes. Standoffs are boring. Parking myself by the door to Trajan's room, I decide to wait till he comes out.

The first crashing notes of some orchestral nonsense makes me jump about six inches in the air. A couple of the were-bikers shriek, too, so I don't feel too bad about my reaction. Without waiting to see if this is a Wagner day or not, I pound on the door.

"What?" Trajan swings the door open so fast it almost hits him in the face.

"There's a situation," I say. He's wearing low-slung jeans and his hair is sticking down in front of his face like Norman Reedus's and lord have mercy this man does something for me.

Connor does something for me, too, so I squash my amorous thoughts and deal with the matter at hand. "You want the good news first, or the bad news?"

He growls in response. Must be a Wagner day.

"Okay, you got up on the wrong side of the bed. Noted."

He bares his teeth at me, the incisors already lengthening.

I've about run out of patience with all of them. "Look, chillax. I said we've got a situation going on and your petulant vampire act is not appreciated."

He plants his fists on his hips and scowls. "What?"

"Let's start by turning the music down."

"No."

OMG he's going to make me hurt him. "Turn down the goddamn music before I shift and my wolf bites your 'nads off."

He gives me another long look, then steps away from the door. The volume drops enough that I don't need to scream to be heard.

"Thank you," I say. He saunters to the doorway, chin cocked with all kinds of attitude.

Oh sugar bear. I can match your attitude and raise you a hundred. "Okay, listen. The house is surrounded by the LAPD SWAT team and we're hoping Brodie will come up with the right police report so the cops will know Smith is the killer."

Trajan blinks. Once. Slowly. "I feel as if I've entered the Twilight Zone."

"Welcome to another dimension. What's important is that Connor's in trouble and he needs our help."

The attitude drains out of his expression the way rain washes a chalk drawing off the sidewalk. He ends up frowning, a little bit lost, gazing at the floor. "I'm not sure he'll want my help, but maybe you should start at the beginning."

"And maybe you should put a shirt on and come downstairs. Sheena's here and so are Lydia and a bunch of her girls."

"You're serious."

"Hell yes. Stone's here, too, but he and his guys can't get through the police blockade."

"Wow."

"I'll see you in a few minutes." Heading for the stairs, I give a final glance over my shoulder. Trajan's still in the doorway, expression still shocked. Before I hit the bottom stair, though, he's turned the music off.

Good.

It's dark enough that the SWAT team turns on a pair of search lights and aims them at the house, making it impossible to see anything out all the windows on the street side. Trajan comes downstairs wearing jeans and a grey hoodie, his hair slicked down. I can tell at a glance he's only used water, which means he'll be playing Norman again in five minutes. Still, he uses his manners to greet our guests and gives Sheena a kiss on the top of her head. The long look he gives Connor would take too many words to describe, and when it's over, we all scoot our chairs around so he can pull another seat up to the table.

"Would one of you like to explain how we got here?"

Connor starts talking. He begins with a meeting between him, Poole, and someone named Ananda Pendragon and finishes up with marching Joey in here. And then he reaches across the table, almost but not quite touching Trajan's hand.

"I'm sorry, *mo shíorghrá*. I should have ignored Poole's request that I keep the investigation a secret."

Trajan covers Connor's hand with his own. "If you hadn't, more than likely when I met with Jacques, he would have forced it out of me."

"As it is…" Connor interlaces his fingers with Trajan. "David says the three of us will have to come up with a plan—"

"Because I won't obey my maker."

"I believe you."

I swear to goddess I exhale for the first time in about six hours and flop back in my chair. "Sweet Jesus on a breadstick. Can we preserve this moment for future reference?"

"Hush, puppy," Trajan says, one side of his mouth flickering into something like a smile.

Connor's shoulders drop, too, as if he's let go of something really heavy.

"Hate to interrupt your little Hallmark moment," Sheena says, "but I think I have a plan."

We all look at her, though I'm gratified to note that Trajan doesn't let go of Connor's hand.

"So the LAPD wants Connor to come out, and our assumption is that Smith has set him up for arrest."

"Yes," Connor says, and Lydia and I both nod.

"What if we all went out and demanded to talk to the supernatural liaison?"

"Smith?" Trajan asks.

"Yeah, Smith. I mean, we live in LA, so we're under the authority of the LAPD, but we're not ordinary citizens. We demand that they pull their troops back and that Smith meet with us."

"Assuming he agrees, what then?" Connor's expression is too weary for hope.

"Then we let him know that as representatives of the supernatural community, we're going to make sure he suffers consequences for the games he's playing."

She says it casually, as if the *consequences* are no more serious than being forced to drink cold coffee.

Coffee? I could totally use some coffee. Since I'm playing hostess, I run to the kitchen to brew another pot. When I come back, they're drawing straws for who'll approach the SWAT team.

Lydia wins, but Trajan snatches the straws out of her hand.

"Of all of us, I'm the most likely to survive a stray bullet. I'll go demand a conference."

He stands, and my heart tries to jump through my chest. "Be careful," I whisper, and he squeezes my shoulder on his way out the door. After two heartbeats the rest of us follow along. I'm on my knees with my nose pressed to the one remaining window by the door. Lydia's bracing herself with a hand on my back, watching the proceedings, and Sheena's got the top section of glass.

Trajan stands alone on the front walkway. The loudspeaker repeats its demand for Connor to come out, the phrasing so precise and so similar to the earlier announcements I wonder if they're a recording.

"We have a request," Trajan says, his voice echoing across the yard.

There's some static and a couple of random bumps, as if people are tussling over the microphone.

"Request denied," a voice says, but it's a different speaker than whoever's been ordering Connor to come out. I might have said the new voice was Smith, but lower pitched and harsh.

Trajan stands there, some six feet away from the house, and waits. There's another crackle and a thump, and the original speaker returns. "What do you want?"

That's our cue. Sheena and Connor walk out together and take their places on either side of Trajan. Lydia, flanked by her weres, is next. She takes a position to Trajan's left and her wolves spread out behind all of us. Even Joey makes it out, in his snake form, draped over the shoulders of the young were who's been with him.

Alone in the hall, I shift, and my wolf strolls out like we're all going on a moonlit walk. I take my seat at Connor's feet, and he rests a hand on my head.

There's a low growl, deep enough to raise the hairs on the back of my neck. Behind the command post there's a moment of confusion, and then there's Stone.

He's only half troll, which means he's only seven and a half feet tall instead of nine feet, and he's built like Jason Momoa on steroids. Between the black leather and the throwing stars strapped to each wrist, he damn near takes my wolf's breath away.

Who knew Trajan's clean-up buddy cleaned up that good?

Behind Stone is an array of shifters, some on two legs and others on four. There must be thirty in all, easily as many as the SWAT members. Our team might not have body armor and fierce black masks, but you wouldn't know it based on the SWAT members' response. The stink of fear rises so far and so fast it almost gags me.

"As I said before," Trajan says, his voice cutting through the miasma of murmuring anxiety among the SWAT team members. "We have a request. We want to talk to Smith before this goes any further."

An argument ensues among people who are just out of range of the microphone. The only thing that comes through clearly is an especially potent, "No, I will not," from someone who sounds like Smith.

A car pulls up, closer than they should have gotten, given the circumstances. My wolf makes note of the arrivals, and apparently so does Smith, because he grabs the microphone and demands that Connor meet him in the center of the yard.

Connor looks weary, his leather jacket scuffed and worn, his shoulders at half-mast. Still, he takes hold of Trajan's hand and the three of us share a smile. Well, they smile and I yip in agreement.

Then Connor steps away from us, heading for where Smith is waiting.

He stops just outside of arm's length. "What do you want?" Connor's voice is clear and calm, his stance firm.

"You think you can frame this on me, don't you. I know you killed those women, and I can prove it."

Something in Smith's voice grabs my wolf's attention, something wild and dangerous. I crouch, ready to spring.

"I didn't kill anyone, Smith. You did."

"Prove it," Smith says, and in a flash, the man is gone. Instead, his head is that of an enormous shark, his mouth open wide to show off a double row of razer-sharp teeth. His shoulders broaden, the skin gone smooth and grey, and he's holding a dagger in each hand. "Take me down and I'll confess," the shark-man says, and I instinctively growl. The rest of the supes around me surge forward a step or two, ready to jump in.

Trajan grabs my ruff. "Don't even think about it, puppy. If any of us move, those SWAT idiots are going to start shooting."

The shark-man makes a move toward Connor, who steps aside. The shark-man takes a swing, the blade slicing through the air. Connor dodges, but not quite fast enough. The blade catches the hem of his jacket and punches a hole through the leather.

Backing away, Connor leads the shark-man around the yard. His hands are raised, palm out, as if to show he doesn't intend to fight. I wonder if his aim is to exhaust the creature and then make a move, but unless he's got some trick hidden in a pocket somewhere, I'm not sure what his *move* will be.

Connor's doing fine – he even manages to knock one of the shark's daggers to the ground – until the creature lunges twice in quick succession. Connor loses his footing and goes down in the grass. I howl, and Trajan's grip on my ruff grows tighter.

"Don't do it, David," he says, although I sense his desire to leap into the fray, too.

Sheena gives a war cry, one echoed by Stone, and Smith has to know if he does anything to Connor, the rest of us will be on him. Still, the shark-man raises his remaining blade in both hands, pausing dramatically over Connor's supine form.

And with a terrible scream, the shark-creature leaps away from Connor.

Who's not Connor anymore. In his place is a dark figure, taller and broader than Connor had been, with no discernable facial features.

"Bodach," one of the weres whispers. "It's a bodach."

My wolf crouches lower still, torn between the need to defend Connor and the deep-seated, instinctive fear of whatever he's become. Trajan lets go of me, as if he needs both hands to believe what he's seeing, and even Sheena looks doubtful.

The shark-man scrambles away, coming to a stop at the line of SWAT team members. They shy away from him, but rather than run, he growls a command. "Kill him."

No one responds. The bodach – Connor – moves toward the shark without seeming to move at all, the way a shadow chases a runner. The shark creature stumbles and cries out. The bodach makes its inexorable way forward. The shark-man screams again, an otherworldly sound, and then it's Smith, on the ground, scuttling away like a crab.

The bodach keeps coming, close enough to touch. When the shadow covers Smith's feet he makes a sound that'll punctuate my nightmares from now until forever. The bodach moves over Smith, covering him in shadow.

Smith's screams dwindle and then fade away.

It's Connor who falls to his knees beside Smith's stricken form, and it's Trajan and I who get to Connor first.

CHAPTER TWENTY-EIGHT

Learning your lover can turn himself into the specter of death would shock anyone, so I don't beat myself up too much for my reaction.

Shock, yes, and also fear, frustration, and, surprisingly, understanding.

"I mean, I guess the bodach thing wouldn't lend itself to casual conversation."

Connor's smile is subdued. We're out by the pool, buffeted by the intermittent wind, and the night sky has turned a lighter grey. All of our many guests – Sheena, Lydia and her weres, Stone, and Joey DelMarco – have been sent home with as much gratitude as we could muster.

Which is far less than they deserve.

David's in the water, forearms on the deck, chin resting on his hands. A few persistent police are still out front. They've threatened us with interviews and statements, but so far have left us on our own.

"Honestly," Connor says, "I've only found that form once before. It comes from a place of extreme fear or emotional distress…" His voice trails off, then he shakes himself and continues. "So even if you obeyed Jacques and tried to kill me, I'm not sure that you could."

David squints at us from the water. "You mean you're immortal?"

"Hell if I know. The Tuatha Dé Danann tend to be fairly long-lived, but other *meascach* take after their human side. Since I don't know who my father is" — he shrugs — "I have no idea what my lifespan will be."

David nods like he understands, but there's still a crease in his brow.

"It's okay, puppy. Wolves live a long time, too."

David laughs it off with a spray of water in our direction, but I can tell he's going to be chewing over Connor's announcement for a while. So will I, to be honest.

"You were the horse the night my uncle's creeps firebombed the cabin," David says, his grin almost normal.

"Yeah, that was me." Connor gives him a small smile. "Your phouka guess wasn't that far off."

"I knew it!" David reaches out and flips more water in our direction. From my recliner, I'm close enough to catch a few drops. Connor's recliner is on my other side, so he stays dry.

I hate what I have to say next. "We need to leave this place."

Connor finds something to pick at on the chaise's pillow. "We probably should have left already."

I reach for his hand. "Been a little busy."

David pulls himself halfway out of the pool. "Except I keep waiting for one of Jacques' minions to start shooting at us again."

"Good point."

Connor sits up straighter. "Let's get inside, at least."

"There are enough cops around that I think it's unlikely Jacques would do anything now."

David hops out of the water. "What if you're wrong?"

Scooting to the end of the chaise, I grab hold of David's hand, linking the three of us. "I think we're okay for now, but once the cops leave—"

"Wait." David interrupts me. "If Smith was your contact with the cops, are you still going to get paid for helping him?"

That makes Connor laugh. "For god's sake, David. I just fried their liaison. I'll be lucky if I don't end up behind bars."

"No fear of that," a new voice says. An older gentleman with white hair and a salt and pepper beard shadow strides through the open sliding glass door. Connor introduces him as Colonel Poole and his sidekick as Brodie Kerr. David slides back into the water so they don't know he's swimming in his birthday suit.

"The LAPD send their regards," Poole says. "Between DelMarco's statement and the false police report Smith filed, they have the leverage they need to initiate a forensic examination of all of his work on the murders. Their main concern now is finding a replacement for their liaison."

"Seriously?" Connor sits upright, feet planted on the ground. "What happened to innocent until proven guilty?"

Poole gives him a *bless your heart* smile. "I think that only applies to ordinary people. We're special."

David's sputter is cut off when he dunks himself. For my part, I can't disagree. Humans may tolerate their supernatural neighbors, but they seem happiest when we police ourselves. And *damn,* Connor makes a helluva judge and jury.

"Anyway, they've wrapped things up and should be out of your hair until at least noon."

"What happens then?" David asks.

"They still need statements." Brodie waves a hand in my direction. "Although they know they'll need to wait till after sunset for you."

The pieces fall into place. The cops hadn't been all up in our faces because Poole and Brodie ran interference. "Thank you." Another debt of gratitude I won't be able to repay. "I appreciate what you've done."

Brodie shrugs and Poole laughs it off. "You guys get some rest," Poole says, "and Mack, I'll be in touch sometime this afternoon."

Connor pushes off the chaise and shakes Poole's hand. "Yes sir. Thank you, sir."

Brodie extends his hand and Connor smacks it, like a misdirected high five. "And thank you too, asshole."

Rather than cut through, the two members of the Elites circle around the outside of the house. Connor watches them go, still standing. Once I no longer hear their footsteps, I stand, too.

"Let's go to bed, *amore mio*."

David pushes himself out of the water and shakes like the puppy I accuse him of being. "Yeah, pookie," he says. "Let's go to bed."

Connor meets my gaze, his expression guarded. "I can't promise I won't work with them again, but if and when I do, I'll tell you, no matter what Poole makes me promise."

"Thank you." Connor's motivated by loyalty and I can't fault him for that. "I might bitch and moan, but I'd rather hear the truth."

"Hey Santa," David says, wrapping his arms around me and pressing his wet body to mine.

"Yes?"

"While you're handing out treats, can we agree that restaurant management isn't in my future?"

I twist around to scowl at him. "I never said it was."

Connor chokes on a laugh, and David jams his knee into mine, nearly tipping us both over. Regaining my balance, I wrap my hands around his wrists. "Okay, maybe I did say that, but it's only because I figured then we'd have something in common."

"Oh man, Guido, way to cut a guy's heart." David knocks his forehead against my spine a couple times. "Okay, you wanna know what we can have in common?"

"What?"

"You can teach me to do that thing you and Sheena did, the night you needed to feed."

"Jack guys off in public?"

He rocks his hips against me, letting me feel how his cock is swelling. "More like stride around the room like you own the damned place."

"I do own the damned place."

He knocks his forehead harder. "I mean you and Sheena both have so much attitude, like you could point at anyone in the room and order them to come, and they would."

I tug him around so we're face to face. "You want to be a baby Dom?"

He smirks. "Maybe."

"That can be arranged." I glance up to meet Connor's gaze. "But for tonight, why don't we just go to bed."

"In separate rooms?" David pouts.

"Not unless you want to sleep alone."

David reaches out to draw Connor into our embrace. "Nope," David says. "I want to be the filling in a Connor and Trajan sandwich."

My own cock starts to swell. "That can be arranged, too."

"Will you be bummed if I keep working with Connor?" David rubs up against my now-soggy jeans.

Connor still looks guarded. "What are you thinking, David?"

He slides around me, settling with my arm around his shoulders. "You need a partner, and when people weren't dying, helping you was kinda fun."

"Yeah, all right," Connor says. "But most of the time, all we have is scut work like chasing revenants off a rich guy's lawn."

"As long as you spring for a decent ride, I'm good with that."

Humor glints from Connor's eyes. "I told you. I want a Mini Cooper."

David groans and I pull him closer. "What if the LAPD calls, Connor? I mean, they need another supernatural liaison."

David reaches for Connor's hands, and the three of us move toward the glass doors. Connor doesn't answer my question. He just shakes his head and laughs.

It's close enough to dawn that I drag them both into my windowless room. I turn on a small lamp that throws an amber wash over the space. David's already stroking himself, and Connor's got both hands on the hem of my shirt. He strips it off over my head, and I return the favor. In short order, the three of us are down to our skin; David glowing golden in the semi-darkness, and Connor shining copper and cream.

David pulls Connor in for a long kiss, and there's nothing more erotic than watching the two of them together. I take my own cock in hand, waiting my turn, and in a moment, David reels me in, his lips swollen and his pupils blown.

"I don't deserve the two of you," Connor murmurs, and I break off kissing David to respond.

"Of course you do. There's a reason I call you *amore mio*." I tug David close, relaxing against his warm body.

"We belong to each other, and we belong together," David says, pulling Connor closer, then sliding to his knees. "I truly believe that." He rests his cheek against my thigh. "If any of us is undeserving, it's me. I mean, you two have history and—"

Connor and I both shout him down. "The only history I care about is what happens between the three of us," I say.

"Agreed." Connor gasps when David takes hold of his dick.

"Good," David says. "I've got you." He gives my cock a long lick. "And I've got you." He does the same for Connor. "And that's more than I ever knew I wanted."

I pull Connor in for a kiss and David takes turns, sucking on each of us. We've still got things to sort out, but this, right now, is very, very good.

I wake up about an hour before sunset, surprised – no, shocked – to have slept that well and for that long. David's on one side of me, propped on a pillow, playing a game on his laptop. Trajan's still out, but I'm not surprised.

"Your phone keeps buzzing," David murmurs without looking up from his game.

"Neat."

He grins and I do too, though he doesn't see me because he's too busy whacking zombies or whatever. I reach over him to the nightstand, planting a kiss on his shoulder on my way by.

"Hey, you made me miss a shot."

Rolling onto my back, I laugh at him. "Sorry not sorry."

"Hmph."

Still smiling at his pretend pique, I swipe my phone's screen. A message from Sam Kowalski comes up.

Went by the address you gave me but no luck. Looks like someone burned the place to the ground.

"David?" I do my best to hide my bad feeling, but it's a very bad feeling and I'm not sure I'm successful.

His hands go still. "Hmm?"

"How long do you think it'll take us to pack up and get out of here?"

There's no disguising it now, and he looks up from his game. "Depends on how bad we need to get gone."

I glance over at Trajan, then back at David. "Sounds like Betancourt is in the wind, and I have the feeling we should be, too."

Shutting his laptop, David swings his legs to the side of the bed. "We can have our stuff in the Range Rover by the time Trajan rises."

"Good." I scramble behind him, sliding to the side when he stops dead.

"If Jacques isn't around, will Trajan still feel like he has to kill you?" David catches his bottom lip in his teeth, a surprising show of uncertainty.

I right myself. "In the first place, I don't think he can, but our only other option is to separate, which sounds even more dangerous."

David nods, his expression firm. "Then let's bounce, babe."

I squint at him. "Did you just call me babe?"

"Aw why, do you like pookie better? Okay, I'll call you pookie."

Shaking my head, I wave him toward the door. Trajan's still out, but David's right. If we apply ourselves, we can be ready to leave when he rises.

Though I'm not at all sure where we're going to go. Between the three of us, we'll think of something, because yeah, while I can't say why, down deep I know we were meant to be together.

About the Author

Liv Rancourt is a multi-published author of m/m romance. Because love is love, even with fangs.

Liv likes to write stories about vampires, either contemporary or historical. Sometimes she branches out into other paranormal realms, but there's always magic, and there's always romance. She also co-authors two m/m paranormal romance series with Irene Preston. Their partnership works because Liv is good at blowing things up and Irene is good at explaining why.

When Liv isn't writing she takes care of tiny premature babies in the NICU. Her husband is a soul of patience, her kids are her pride and joy, and her cat Praline (pronounced PRAH-leen) is endlessly entertaining. Happy reading!